DRAGON HORSE WAR: THE CALLING

What Reviewers Say About
D. Jackson Leigh's Work

"*Call Me Softly* is a thrilling and enthralling novel of love, lies, intrigue and Southern charm."—*Bibliophilic Book Blog*

"D. Jackson Leigh understands the value of branding and delivers more of the familiar and welcome story elements that set her novels apart from other authors in the romance genre."—*The Rainbow Reader*

"D. Jackson Leigh has created very likeable characters in the throes of making very realistic life decisions. She's also written an enjoyable novel full of humor and great love scenes."—*Just About Write*

"Her prose is clean, lean, and mean—elegantly descriptive…"—*Out in Print*

Visit us at www.boldstrokesbooks.com

By the Author

Bareback

Long Shot

Call Me Softly

Touch Me Gently

Every Second Counts

Hold Me Forever

Dragon Horse War: The Calling

DRAGON HORSE WAR: THE CALLING

by

D. Jackson Leigh

2015

DRAGON HORSE WAR: THE CALLING
© 2015 By D. Jackson Leigh. All Rights Reserved.

ISBN 13: 978-1-62639-240-3

This Trade Paperback Original Is Published By
Bold Strokes Books, Inc.
P.O. Box 249
Valley Falls, NY 12185

First Edition: February 2015

Credits
Editor: Shelley Thrasher
Production Design: Susan Ramundo
Cover Design By Sheri (graphicartist2020@hotmail.com)

Acknowledgments

First, I want to thank my awesome editor, Shelley Thrasher. I was so uncharacteristically discombobulated when I took the podium to accept a 2014 Golden Crown Literary Society award in the romance category for *Every Second Counts* that I forgot to do that. The vast improvement in my writing since my first book is because of Shelley's gentle hand and incredible patience. Improving a writer without changing her voice takes great skill. We've edited seven books together, including my upcoming anthology that will be released a few months after this book. I hope there will be many more before she tires of me.

This was my first attempt at writing fantasy. World building is hard. This book was also difficult because it explores some controversial issues—diversity, afterlife, reincarnation, and the politics of socialism vs. survival of the strongest. As if that wasn't enough, a third gender character unexpectedly jumped in the mix and begged to be explored further. The Dragon Horse War Trilogy (yes, there will be two more books to complete the overall story arc) is meant to be a question, not a judgment. If there's any judgment, it's my strong belief that all people should be treated equally—regardless of gender or sexual orientation or race or ethnic origin.

So, secondly, I owe an amazing debt to my beta readers Jenny Harmon, Ellen Greenblatt, Carol Poyner, and Henrietta Bookgeek. I leaned heavily on their feedback to help me hopefully find and use the right words for these sensitive subjects. The unique opportunity to sit down with Jenny and Ellen in person at the summer 2014 Bold Strokes writers retreat to discuss certain points was invaluable. You guys rock!

I also have to give a shout out to BSB fantasy author extraordinaire Jane Fletcher. When dragon horses were still just a grain of sand irritating my imagination, Jane took time to read over a synopsis of my fledgling idea and point out a few gaping holes in my premise. That armed me with better tools to get started. Jane Fletcher's work is a standard I hope to one day achieve if I continue to indulge in the fantasy genre.

As always, none of this could be possible without the supportive environment envisioned and nurtured by the amazing Len Barot and her very professional staff at Bold Strokes Books. I've never regretted or second-guessed my decision to sign with BSB.

Finally, thanks again, Shelley. Your patience with my constant self-editing during your editing of this book was more appreciated than you know.

Dedication

This book is dedicated to my writing companions, my trio of terrors, uh, terriers. They are the very throb of my heart and let me know every time dragon horses are flying about by running out the pet door at four a.m. and barking at the sky.

A second, very special dedication goes to my "adanin," my kindred author Cate Culpepper, who followed her wee warrior Westie, Kirby, over the rainbow bridge on October 25, 2014. May there always be wind in your sails, my captain.

PROLOGUE

Professor, are you saying that people hoarded food and refused to share while others starved? How could they do this?"

His students' expressions were incredulous. Cyrus smiled. He loved teaching. They were blank slates, and he held the chalk to write on them.

"The world was viewed very differently then. There was an entirely different social order. The races were still mostly pure, and nationalism rather than world order ruled. Obviously, some countries had greater natural resources, as some regions still do today, and there was no common vehicle, no laws to enforce distribution of food and other essentials to less productive areas."

"It sounds barbaric," one young woman said, frowning.

Cyrus shrugged. "Some historians would contend that competition for wealth and resources spurred ingenuity and rewarded ambition. It was a time of great advances in medicine, industry, and technology. Over the past century, we've become a complacent society of thinkers rather than doers."

"Surely you aren't suggesting that violent divisive era before The Great Religion Wars was better than The Enlightenment that has followed." They stared at him, disbelief written on their young faces.

"Of course he's not." The handsome, brown-skinned man who descended the stairs of the amphitheater-style classroom was young, but his intelligent eyes held an old soul of many incarnations. "Professor Cyrus is simply trying to help you gain insight into why people acted as they did before The Enlightenment."

"Dean Furcho. What a surprise." Cyrus hated to have his class interrupted, especially by a man half his physical age yet chosen over him to lead the college. Furcho was nearly a pureblood, as was he. In a different time, Cyrus's Caucasian ancestry would have given him immediate preference over Furcho's Hispanic bloodlines. It wasn't the first time he'd wished The Enlightenment had never happened. "Is there something we can help you with, Dean? As you can see, we are in the middle of a class discussion."

Furcho dipped his head in acknowledgment. "I apologize for the interruption, but the matter is urgent. I must dismiss the class immediately."

Cyrus grudgingly made room for him when he stepped onto the speaking platform and turned to the students.

"We must evacuate the town. The rains have weakened the mountainside to the point that the Corps has detected an imminent danger of massive mudslide." Furcho's demeanor was casual, but the authority in his voice quieted the paper-shufflers. "If you have families here, go straightaway to gather them. If you do not have transportation, they will be loading transports at the main gymnasium to carry you to safety."

A few students began shoving their tablets into shoulder bags, but many sat stunned.

"Do not waste time collecting household belongings. Nothing is more valuable than your lives. Stay calm, but go. Go now." The urgency in Furcho's command sent them scrambling for the building's exits. He turned to Cyrus. "Your mate, Laine, was the Corps representative who called the university about the evacuation. She also asked me to pass along a personal message. She's leading the unit that's evacuating the east side of town, and your son is assigned to her group. Your youngest daughter is with your sister, and they are headed to her home in the flatlands where they'll be safe. Laine said you should go there, too, until the town is considered safe again or she and Thomas can join you." Furcho started up the steps of the amphitheater classroom, then turned back. "Oh, and she wasn't able to get in touch with your oldest daughter since she's on a research trip…to let her know to go to her aunt's house, rather than here when she returns."

"I won't leave here without my son—"

A great rumbling cut his refusal short. The floor under their feet bucked and heaved.

"Out! Out of the building." Furcho pushed Cyrus toward the exit.

They stumbled and half crawled up the steps of the tiered seating, struggling to find their balance as the building groaned and chunks of the ceiling fell around them. Cyrus stumbled and fell, slamming his head against the metal arm of a chair. Pain exploded around his left ear and his vision dimmed. When the darkness receded seconds later, he wished for it again because the room spun crazily and his stomach heaved. Furcho was pulling at his coat, dragging him up toward the door.

He regained his feet enough to lean heavily against Furcho the final few steps before they burst through the door and into a torrent of rain. The chill of it began to clear his head.

"You're bleeding," Furcho said. "We should go to the clinic."

"No. I have to find Thomas and Laine." He gingerly felt around his ear, but the downpour made it impossible to judge how badly he was bleeding.

Furcho peered at him. "You have a cut above your ear, but it doesn't look too bad. I'll go with you."

The streets of the small university town were clogged with people fleeing from danger and emergency vehicles moving toward it.

"This way," Furcho said, directing them down an alley to a street less congested.

Ten blocks later, they hit the outer edge of the emergency-response force. Fire trucks ringed an east-side neighborhood that had been flooded by a slide so massive the houses protruded from a deep sludge of mud and forest debris like candles on a birthday cake. As if the constant rain wasn't enough, firemen were streaming water onto the sludge, washing it toward the huge metal scoops of bulldozers that in turn deposited the mud into massive transports to be hauled away. An army of ambulances darted along the edges of the rescue like gulls, snatching up victims as they were carried out and flying off to the clinic with lights flashing and sirens blaring.

The cacophony of shouts and sirens and machinery competed with the pounding in Cyrus's head as they picked a path through the jumble of vehicles. He grabbed a grim-faced fireman who protectively cradled a mud-covered child against his chest, even though the girl's eyes were open and fixed in the cold stare of death.

"I'm looking for my mate and son," Cyrus said. "She was commanding a Corps evacuation unit."

The fireman shook his head. "The streets were filled with people trying to leave when the mountain gave way. That's why we're using the hoses rather than digging. We don't know how many are buried in the sludge and can't risk injuring someone who could still be alive in a pocket of air. There are only two places to look for your family. Those who survived are being taken to the clinic." He hugged the dead child closer to his chest. "Those who didn't are being taken to the football stadium until we can set up a temporary morgue."

"We'll go there first since it's closer," Furcho said gently. He turned to the fireman and held out his arms. "I'll take the child so you can go back and help find survivors."

Tears filled the man's eyes. "She's my brother's child, Sophie. She's only seven."

Furcho nodded. "I'll take very good care of Sophie."

"We have to go." Cyrus was impatient, frantic to find his own child.

The fireman handed the girl over but touched her cheek one last time, his eyes searching her face. "She will live again."

"She has many lives ahead of her yet."

The man searched Furcho's eyes and seemed relieved by his certainty. "Thank you," he said.

The fireman's response irritated Cyrus. He had doubts about those who claimed many incarnations. His mate insisted she could recall other lives, but he couldn't remember anything further back than his toddler years. It was probably because he was a newling, she said, assuring him that at some point he would have lived enough lives to remember, too. But he resented people like Laine and Furcho. They paraded around spouting their advice and acting like they knew everything. He didn't believe a word of it.

"If you see a tall woman with a scar on her chin ordering people around or a boy about eighteen with red hair, tell them Cyrus is looking for them," he said gruffly. Without waiting for an answer, he headed for the stadium at a fast clip, not caring if Furcho, with his tragic burden, could keep up.

The football field was a surreal nightmare. Row after row of muddy figures lay on the sodden turf. The persistent drizzle washed the mud from their bodies in rivulets, gradually revealing slack faces. Wails of grief rose from equally muddy survivors hunched over many of the still forms.

Cyrus walked slowly among them, searching each face for that of his mate or son. He was midway down the field when his gaze fell on the figure near the end of the row. Even soaked with rain, the carrot-colored hair was a beacon in the dreary landscape. With an anguished cry, he ran and fell to his knees next to his son's prone body. The boy's eyes were closed, as if sleeping, but his skin was cold as Cyrus brushed the mud away from his cheeks.

"No, no, no. Not my son." He raised his face to the sky and cried out. "You can't have him!"

He didn't care how long Thomas had lain there; he had to try. He thumped hard on the boy's chest, but his sternum felt like shattered glass under his fist. He pulled at his chin, intending to inflate the slack lungs with his own breath, but his son's mouth was filled with grit and twigs. He dug at the debris with his fingers, but it was no use. Mud oozed in the boy's throat. He screamed at the sky, roiling and black with the unending rain. "He was my son."

He blamed himself. He was one of few experts in the ancient texts. He knew the real truth, had known it for some time, yet failed to heed it. Like the ten plagues of Egypt noted by several major religions, the weather had been a plague for the past two years. Perpetual rain, flooding, mudslides, hurricanes, tornadoes, wildfires started by bolts of lightning had been tearing at the planet, taking lives, destroying homes and crops. This could only be the work of a powerful and vengeful omnipotent deity impatient with the homage paid to The Collective and the prevailing belief in rebirth and multiple lives for common souls.

A mud-caked figure knelt opposite him, and he looked up to see his agony reflected in his mate's eyes. Tears streaked the muddy film that covered Laine's face.

"He ran back to help an elderly woman," she said softly.

Cyrus stared at her, his anger rising. "And you let him? My only son and you let him?"

She seemed startled at his harsh tones. "We were there to help evacuate people. The woman was a widower, alone with only her small dog. There was no one to help her. Thomas went to her because it was his duty, because he was a good man." A sob escaped her throat as she caressed the face of her son. "His selfless deed surely will benefit him in his next life."

He blamed her. She had filled their son with ridiculous stories of future lives that stripped him of the natural instinct of self-survival.

He stared at her and wondered how he could have ever married such a woman. Her beauty had captured him when he was a young man, but her natural leadership and seemingly constant heroic deeds as an emergency responder had overshadowed, emasculated him over the years. After Thomas, he'd only been able to produce daughters with her. To add insult, their only son was enthralled by her fantastic tales of heroic deeds and joined her as an emergency responder rather than follow him into the teaching profession. It had been a wedge in their already crumbling marriage. He rose to his feet.

"There is no next life," he shouted. "You are all fools."

The sluggish movements of the other grief-stricken stopped, and the steamy stadium became still. Even the rain had ceased and he drew purpose from it, raising his voice so all could hear. "Read the ancient texts and pay heed. This is no coincidence. This is punishment dealt by the one true omnipotent being who has power over all things. This plague of nature that has stolen our children, our mates, our brothers and sisters is the price for departing from the true nature of things. Heed my words. There is no Collective. There are no future lives. You have wrought this upon yourselves with your disbelief, your disobedience."

He whirled around at the prick and hiss of an injector pressed against his neck. His limbs were instantly leaden, and he felt hands lower him carefully to the ground.

"He's distraught, overcome with grief," Laine said, her voice sounding far away.

"You should take him to the clinic."

That bastard Furcho always seemed to be around for his worst failings—when he was passed over for promotion and now as he lay helplessly drugged.

"I can't leave. I'm needed here," Laine said.

"Then I'll take him before I seek out the town chancellor to offer any university facilities that can be utilized for the displaced and injured."

His vision began to dim, and he used the last of his strength to turn his head and focus one final time upon the muddy profile of his dead son. His lips worked around the words, but the drug paralyzed his voice. He would be the modern prophet to this misguided world. He'd lead them back to purity. His son would not have died in vain.

CHAPTER ONE

Jael crept silently along the edge of the woods. She had heard her thoughts the moment the intruder left her transport and climbed over the gate blocking the four-klick corridor to her quarters. It was unusual for her to hear thoughts from that distance without focusing, but this woman had an amazing projection for someone who wasn't trying. And she knew it wasn't deliberate because the visitor was babbling uncertainty—thoughts you would not choose to broadcast.

So she saved her work, shut down her digital tablet, and slipped out the door. The scout trail that paralleled the drive corridor was lined with brambles for concealment and padded with sand so that her bare feet made no sound even at a dead run. The precaution really wasn't necessary, but the habits of more than twenty lifetimes were hard to break. The trespasser had gone less than a quarter of the distance to the house by the time Jael had circled around to tail her.

Anyone who could broadcast that strongly might also be able to probe, so she was careful to raise her mental shields. The effort was almost laughable. The woman appeared to be little more than a lost teen. She was ill dressed for hiking in a white gauzy tunic and linen pants that reached to mid-calf. She carried no bag—meaning no water or food or animal deterrent—and her sandals slapped against the hard-packed dirt of the corridor loud enough to rouse the entire forest. She stopped several times, hands on her hips, to peer forward, then back toward the gate as though she was contemplating whether to continue or return to her transport. Each time she heaved a huge sigh and resumed her trek.

With only a klick to go, the woman stopped and sat on the thick root of an ancient oak at the edge of the road and slumped against its gnarled trunk. She began to mumble, and Jael crept closer as her grumbling gained volume.

"Stars above! I know one lifetime doesn't give me much rank, but you'd think that if I'm important enough for them to send on a mission, they could have at least messaged ahead to let this person know I was coming." She grimaced and slapped at a mosquito that was feasting on her neck and pulled the collar of her tunic up to wipe the sweat from her face. "I'm going to look a mess by the time I reach his house, if I ever do." She stood and looked up and down the path again. "There's no telling how far this road goes. They said he owns the entire mountain. I could still be walking this time tomorrow."

Jael felt, for the first time, tendrils of a mental probe. She relaxed. Ah, an empath. They were much easier to block than a telepath. She was tempted, as an amusing distraction, to leak a fierce image past her shields. She was still contemplating this when she saw her quarry stiffen.

"Who's there?" The woman jumped to her feet.

Curious. Could she feel Jael's shields? Had she said one lifetime? It was rare enough to meet an empath who could project, but this fledgling had the skills of a much older, more experienced soul. Still, she didn't worry about detection. Her perfect stillness and the earthy colors of her clothing concealed her sufficiently from the naked eye. Besides, this lifetime of peace afforded little opportunity for a warrior to practice her skills, and she was enjoying the stalk. She wasn't ready to reveal herself.

The woman turned slowly in a circle and scanned the forest. She stopped, put her hands on her hips, and lifted her chin. "I know you're there. I mean you no harm."

A warm, welcoming thrall washed over Jael. This empath was good. Very good. Skilled enough to entice almost any soul from hiding. But Jael wasn't just anybody.

After a few heartbeats of silence and no response, the woman cocked her head. "I guess you're shy then. No matter. Follow along if you must."

Jael smiled to herself. Whether the woman's bravado was bravery or stupidity, she liked her spunk and full, melodic voice. A singer, perhaps? She frowned. Dung. She hoped it wasn't that person who had been d-messaging her about putting music to her book of poetry that had released last year. She should have stuck with her usual intrigue novels.

She waited until the woman moved farther up the corridor before she slipped among the trees to shadow her.

❖

Alyssa felt a bit stupid talking to the trees, but she was certain—well, almost certain—that she felt someone, something close by. Maybe it was an animal rather than a person. Were there bears or wolves in these mountains? Maybe a cougar? She'd never tried her skills on a predator, but she had calmed a nervous or injured animal on more than one occasion in her role as a healer. She didn't like using her empathic gift to manipulate, but it was a tool of peace she was coming to accept.

She swatted at another mosquito dining on her neck. Fireballs and ice cream! She wished she could project something that would keep the nasty bloodsuckers off her.

So, anyway, if it was a beast, what was the worst that could happen? Death? Was it wrong that the idea filled her with anticipation? Wouldn't it be amazing to have past lives, millenniums of wisdom to call upon? She snorted. First she'd have to experience some wisdom to make this life worth recalling. Then she sighed. Perhaps she'd find a soul mate to bond with so completely that they'd immediately recognize each other in their next new life, and every life after. She threw her hands up in an impatient gesture.

"Yeah, well, you're not going to find a soul mate when you don't even date." The sound of her own voice was a bit of comfort in the absolute quiet of the forest, so she continued her muttering. "But who has time for dating. It's Alyssa do this, Alyssa do that. Alyssa, can you fetch a poultice? Alyssa, can you calm these children? Alyssa, can you sweep the temple? You'd think I was still an acolyte."

She swatted at still another mosquito, then frowned at the blood on her hand. "Nasty." She stopped and stared longingly back the way she'd come, but she couldn't see much. The trail switched back and forth to lessen the incline of the mountain's elevation. She shook her head and continued forward. "Finally, I'm assigned my first real mission as a full Advocate, and it turns out to be as messenger girl to some recluse of a writer. J. El. Why doesn't anybody know what the J stands for, anyway? He's probably some bald, grumpy old man who can't stop living in his past lives. I mean, what kind of person spends their time writing historic fiction about war and espionage? It just doesn't seem healthy to glorify such a horrific time in history. And why do I have to deliver this message in person? Surely this J. El has access to d-messaging. I mean, who isn't tied into digital these days?"

Souls above, how much farther? These new sandals were proving to be a poor choice. But, then, she hadn't anticipated that she'd have to hike a million klicks just to find this J. El person. She stopped and pulled at the leather strap circling her left heel to reveal raw skin where a blister was draining. The burning of her right heel was a sure sign she'd find the same on that foot, too. She straightened and peered ahead. There! A beacon piercing the gloom. Relief washed through her and she slipped off the sandals. The dirt was cool against her feet and she broke into a jog. She was so intent on reaching her destination, any destination, that she was jarred when the forest released her into blinding sunlight and a riot of color.

The mountaintop was gently sloped and nearly covered in wildflowers of every variety. Alyssa was relieved to also see a large log cabin at the meadow's edge opposite her. She glanced at the sun. Her walk from the entry gate had taken longer than she realized. It was well past midday and she hoped that, after she relayed her message, this J. El person would take her back to her transport. She wasn't keen on spending the night as the guest of a stranger—a male stranger—no matter who he was.

In spite of her need for expediency, she couldn't resist stopping several times to sniff or touch a particularly pretty or unusual bloom. How could someone who lived among such beauty write the horrific novels of battle and physical violence penned by J. El?

She climbed the stone steps to the high, wide porch and knocked on the elaborately carved door. She waited the appropriate length of time for someone to respond, then raised her hand to knock harder. She hesitated, studying the carvings on the door. They were winged horses. She looked closer. No. They were some sort of dragons. She was a fan of classic fantasy novels and had spent much of her preteen years determined to write such a novel herself. Then the full strength of her empathic abilities began to manifest at the onset of puberty, and she was called to serve The Collective. But she hadn't forgotten the dragons. Or maybe she had. These figures weren't exactly what she had pictured. She almost laughed at herself. Dragons weren't real. Obviously, the artisan who carved this door had just imagined them differently. She traced the figures with her fingertips, and the wood felt as though it warmed under her touch. An unusual sensation filled her, like a whisper too faint to distinguish. She jerked her hand back and shook herself. Her brain must be fuzzy with fatigue.

She knocked again and waited. Still no response. She tried to peer through one of the huge plate-glass windows that flanked the door, but she could only see her image reflected back at her. She knocked again, this time pounding with the heel of her hand. "Hello? Mr. El?" Her shout was met with silence and she let out a long breath. What should she do if this guy wasn't home? She took a deep breath and bellowed. "Hello? J. El?" She turned at the sound of a piercing cry. A hawk, apparently disturbed by her noise, leapt from his perch at the edge of the woods, and she watched him soar away.

Jael paused at the edge of the woods, watching the trespasser ignore the vehicle path that skirted the meadow to wade through the knee-high wildflowers in a direct path to her quarters. Her stealth wasn't necessary. She probably could have been riding an elephant and the woman wouldn't have noticed. If this was the singer-song writer who had been pestering her with persistent d-messages, she intended to scare a lifetime out of her so maybe the woman would finally leave her alone.

It wasn't obvious from this side of the meadow, but the terrain behind her quarters was a sheer drop of several hundred feet to a wide ledge. Then the mountain continued down at a much steeper slope than the side her visitor had traversed. Jael skirted along the edge of the woods and slipped over the precipice. Finding nearly invisible hand- and footholds, she free-climbed sideways along the rock face to the rear of her quarters. She hadn't had this much fun in nearly a lifetime and was reluctant to end it by entering her rear door and going through the house to confront the trespasser banging on her front door. So she crouched low beside the tall stone foundation and crept silently around to the front stairs.

"Hello? Mr. El?" Loud pounding. "Hello? J. El?"

Dragon's teeth. She'd never suspect one small woman could make that much racket. Was she trying to pound the door in? She was loud enough to wake a hibernating bear. It was certainly disturbing enough to make the hawk that was watching the meadow for a field-mouse meal decide to hunt elsewhere. She froze when the woman turned toward her as the predator screamed his irritation and rose into the air.

Alyssa turned back to the door, resigned to the fact that the bird might be the only inhabitant present. Should she wait on the chance that the property owner would return? What if he was away for days? She couldn't stay on his porch forever. She hadn't brought any provisions. Her feet throbbed and weariness seeped into her bones as she contemplated the hike back to her transport. She closed her eyes and rested her head against the wood. "Can't anybody hear me?" she muttered.

"I suspect anyone two mountains over can hear you."

Alyssa screamed and whirled to face the low voice that sounded only inches behind her and was slammed by a wave of aggression so strong and foreign to anything she'd ever experienced that she instinctively threw herself backward to escape the intimidating figure towering into her personal space. Her head rapped sharply against the hard door. Her vision swam and her knees buckled as everything faded to…blue?

Chapter Two

The town lay in shambles. The houses, churches, stores—rooftops that had two days ago filled the landscape—were a heap of splintered wood, crumbled bricks, and twisted metal as far as the eye could see. Nothing rose from the devastated landscape except smoke from the fires that burned freely because even the firehouses had been flattened.

The injured—those readily discovered—already had been transported to nearby towns that had escaped the band of tornadoes that had mowed a path of horrific destruction across the heartland of the Third Continent. Still, stunned survivors wandered through the rubble while others frantically dug through the debris, calling the names of missing loved ones or beloved family pets.

The suffering wouldn't stop here. Beyond the town's borders, miles and miles of fields planted with corn and wheat were flooded, the crops torn from the ground. There'd be no harvest in one of the world's greatest bread-belts. People worldwide would have less to eat.

Cyrus climbed onto the low wall, one of the few left standing, in front of the elementary school. Authorities had corralled a large group of parents there while a crane carefully lifted away several heavy beams impeding their search for the children who were in class when the tornadoes hit. He raised his voice to carry over the whine of the crane's motor.

"Earthquakes on our western coast and in the First Continent have claimed thousands of lives. Typhoons across the tropics have drowned entire island populations. Drought has killed more than half of the Second Continent's wildlife and made their human population dependent on the rest of us for food." He swept his arm in the direction of the sodden fields that surrounded the wreckage of the town. "And now we won't have enough food to share because our own children will soon go hungry, too."

Much of the crowd turned toward him, easily distracted from the slow process of determining which beam to lift first and how to best secure it to the crane.

"Authorities tell us these are freak weather disasters, accidental to a convergence of galactic events and our legacy of environmental abuse." He made eye contact with several. "I believed that, too, until the Appalachian mudslides claimed my son, and in my grief, I refused to accept his death as happenstance. I began to search for real answers." He paced the length of the wall. "Do you know what I found? There are reasons for these disasters. We can do something to right our world again."

He had their full attention now. "All of the ancient religions knew what we refuse to recognize. There is only one true power, one creator, one omnipotent being. And he is angry."

The crowd shifted uneasily, and a few people turned away shaking their heads.

"I am a professor of ancient culture. I know what I speak about." He paced the length of the wall. "This isn't the first time The One has evoked nature to purge the world of those who would deny his existence. The great flood and the plagues of Egypt were similarly recorded in the histories of nearly every one of the great religions." He tapped his finger against his temple. "Think. What does this tell you? These were real events of history. Deny it if you want, but ancient texts record prosperity following each period of natural disaster—but only after the people acknowledged there is only one true power, the maker of the purebloods at the beginning of time."

"Nutcase," one man said, turning back to watch as the crane slowly lifted a huge beam from the wreckage. Many of the others also dismissed Cyrus now that something was actually happening in the recovery effort.

Imbeciles. He flushed with anger. Cyrus bellowed at the group of waiting parents. "How many of your children are lost, likely dead in that rubble?" The shifting crowd stilled at his words. The beam was resettled out of way, and the crane's deafening engine shifted into a quiet idle. "Your babies are dead, and you are responsible. My son is dead, and I am responsible because I knew the ancient texts and yet paid homage to this fictitious Collective that mankind has dreamed up to justify straying from the hard truths. Heed my words. Continue to ignore the power of the truth, and the children you have left will pay for your refusal. The One is tired of waiting."

An older man separated from the group and hopped up next to Cyrus. He wrapped an arm around Cyrus's shoulders and gently, but firmly guided him off the wall. "Brother, I know you are grieving, but use this time to find your place in The Collective and peace in the knowledge that your son will live again."

Cyrus jerked away from the man, his anger roiling as he recognized the tribal-like tattoo that marked him as an Advocate of The Collective. "You speak blasphemy against The One." He turned to the crowd. "I am camped for the rest of the week in the park at town center. If you want to know more about the truth, if you want to save the lives of your remaining loved ones, come there tonight and I will tell you all that I know."

A wail rose from a woman at the edge of the crowd as the recovery team began carrying small bodies from a newly exposed classroom. Cyrus smiled to himself. He would see some of them tonight. This town was the fifth disaster he'd visited, and more joined his cause at each location. He'd hang around for a few more days to give the grieving time to respond.

His message was spreading exponentially. He had teams of followers who were sharing his views at three other disaster areas on this continent and several others attending an avalanche and a flooded city on two other continents. He would need to find a town soon where the global digital-network towers were working because he d-communicated with each team at least once a week.

As he approached the park, three women sat in camp chairs waiting while Ruth warmed last night's stew on the solar stove. She had been his first recruit after she lost her mate and two children in the same mudslide that claimed Thomas, and she had proved her worth many times over in the months that followed. Women were the toughest for him to sway toward his cause, but they listened to Ruth. Now, while he'd been at the school, she'd found three more seeking answers… answers that he could give them.

"That smells good," he said as he approached.

Ruth turned to him. "Cyrus, I didn't expect you back so soon. I was warming the leftover stew for a few new friends. They lived on the west side of town where everything was destroyed and are hungry."

He nodded to the women, their bleak faces streaked with grime and their clothes coated with dust of the destruction surrounding them. One was little more than a girl, maybe thirteen or fourteen years old. "We're happy to share. We have an extra tent and blankets, too. We are survivors as well, and you are welcome to join up with us." He smiled at Ruth to let her know he was pleased. They could offer comfort that the women wouldn't find in long, impersonal lines at the disaster refugee camp. Even better, Cyrus could offer them purpose when they had to feel like they had none.

Ruth beamed at the women. "I know it won't replace your loved ones, but you have a new family with us."

Chapter Three

Well, balls. She hadn't meant to scare the woman that badly. Jael stared down at the crumpled body for a long minute. When it became apparent she wasn't going to stir right away, she sighed and bent to gather her up.

At least six inches shorter than she and whip thin, she'd expected the woman would feel light as an arrow in her arms, but she was surprised at the quiver of energy that hummed through her as she carried her visitor inside and laid her on the lounger.

Not as young as she'd initially thought, the woman had short, spiky deep-red hair and pale skin, unusual among today's population. Her flawless cheeks streaked by a natural blush only a shade lighter than her full lips mesmerized Jael, but the flutter of thick eyelashes stopped her sudden impulse to test the softness of one creamy cheek. A soft moan and twitch of fingers followed, but the woman did not awaken.

Still, Jael recognized that reanimation was imminent, so she quickly logged a more professional assessment. She was slender but not frail. The long-fingered hands were soft. She definitely wasn't in a profession that required manual labor. She frowned. Maybe this wasn't the pesky musician. There were no calluses on her fingertips. She could be a pianist or flutist though.

The woman moaned again and rolled her head toward Jael. Why hadn't she noticed this before? The tattoo that wended its way from the woman's neck to her left temple was new, the skin around it still slightly irritated, but it was undeniably the mark of a Collective Advocate.

Jael's blood sang, her eyes fixed on the intricate design. Could it be? No. Surely they wouldn't have sent a novice to summon her. She was probably lost. Their newly anointed often wandered for a few years, offering service to random groups in need and learning what they needed to find their place in the world. That was probably the case of this neophyte. But then, she had specifically called out for her as she stood at the door. A gasp tore Jael's gaze from the tattoo, and she was swallowed by eyes the color of lush grass.

They both froze, and then the woman suddenly crab-crawled backward and would have fallen off the end of the lounger if Jael hadn't clamped her hands firmly around the woman's forearms to hold her in place.

"Let me go!" The woman struggled, bringing her feet up to kick hard at Jael's chest.

Pain shot through her unshielded breasts and numbed her arms, but she gritted her teeth and held tight. "Dragon's balls. Stop struggling. I won't hurt you. I'm trying to keep you from falling off the lounger and hurting yourself."

The woman stilled, but her eyes were wary. "Who are you?"

Jael cautiously relaxed her hold and sat back. She'd been leaning over the woman in the same way she had at the door. She hadn't intended to intimidate. Well, not once she carried her in the house. She rubbed a bruised nipple. "Shouldn't I be the one asking that question? You are here without an invitation."

"Alyssa." She touched the back of her head and frowned. "You assaulted me."

Not the pesky musician. She couldn't remember that person's name, but it wasn't Alyssa. "I did not."

"Then how do you explain the lump on the back of my head?"

"You did it to yourself when you backed into the door."

"Because you scared a lifetime out of me." Alyssa's green eyes radiated with unfocused intensity, then cleared. "Who are you?"

Jael wasn't sure if the whispered question was meant for her or if it was only a thought spoken aloud, but she saw no reason to withhold her identity. "You can stop trying to read me. I'm Jael and this is my mountain you're trespassing on."

"Mr. El?"

"J-a-e-l. Not a mister." She stood and rubbed her breast again. "Though I wished I was when you kicked me. It might not have hurt as much."

The splotches on Alyssa's cheeks flared a deeper red. "Sorry." She smiled slightly. "You're obviously not a man. I was asking if you're the author—generally assumed to be male—who writes as J-period-E-l."

"That's me." Jael went to the food-prep area and pulled a cold pack from the storage. She cracked the activation capsule and returned to the common room to offer it to Alyssa. "For the swelling. It will numb the headache, too."

"I'm fine," Alyssa said, staring at the cold pack but not taking it.

Jael grabbed her hand and put the cold pack in it. "You're broadcasting pain so strongly, it's almost making my head hurt."

Alyssa narrowed her eyes but obediently slipped it behind her head, where it rested on the back of the lounger. "You're an empath, too?"

"Telepath. You read emotions, I read thoughts. By the way, I have to congratulate you on your colorful and original curses."

Alyssa scowled. "It's very poor manners to read someone's thoughts without their consent."

"Hard not to hear your thoughts. You just chatter away in that pretty head of yours." Jael shook her head. "Didn't they teach you to shield at all?"

Alyssa stiffened. "I know how to shield. I wasn't doing it before because I thought I was alone. And now, it makes my headache worse to shield."

Alyssa's thoughts went quiet, but Jael could see that pain still dulled her eyes.

"Don't. Wait for the swelling to subside and you can shield without pain. If your mind chatter becomes too noisy, I can block you out." Alyssa closed her expressive eyes, but the quiet remained. "Really," Jael said more gently. "It's okay." She took a chance and raised a block she thought Alyssa could sense. Alyssa's face relaxed. "Better?"

Alyssa sighed and slowly opened her eyes. "Infinitely."

Jael felt unreasonably pleased that her guest's pain had eased a little. She hadn't completely forgotten how to be civil. "I have some ginger. I usually just chew it, but I can make some tea if you'd like."

Alyssa stared up at her host and realized those eyes were the last image she could recall before she hit her head. They were the brilliant blue of a cloudless sky. She'd have thought it a glimpse of the hereafter except for the fierce anger she had felt when that blue filled her vision. Then, when she awoke, the same cerulean view was eerily tranquil. She shivered at the contrast. Could she trust the calm? Or was it the eye of a storm ready to unleash again?

"It's just tea. I won't poison you."

"You said you wouldn't listen in on my thoughts."

"I don't have to listen in. They're written on your face." The smile was little more than a crinkling of skin around the eyes and a slight tightening of the cheeks, but Alyssa felt her amusement.

Alyssa smiled as much as the pounding in her head would allow. "I'm glad you find me entertaining."

One eyebrow rose.

"Your eyes speak as loudly as my face." The words were barely past her lips when she regretted them. Jael's eyes instantly shuttered.

"I'll get that tea for you," she said, striding back to the prep.

Alyssa watched her cross the room. Tall and leanly muscled, Jael moved like a big, sleek cat. Her blond mane draped carelessly across her shoulders. Her T-shirt was a dull olive, and the cargo pants that hung loosely from her hips were the same, only a few shades darker. Her hands and bare feet were dirty, and Alyssa wondered if she had been the invisible stalker she had sensed in the forest.

While Jael washed a root of ginger to crush and boil with a few other tea leaves, Alyssa took advantage of the silence between them to close her eyes and empty her aching head. Even in the midst of her relaxed meditation, she felt Jael move closer and opened her eyes to accept the mug of steaming tea she held out. Jael sat on the low table next to the lounger to face her.

"Thank you." She took a few sips.

"I need to look at your head to make sure you didn't break the skin."

Alyssa nodded and turned. Jael was surprisingly gentle and quick.

"The skin is intact, but you have a good-sized swelling. You should be careful not to exert yourself for a couple of days, and let me know immediately if you feel nauseated or dizzy or if your headache gets worse."

Alyssa turned to resettle on the lounger, hyperaware that Jael's legs were mere inches from her own. She'd expected her to move back out of her personal space and sit somewhere else now that the inspection of her wound was done, but Jael didn't. She looked up, then glanced away from the intense stare. "You're wondering why I'm here."

Jael canted her head, then nodded slowly. "That is the big question, yes. But I'm more immediately curious about your empathic ability."

Alyssa stared into her cup. There were very few, even among the temple elders, who were privy to the extent of her power. "I'm not sure what you mean."

"I felt you projecting the minute you climbed over my gate, which we'll talk about later. A closed gate means keep out, not climb over."

"You're a telepath. It's not surprising that you could hear me. I'm probably the only other human on your mountain."

"But I didn't just 'hear,' I felt you. I'm not empathic, but I've lived enough lifetimes to recognize the sensation. When you were in the forest, I felt you deliberately project."

"You must be mistaken." The denial died on her tongue. The eyes that now held hers were old, centuries old. She was but a fledgling in comparison and instinctively lowered her eyes.

"And, even though I blocked, you could detect me. I've known one other empath who could project emotions, but even he couldn't do that."

Alyssa had learned early that she should keep the extent of her talents secret. Once someone knew, they never again trusted their own feelings around her. They avoided touching her for fear she would dig into and manipulate their emotions. She didn't want to chance how they'd react if they discovered she didn't need to physically touch them to influence their feelings. "I would never misuse the gifts I've been given. I'm sworn to serve The Collective. I was just scared and protecting myself. For all I knew, it was a beast stalking me."

I've been called a beast before, but the lady meant it as a compliment.

Startled, Alyssa realized the whisper in her mind wasn't intended as an intrusion, but a joke to defuse her defensive response.

She was only seven when she was sent home from school with a note telling her parents that she was a distraction to the other students and should be taken to The Collective temple. Even in this age of enlightenment, only a small percentage of the population actually manifested special abilities. Those who did elicited a wide range of response—fear, skepticism, reverence. She'd cried herself to sleep those first nights in the temple dormitory. But before long, her birth family became nothing but an uneasy memory. She realized she fit much better into this new family where everyone had special talents. And, although they'd just met, Jael was part of the same family.

She smiled at the jest and shook her head. "I'm sorry. It was such a relief to be out here where there was no one. The freedom to drop my shields without being inundated by others' emotions was too tempting." She drained her cup, realizing that her headache had already begun to ease, and raised her eyes to Jael's again. "That's why you live on this mountain, isn't it? You must be swamped with people's thoughts the way I am with their emotions. You've found peace here."

Jael nodded. "It's one reason."

They regarded each other.

"You have a message for me?"

Alyssa blinked. Did she? "I…I don't know. Honored Advocate Han sent me." She reached back and winced when her fingers found the swelling on her tender skull. "But I don't remember what I'm supposed to tell you." She shook her head to clear it, and her stomach roiled with the movement. She groaned and held her head. "Bad move. I think I might be sick."

Jael watched the color drain from Alyssa's face. The tattoo along the left side of her face seemed to vibrate against the pale skin. "Sit back for a minute and close your eyes." She grasped Alyssa's slender wrist and found the pressure point. "This is an old sailor's remedy for seasickness. There's a trigger in your wrist that will relieve nausea. Rather than constantly swabbing the decks of vomit when they transported seasick Roman troops, the sailors would show the soldiers how to place a pebble there and then bind the wrist tightly with a strip of cloth to keep the pressure constant."

After several minutes, color flooded back into Alyssa's cheeks and Jael released her.

"Thank you. I feel much better," she said, though her emerald eyes had clouded gray-green with fatigue. "The message is, um…" She closed her eyes for a few seconds, then looked up at Jael. "Look inside to learn your destiny. That's the message. I'm guessing you know what it means."

"That's all he said?"

Alyssa nodded.

"Tell me what happened when he gave you the message."

"I don't see how—"

"Humor me."

Alyssa rubbed at her temples. "I recall sitting on the garden bench with Advocate Han while he explained how to get here." She blinked several times, frowning. "He took my hand and said I was to deliver an important message. I thought that was odd because he rarely touches anyone. Then he was telling me to be careful and come directly here." Her eyes were apologetic. "I'm sure that isn't much help."

Jael drummed her fingers against her thigh. She should have realized. Of course they wouldn't have revealed The Guard to her. That secret was held so tightly even very few of the priests knew. "You wouldn't remember, because he didn't tell you. He embedded the message in your mind when he took hold of your hand."

Alyssa stared at her. "Embedded—"

"—in your subconscious," Jael said. "It's an unbreakable encryption because I'm the only one with the ability to retrieve it."

"Retrieve it?" Alyssa frowned. "How exactly?"

"The same way Han stuck it in your head."

Alyssa's brow furrowed with this information, and Jael carefully lowered her shields, allowing Alyssa to feel the sincerity of her intent.

"We can wait until tomorrow, after you're rested." *But you won't even feel as much as this whisper in your head.*

Alyssa smiled at her telepathic reassurance and shook her head, more carefully this time. "It could be urgent."

Her fingers were soft in Jael's callused hands. She reached up to touch her even-softer cheek. "Close your eyes. You can trust me."

Alyssa nodded slowly and settled back into the lounger and took a deep breath.

Jael closed her eyes, too, and began to search for the embedded thought. She moved quickly, skimming as shallow as possible because she didn't intend to invade Alyssa's privacy. She lingered, however, over Alyssa's memory of her walking to the prep to make the tea. She smiled. Alyssa was definitely female-oriented. She'd spent a significant time checking out Jael's gluteus maximus. She reluctantly resisted reviewing Alyssa's entire memory since she had arrived on the mountain and moved deeper. She immediately recognized Advocate Han's imprint and plunged in.

The Calling has already begun. The Collective Council awaits you.

She ran through the message several times and then carefully backed out. She'd need a bit of subterfuge to facilitate her departure.

"Your injury's a bit worse than I expected, so I need to prepare another dose for the swelling." She wasn't capable of detecting physical problems as she plundered through thoughts and memories, so she carefully shielded the lie from Alyssa. She sorted through various small bottles in the storage. She wouldn't bother with the pretense of tea this time, just a potent dose that would go down in a gulp and work quickly.

"Is everything okay?" Alyssa asked when she returned with the small glass of dark, syrupy liquid.

"Drink this. It will make you groggy, but you need to sleep to allow your brain to heal."

Alyssa eyed her. "How do I know you aren't just killing the messenger?"

"I promised that I wouldn't poison you, and I always keep my promises. It's simply a stronger anti-inflammatory mixed in amaretto to make it more palatable. But don't sip it. Toss it." She gestured as if she were gulping down the medicine in one swallow to demonstrate how it should be done.

Alyssa hesitated and then followed her instructions. She smacked her lips. "Very tasty."

Jael found the lip-smacking and the way the liquor flushed Alyssa's cheeks darker very distracting. She stood and took the glass to rinse it. She needed a bit of distance between them. She was well past the age when her ovaries did her thinking and had no idea why this neophyte was affecting her so. Perhaps it was just the adrenaline triggered by the message. It must be sharpening her other senses. Or maybe she'd been alone on this mountain too long.

When she returned again to the common room, Jael paced in front of the mantle, glancing occasionally at Alyssa, who appeared comfortably—attractively—sprawled on the lounger. Her eyes were drooping, but she could not summon Specter until Alyssa was soundly asleep. She wrenched her thoughts back to the task at hand. She hadn't communed with The Collective Council since she came of age and bonded in this lifetime. Her blood quickened at the thought, or was it because she could feel Alyssa watching her?

"So, did you find your message? Is everything okay?"

Was it? How could she explain that she'd spent many, many lifetimes in anticipation of this day? It was her soul's purpose.

She had suspected this would be her last incarnation before she was absorbed into The Collective, but now she was sure. She had been born a warrior many centuries ago when armies fought with sword and arrow, then reincarnated each time to more wars, the last fought with high-tech weapons fired from sterile distances. Bloody and brutal as all battles were, she had missed the dark-and-light certainty of life and death, good and evil. This century of peace had been disorienting for her. Her only battles in her last life had been against fires, hot and deadly but an unthinking enemy. The strategy for victory was predictably the same and soon grew monotonous. Still, it wasn't as bad as this incarnation where her battles were simply memories put to record for others to read. She had been treading water, training every day for war in a time of complete harmony.

All that had instantly changed with one neophyte of an Advocate and one embedded message.

"I need to go somewhere for a few hours. You'll have to stay at least until morning or until you've recovered sufficiently."

"You're leaving me here alone?" Alyssa's words were slurred by the sedative.

The Calling has already begun.

"You won't be alone long. I have friends who will be arriving." Her last words were lost, because Alyssa was fast asleep.

Jael gathered her up again, enjoying the loll of Alyssa's head against her shoulder, and carried her to the bedroom. She slid her under the light covers. She stood to go and then pulled the covers back. The Advocate would be more comfortable sleeping in her tunic and underwear. She unfastened Alyssa's linen pants and slid them down the well-muscled legs. Jael sucked in the scent of her and then steeled herself against it. It was a good thing that Tan would be arriving soon. She apparently needed a jump to clear her head for the task ahead. She pulled the covers up but allowed herself one indulgence. She sat on the side of the bed and brushed her fingers through the dark flames of Alyssa's silky spikes. She bent close enough to feel her warm breath, sorely tempted to taste her amaretto-sweetened lips. A gift stolen, sure enough, and a theft she'd never commit.

There'd be time later for the spoils of war. The Calling had barely begun.

CHAPTER FOUR

The flare she tossed skyward glinted against the rock face behind the wide ledge, and she shot out a telepathic imperative to accompany the fiery signal. She tugged at the neck of her battle skin and brushed a speck of dirt from the red emblem emblazoned across the chest of the silvery tunic. Good thing the material could stretch to triple its original size. She hadn't worn it since her bonding, and she was but a juvenile yearling then. She was a foot taller now and carried a lot more muscle.

She stepped back against the rock when the air began to pulse in great gusts that whipped her hair about her face. She mentally berated herself. Braiding back her hair was a small detail, but she'd spent many lifetimes schooling her mind to be methodical despite the circumstances. A minuscule detail forgotten could get an entire army killed.

His landing was a muted *swoosh*, minus the usual dramatic show. He had heard as well as seen her summons and now stood before her, his eyes bright and body quivering with anticipation.

"Our destination is the portal. We have been summoned to The Collective," she said unnecessarily. His kind communicated in pictures, and he would read the scene that formed in her mind rather than understand her words. But she needed to hear her own voice, to reassure herself this was real and not some dream.

Her destiny was beginning to unfold.

❖

The portal was a tall peak several mountains away from hers that appeared as if its tip had been lopped off by some great sword to create a circular platform some thirty meters in circumference. Leading up to it on all sides was at least a klick of steep, loose shale so that the only access to this portal was by air.

Jael dismounted and took a minute to absorb its magnificence. The moon was only a sickle, but the velvet black sky above her pulsed with a billion stars. Olympus, she had jokingly labeled this portal years ago. She had been there many times to meditate and occasionally received a telepathic communication concerning a task for The Guard to complete, but she'd never been summoned. The only time they'd ever appeared to her was at her bonding, and she wondered if they would appear tonight.

She knelt on one knee, raised her arms, and spoke to the stars. "I am Jael, First Warrior of The Guard. You have summoned me."

One by one they began to manifest in a semicircle around her, and Specter protectively extended his great wings behind her. They materialized as human images, nearly flesh but flickering slightly in the starlight with each movement of their limbs. When the seventh and last of The Collective appeared, she lowered her arms and her head. "I am here to serve."

"Rise." They spoke in an odd chorus, one voice but many.

Jael stood and studied them. All robed in flowing gauze, they were genderless, ageless composites of their multiple past lives. One robed in a faint tint of green was square-jawed and bearded but had dark curls that draped over full breasts. Another, robed in silver, had a youthful, heart-shaped face and severely short, gray hair.

She recognized Saran-Sung-Josh—at least those were the names of the entity's most recent lives—soul mate to her cousin Danielle, the Second Warrior. The Elder's gaze lingered over her like a caress. Even in this spiritual realm, the essence of Saran-Sung-Josh was drawn to Jael's physical resemblance to Second. She was honored that perhaps her presence brought a few minutes of comfort while the mates were currently parted. At the same time, the reminder that she'd never found a soul mate in all her incarnations pierced her. It was rare for a soul to have no match, but she told herself that it was best because of the secret and dangerous lives she had led.

The Collective hummed in a nearly undetectable expression of empathy for the separated mates, but Saran-Sung-Josh spoke for them. "Glorious will be the day when all is as it should be, and we are reunited."

Jael wasn't sure if the Elder spoke of Second or of The Collective belief that all souls were just shards of one soul. If complete harmony could ever be achieved on the physical plane, those shards would reunite as one soul on the spiritual plain. What would happen after that was unclear. The end of time, Elysium, a new shattering to restart the chaos of life and opportunity to return it to order? But she was a soldier, a warrior who followed orders and did not question, so she echoed the mantra. "Glorious be the day." Specter, apparently appeased by her calm, folded his wings. "How might The Guard serve you?"

The Elder with the gray crew cut stepped forward. Jael recognized this soul, too, from previous lifetimes. Morgaine-Viktor-Paola had lived more lives than most before ascending—experiencing the physical realm as a healer, a general, a politician, and a spiritual leader, among others. "There is a significant tear in The Collective fabric, and it is growing. It already has ripped far beyond what The Guard could repair."

"In the chaos of a natural misfortune, a badly born has escaped the watch of The Guard and is swaying weakened souls toward ancient legends of an omnipotent power who deals out punishment and reward to those who are obedient," Saran-Sung-Josh said. "This is a doctrine very dangerous to The Collective because it is based on conformity and discourages the diversity of parts that make us one whole."

As leader of The Guard, Jael was well versed in The Collective doctrine. "Why not just send The Guard after this one soul?"

The constant underlying hum of The Collective rose to sound like the murmur of a thousand voices. A third Elder with Scandinavian blue eyes, the dark complexion of a Moor, and a smooth, hairless skull raised a hand to quiet the din. "The recent cycle of the sun has greatly affected natural phenomena, presenting many trials for those currently existing in the physical world. The Collective and its earthly counterparts have been constantly engaged in arranging relief for the survivors and receiving those whose earthly existence has been ended by the mishaps."

Morgaine-Viktor-Paola nodded. "This badly born of whom we speak went unnoticed for too long. He has raised a plague of followers, and they are spreading with the speed of an airborne virus. He calls himself The Prophet and advocates the old, misguided practice of burial rather than cremation."

"So, the only solution is incineration of these badly born, so that they can reincarnate pure again and rejoin The Collective," Saran-Sung-Josh said. "Since the first of your lineage discovered and bonded thousands of years ago, it has been the duty of The Guard to keep track of the badly born and incinerate their bodies upon death. It is an unthinkable duty in a time of peace, but this prophet's army is so many in number, we no longer have the luxury of waiting for each to die naturally. The Guard must incinerate them on sight. Are you up to the task?"

Jael stiffened. Did The Collective Council doubt The Guard? "I should not need to remind you that The Guard all have been warriors for many lifetimes. We have seen and done much worse."

Saran-Sung-Josh bowed slightly in apology. "As mate to your second, I know that better than most. I did not mean to question the ability or loyalty of The Guard, only to express concern for the emotional toll demanded by the task."

"It is our destiny," Jael said. There would be no room for regret.

"The numbers joining this cult on the Third and Fourth Continents already are greater than The Guard of seven can stop. The Calling has been issued," Morgaine-Viktor-Paola said. "The point of reckoning will be in the southern portion of the Sierra Madre so that you are close to a nest."

"While The Collective has grown strong during these years of embracing diversity, it has greatly diluted the lineage from which I can draw warriors," Jael said. She was already forming lists in her mind. "It will take months to screen and train an army. In that time, the badly born will grow in strength and number. The Guard stands ready now."

The seventh Elder, whose long dreadlocks matched stark-white pupil-less eyes, spoke in a language so ancient even Jael didn't recognize it. Five of the council bowed their heads in respect, while the sixth translated.

"A protracted mission with a small force would prolong the wound on our peace. The threads of your destiny are entwined with what is to come, First Warrior. It is a difficult path, but you will not take it alone. Just this day, you have greeted the one who will take up the mantle of duty with you."

"The novice Advocate? She wasn't just a message vessel?" That was just plain insulting, not to mention distracting. "I have a war to plan. How can a first-life with no experience do anything but get in the way? Maybe you've been away from the physical realm too long and have forgotten a few things."

Morgaine-Viktor-Paola growled and a great pressure forced Jael to her knees. Specter screamed a warning and two others moved toward him. He struggled against an invisible force that had pinned his wings. "All of those lifetimes and you have yet to learn humility."

"Forgive me," Jael choked out against the force holding her. She could not let Specter be harmed while defending her ego.

The ancient Elder raised a hand and all stopped. The ancient spoke again, waiting after each sentence for its translation.

"The Advocate is a first-life, indeed, but her gifts are unique and surprisingly powerful. It is not clear, even to The Collective, what her role might be, only that her destiny is closely entwined with yours. Let this flow as it will, First Warrior. It is not a river you need to dam and control."

Jael bowed her head. "As you command."

The night was suddenly silent, and Jael realized the constant hum of The Collective had ceased. She wondered if she was dismissed, but when she looked up, they all remained. Their eyes were on the ancient rather than her. This time, the ancient spoke in a language she understood. "Open your mind, First Warrior. You will need to look through both old and new eyes for what is coming. We are stronger together."

Their manifestations seemed to go thin, stars punching through their filmy essence, until only a hint of the ancient's image remained. The dismissal was again the chorus that first greeted her. "Rise and go as commanded."

CHAPTER FIVE

Alyssa rolled onto her back and blinked slowly. Sunlight that flooded in through the large window was softened by the warm pine planks of the floor, walls, and ceiling as she took a minute to orient herself. Since she'd traveled nearly half the continent to get here, she was no longer startled when she awoke in a strange place. The pillow, which smelled of rain and pine and musk, conjured an image of her host that made her hum as she stretched—a corn-silk blond mane falling across broad shoulders and buttocks she would like to put her hands on. Hmmm. Something stirred in her peripheral vision and she clamped down on the lascivious rumination. God, she didn't broadcast that, did she?

As if materializing from her thoughts, a tall figure unfolded from a chair in the corner of the room, boots scuffing against the wood floor as she crossed to the bed.

"You're awake."

She had the same athletic build and mane of blond hair, but the eyes were disappointingly brown—a rich milk chocolate but not vibrant blue. Alyssa tried to speak, but only a strangled sound came from her dry throat. Her tongue felt like it was glued to the top of her mouth.

The woman went to a table and poured a tumbler of water, then offered it to her.

"Jael said she'd doped you. That stuff dries your mouth out like a desert."

Alyssa sat up carefully, even though her nausea and headache from the evening before were gone, and drank deeply. "Thank you," she said, once her tongue could function again.

"She said you had a head injury. How do you feel?"

"I seem to be fine. No headache." She eyed the woman. They were nearly twins, except for something completely different—how could she describe it? The air vibrated around Jael, like she was a coiled spring set to release at any minute, even though her emotions were carefully shielded. This woman's emotions were an open book, calm and steady. Alyssa liked her immediately. "You talked to her?"

"I heard from her. I'm not telepathic, but I can hear her in my head." The woman smiled and mock-shivered. "I hate it when she does that." She extended her hand. "I'm Danielle, but everybody calls me Second. Jael is my cousin."

"I'm Alyssa." She returned Second's handshake. "You don't have to be telepathic for her to hear your thoughts," she said absently as she looked about for her pants.

"Much to her consternation, she says I'm too thick-skulled for her to read me." She grinned. "It's actually one of my talents—having a natural shield against any mind probe. Unlike other gifted who have to learn to put up shields, I had to learn to drop mine." She produced Alyssa's travel bag from the floor at the end of the bed and handed it to her. "I drove your transport up from the gate and brought your bag in. Her latrine is through that door."

Latrine? It took a minute, but Alyssa guessed that Second was referring to the personal facility. "Thank you. I could use a shower."

"Then I'll leave you to it." She went to the door. "Jael lives off pro-chow and packaged meals, but I can actually cook and brought some real food with me. So join me when you're done."

Her last meal had been the previous morning. "I am starving, but I'd like to get clean first."

"Not a problem. The food should be ready by the time you are."

"I have sufficient meals in cold storage to feed an army. You didn't need to bring food," Jael said.

Second didn't turn from the eggs and vegetables she was scrambling together. "You're back. Good."

"I'm not cleaning up after you. I eat prepackaged meals because I hate the wasted time cooking and cleaning."

"No one will be eating that cardboard you call nourishment as long as I'm here."

"Fine." Jael leaned over her cousin's shoulder and inhaled the spicy scent of jalapeños and peppers added to the eggs. Her mouth watered. "I have some goat cheese in cold storage."

"Found it already. Go wash up in the guest latrine. It's almost ready, and your visitor is showering in your latrine upstairs." Second opened the warmer and added the contents of the skillet to a large pan filled with the same concoction. A long loaf of flat bread warmed next to it.

"Great morning, you've made enough for an army."

"Furcho, Raven, Michael, and Diego arrived last night. I thought you might have seen them when you came up. They're in the bunks downstairs. Michael and Furcho arrived just after midnight, Raven around three a.m., and Diego trailed in at dawn. Unlike you, some people require sleep to function, so I thought we could eat, and then I'll leave the rest in the warmer for when they stir."

"Tan?"

"Should get here sometime this morning."

Jael was tired and had so much to do. It was a relief to have Second around to take care of the details while she worked out the bigger picture. She grabbed her cousin by the nape and gave her an affectionate squeeze. "It feels good to have you at my side again."

Second grinned at her. "Aw. That's sweet. You've missed me."

Jael released her hold and cuffed Second gently on the back of the head. "I'm still not cleaning up after you."

"Stars. If that tastes as good as it smells, I'll be happy to clean the prep afterward."

Jael scowled at the voice, flashing on the bumbling, mumbling girl that had stumbled up her corridor yesterday…the first-life that the council insisted she drag along on this important mission. But when she turned, her mind filled with the woman and last night's temptation to steal a kiss. The red spikes of hair were a rakish contrast to the soft oval of her face, her creamy skin, and her rose-splotched cheeks. Her lithe frame was covered in a dark-blue, body-hugging unitard visible under a sheer light-blue tunic. Dragon dung, she was too tired to deal with this distraction. "You two eat. I've got a lot to prepare. I'll shower upstairs then be in my study." She paused at the stairway and then turned back to Second. "We'll be deploying in a few days for an extended time. I don't know how long. Can you make indefinite arrangements for John to watch over my mountain?"

"Consider it done."

Alyssa stared after Jael. "Something I said?"

"Nah. That's just Jael. She's probably tired after being gone all night. She'll be better after some food and a nap." Second filled three plates and then handed two to Alyssa and pointed to the eating area. She followed with two cups of citrus juice but didn't sit when Alyssa did. "Go ahead and start. I'll be right back. If I leave a plate of food on her desk, she'll eat it after she showers."

Alyssa's stomach growled as Second bounded up the stairs, and her polite intention to wait evaporated. She dug into her food and groaned with appreciation at the first mouthful. Stars, it was good. She considered the situation as she ate. She wasn't certain what the day would hold. Should she leave now that her message was delivered? Maybe not right away. She would eat, then complete her daily meditative exercise and figure out what to do next. To be truthful, she wanted to hang around. Something was afoot, and the excitement she was reading off the visitors sleeping restlessly downstairs was much more enticing than returning to the monotony of the temple compound. The most exciting thing to happen there was when a black snake got in the chicken coop and scared a novice half to death.

As promised, Second reappeared almost immediately and settled down to her own breakfast.

"This food is amazing."

"Thank you. I work for the Ministry Nutrition Council. It's a losing battle, but I don't believe healthy food has to be tasteless."

Alyssa swallowed her last bite and put her utensil down. "Can you tell me what's going on? I know there are more people here now, downstairs."

Second raised an eyebrow but didn't question her statement. She pointed to her own temple to indicate the area of Alyssa's tattoo. "I can see that you're an Advocate of The Collective, but I don't know if or where you fit into all this. So, I'll leave it up to Jael to decide what to share."

"What do you think she's doing up there?"

Second chewed, her eyes twinkling as she regarded her. "She's probably wolfing down the food I left her, and then she'll go sit on her balcony." Second swallowed and grinned. "She claims to be communicating—she's telepathic, you know—but I suspect she's just mastered sleeping in a lotus position." She winked at Alyssa. "Maybe she's up there checking your references."

Alyssa frowned. "I'm not aware that I've applied for a position here. I'm not sure, after delivering a message to her, why I'm still here. Should I stay or return to the temple?"

"Jael always says you should get all information available before making decisions."

That was enough of an invitation for her. "I guess I should hang around for a while longer then."

Second finished her meal quickly and began to collect their plates, but Alyssa stopped her.

"You prepared the meal. I'll clean up."

"How about you wash up the dishes while I inventory the storage? I need to know what we have on hand, so I'll know what we need to procure when Jael lets us in on what's up."

"Okay."

While they worked, they talked about the simple diet Alyssa was accustomed to at the temple compound, and Second ranted about the provisions shared with lesser food-producing continents. Protein chow could sustain life, but living should be more than just surviving.

Alyssa put away the clean dishes while half-listening to Second's running dialogue from the pantry. Unlike the enigmatic Jael, Second had no shields around her emotions. She was welcoming and self-assured, easy to like. Still, Alyssa's mind wandered to the floor above them. She tried to imagine Jael in her private study. Was she sitting at the desk, sending out d-messages on her digital processor?

Second emerged from the storage, muttering the last item of her list into the individual communicator strapped to her wrist. "Other than some fresh fruit and vegetables, there isn't much she doesn't have. But I have some arrangements to make." She tapped a few commands into the IC. "The others won't be up for a few more hours, so I'm going to make a quick trip into town. Make yourself at home."

"The bedroom I slept in is hers, isn't it? I should move my things somewhere else."

"Take the first room on the left. It's actually mine, but I never stay in it. I prefer bunking downstairs with the others."

"If you're sure. I don't want to put anyone out."

Second smiled, but a wave of deep sadness washed over Alyssa. "You're not putting anyone out. I don't stay there anymore."

"Thank you. You're very generous." Alyssa instinctively projected an uplifting feeling, and Second seemed to brighten again.

"Well, I'm off. Should be back in a couple of hours."

Alyssa opened the tea pouch she'd brought with her and idly stared into the common area while she waited for a cup to steep. Hmm. She was alone for the first time. Second did say to make herself at home, right? She glanced at the stairway. Jael said she was going to shower and then work, so she probably wouldn't be coming downstairs for a while. Her cheeks heated at an unbidden image of Jael naked, standing under a spray of water. She consciously replaced the image with one of Jael sitting behind a desk, talking on a communicator. She did use communicators, didn't she, even though she was telepathic? Her curiosity was a nagging itch.

Her gaze wandered. A person's home usually held clues about them. The three-tiered structure was beautiful, but efficiency was apparently a design priority. A huge stone fireplace took up one wall, but it was fitted with an insert to produce the greatest amount of heat from the smallest amount of fuel. Solar and wind power were the norm since fossil and nuclear fuel had been outlawed for environmental reasons, but the solar windows on this house were so large, she'd bet they collected and stored enough energy to run three houses, even without the wind turbine that sat on the edge of the large meadow out front.

The hand-hewn furniture was handsomely crafted, but fairly Spartan and functional. She wondered if Jael might have been the artisan who constructed it. Although using wood was no longer common, she suspected the surrounding forest provided more than enough deadfall to fashion furniture and have an endless supply of fuel.

So, none of this was particularly unique. It was unusual, however, that instead of holograms or decorative tapestries, a wide variety of ancient weapons adorned every wall—spears, bows, crossbows, swords, and knives. A shirt of mail hung next to a medieval mace. Only the projectile weapons from the centuries immediately before the Great War of Religions were missing. All had been ordered destroyed in the aftermath of that devastating destruction. Alyssa supposed the collection was part of Jael's profession as a historic-war novelist. She touched the gleaming blade of a long, sickle-shaped sword and shuddered. It was very sharp. She couldn't imagine why anyone would want to dwell on war, but perhaps Jael's books were a necessary reminder of those atrocities so that they never happened again. Still, who would want all these dangerous weapons in their house?

Alyssa discreetly peeked into cabinets and opened doors, finding an electrical junction for the solar windows in a room apparently meant for shedding outerwear and boots, judging from the items hanging on pegs and neatly lined against the wall. A door on the opposite end led outdoors. A series of tall, narrow storage units were built into the wall, curiously locked in a building that didn't appear to have any other locks…anywhere. The prep, common, and dining areas were all part of one large open room, but a door between the stone hearth and the stairway led to a room filled with books and maps. It could have been a study or library, except there was no desk or comfortable chair for reading. In the center of the room were seven straight-back chairs around a long table covered by a world map.

In fact, Alyssa realized there also were seven chairs at the dining table and seating for seven in the common area. If she returned to the outerwear storage, she'd bet the stars she would find seven of those locked cabinets. Seven was a sacred number in The Collective, but not even the priests at the temple were that obsessive about it. Maybe her host had some type of mental peculiarity. A lot of the gifted minority had eccentric quirks that were a side effect of their talent.

She opened the last unexplored door and gasped. It was as if the earth had dropped out from under her—the mountain, at the very least. The gentle slope of the meadow in front gave no clue that the house was perched at the top of a sheer precipice. The majesty of the mountains before her stole her very breath. She could think of nothing more completing than having her morning tea on this wide deck every dawn. Oh, her tea. She'd forgotten it.

When she turned to retrieve it, a slight movement caught her eye. A floor above her and five meters to her left, Jael sat on a platform only a meter in diameter. The window at her back was open. Alyssa's heart stuttered. There was no safety rail, not even a lip on the edges of the platform, and nothing but a thousand-meter drop if she fell from her perch. But Jael sat cross-legged, her hands resting on her knees, utterly still. The movement that had drawn Alyssa's attention was the wind rippling across her loose cotton shirt. Jael's sculpted face was tilted up to the sun, her eyes closed, but Alyssa wondered if she had sensed her. It really didn't matter. She felt like an intruder regardless.

She quietly went inside. Her tea had grown cold so she poured it down the drain and washed the cup. She stared at the tea leaves as she washed them from the sink. She didn't know why Jael unsettled her so. She needed to find her focus.

Since she didn't want to disturb her host, she wandered out front. There was a wide expanse of thick grass before wildflowers took over the meadow, and she stood in the center of it and closed her eyes. She breathed in the thick scent of sun-warmed pine, extended her arms before her to form a circle, and relaxed her knees. It took some time to empty her mind of this mountain and the questions that were as plentiful as the flowers around her. It could have been a few minutes or a half hour later, but without a conscious thought she began the precise, flowing movements that both centered and energized her life force, her chi.

Eighty-eight movements later, she took a deep breath and stilled. She felt absolute peace. And she felt that she was not alone. She calmly opened her eyes to the glare of the sun and turned. Jael sat on the front steps, silently watching her. Her blue eyes, jewels in the sunlight, were unreadable, but Alyssa felt something she couldn't put words to. It was as though Jael had slipped into her pool of calm without causing even a ripple and they were sharing its serenity.

"Hi," she said softly.

"Your execution is near perfect," Jael said quietly.

Alyssa moved closer. "Advocate Han taught me when I was young and still struggling to sort and block the barrage of emotions from other people. I had to learn focus before I could learn to shield, and the exercise helps me do that." She gestured to the steps where Jael sat. "May I?"

Jael nodded and Alyssa sat beside her.

"Han is a good teacher," Jael said.

"You know him?"

"He taught me the same exercise." The curl at the corner of Jael's generous mouth hinted at a smile. "But it took me more than one lifetime to get it right. You must be an apt student."

She flushed at the compliment and demurred. "More like a desperate one." She stared down at her hands. "I had no clue as to how I could stop absorbing every emotion around me. My ability to feel others grew as I got older. The noise—happy, sad, angry, joyful—was deafening by the time I was eleven. I was nearly insane with it. I couldn't sleep or eat most of the time. My parents were at a loss until a teacher told them to take me to the temple." She stared out over the meadow. "I begged them not to leave me there. Then Advocate Han took my hands in his and made it stop." The meadow's riot of color blurred, and she blinked back tears. "I remember weeping with relief. He thanked my parents and assured them I would be fine." She looked up at Jael. "And I was. I am."

Jael nodded again but didn't reply. They sat in comfortable silence.

It still bothered her that she couldn't feel Jael's emotions. Other than Advocate Han, she'd never met anyone who could shut her out completely if she opened to read them. Even so, Jael's presence steadied her. Perhaps it was her old soul. She felt Jael stiffen and was surprised to realize that she had been unconsciously leaning against her shoulder. Alyssa rarely touched people. Children, maybe, but not other adults. It was harder to shield against their emotions if she touched them. She discreetly shifted away, pretending to reach down and scratch her ankle.

Jael stood, staring across the meadow and into the woods. She couldn't feel Jael's emotions, but the snapping of their nascent bond was like a slap. She grappled for something to keep her from pulling away. She had questions.

"Second said you were gone all night. Can I ask where you went?"

Jael glanced down at her. "The message you brought was a summons from The Collective. There's a portal near here." She started down the steps.

Portal? Did she mean—"Wait! You *talked* to The Collective. You actually saw them?" She was incredulous. She'd never known anyone who claimed to have seen them.

Jael paused at the bottom of the stairs and turned back to her. "The others are stirring downstairs. Will you show them the food Second prepared? Our last guest is coming up the mountain." Not waiting for an answer, she crossed the meadow in long strides.

Alyssa stared after her. She whispered the words as if she could taste them. "There's a portal?"

Chapter Six

Jael jogged along the deer path, her light moccasins an occasional whisper against the leaves that sporadically littered the trail. When she burst from the woods into a sloping pasture, she smiled to herself. Grazing next to Specter was a glittering chestnut mare. Jael narrowed her eyes. Phyrrhos surely had made it there before dawn, so where was her bonded? The question had barely formed in her head when she instinctively hopped sideways to dodge the body launched at her back.

Her attacker tucked to roll, and Jael flung herself on the woman's back. They rolled down the slope together, each grappling for a hold until the assailant sprang free and circled as Jael remained crouched, calculating her next move.

Jael sized up her opponent. The woman matched her in height, but her russet skin slid over sinewy muscles more pronounced than Jael's. Barefoot and dressed in a sleeveless desert-bush shirt and tattered jeans, she had shaved her head smooth except for a Mohawk of tight, springy curls. But it was the band of black painted from temple to temple and white diagonals slashing across her cheeks that added an exotically dangerous air to the sharp, dark eyes.

Jael held steady against a series of feints, then sprang to the side when her opponent finally leapt at her. She grabbed the other woman's arm and twisted it against her back as she added her weight to their momentum and pinned her to the ground.

Her arm trapped against her back by Jael's weight, the woman growled and dug sharp fingernails into Jael's belly. With an answering growl, Jael bit hard at the base of the woman's neck. She tasted salt and coconut as she tightened her teeth around the sweat-slicked flesh. And then, she released her.

Tan, the seventh and last member of The Guard to arrive, turned onto her back beneath her, eyes flashing with understanding. She rolled her hips to reverse their positions and silently ripped open the closure of Jael's shirt to bare her breasts. She didn't hesitate, falling on Jael's torso like a starved dog on food, licking and nipping her skin, sucking then biting her nipples as she worked her way down. She looked up a long second, then yanked Jael's pants over her slim hips. Her mouth was hot and her attentions were not gentle. Jael's body sang as hard teeth raked across the swell of her craving again. She grabbed a handful of Mohawk, and her body bowed with her climax as Tan's mouth released the knife-like need that had been riding her since that first-life Advocate had stumbled onto her mountain. She jerked with the aftershock and blinked up at the cloudless sky. She was still wired, but the burn in her gut had retreated to a simmer. She took a deep breath. "Thanks, Tan."

Tan lifted off and crawled up to lie on her side. She propped up on her elbow to stare down at Jael. "That didn't take long, eh? Whatever has you wound up must be important to have you that close to the edge." Her eyes shone with anticipation.

Jael sat up to pull her clothes back into order. "Do you—?"

"Nah, I'm good. Just had a jump last night with a very energetic sub." She grinned. "His girlfriend was a tasty side dish this morning."

"So that's why we're all waiting for you to get here?"

"I'm here now." She cocked an eyebrow. "And, since you took the time to waylay me, I'm guessing that nobody's hanging from a cliff. What's up?"

Jael shook her head. "I'll tell you when I have everyone together." She stood and offered a hand to pull Tan to her feet. She studied her as they stood together. "That's a fierce look you've got going there."

Tan's grin was feral. "You like it?"

"Mmm. Better than the shrunken heads you had dangling from your earlobes in the first lifetime I met you."

They walked to the trees, and Tan reached under the boughs of a spruce to retrieve her duffle. "Yes, well, shrunken heads have been frowned upon the last couple of lifetimes."

They paused to look back at Phyrrhos and Specter.

"I hate many things about war—the women and children and old people who were caught in the crossfire when armies slaughtered each other," Tan said quietly. She turned to Jael, her eyes searching. "But I miss some things about it, too. Is that wrong?"

She didn't have to spell it out. They all missed the blood that sang through their veins when the battlefield lay before them. They longed for the rush of battle lust that followed. They each needed the physical test of stealth and sparring and the mental challenge of hunt and strategy. Jael clasped Tan's shoulder and gave it a reassuring squeeze. "We are born warriors over many lifetimes for a reason. It is no shame to accept who you are."

Tan nodded and shouldered her bag as they started up the trail to Jael's quarters. "How is it, by the way, that you always get the upper hand?"

"Easy. You always fake three times, then attack on the fourth."

"Guess I need to revise that tactic."

"It would be advisable."

❖

Jael's request had been a ploy to ditch her, Alyssa realized, when she went inside and found three men and a woman already sitting at the dining table. The empty pan in the middle of the table and the crumbs on their plates were a sure sign they'd had no trouble locating the food. Their conversation stopped and they eyed her suspiciously.

She stared back.

The woman was slender and had long, shining black hair. The reddish-brown hue of her skin could be First People, but a pureblood from those ancient native tribes was so rare these days, Alyssa couldn't be sure.

Two of the men also had black hair and dark features, but one was slender and handsome, with a deep-brown complexion. The other was lighter-skinned with rugged features. He was stocky with shoulder-length hair tied back at his nape and a goatee that he stroked as he stared at her.

The third was an androgynous, smooth-faced man with mismatched eyes of blue and green, a soft blond crew cut, and a sparse beard over pale skin. A dark, angry burn scar rose from the collar of his tight T-shirt and stopped just short of his ear. He hunched over the table, his arms on either side of his plate as though he was trying to take up more space than his lean body required. Defensive and wary, he was the easiest to read but the hardest to decipher.

The handsome man stood, his eyes flicking to her tattoo. "Advocate." He gave a slight bow of respect. "I am Furcho. How might I be of service?"

"Please, I'm not on duty at the temple. I'm Alyssa." She moved farther into the room and smiled, sending out an emotion she hoped made her seem non-threatening. "Actually, Jael had asked me to let you know that Second had prepared food for you, but I see my assistance is unnecessary."

The stocky man scowled. "Where is Jael?"

Furcho held up a hand to silence him. "Allow me to introduce my friends." He indicated the woman. "This is Raven." The woman smiled, but her eyes remained solemn as she nodded. Alyssa read her as curious but not guarded.

"This is Diego," he said as the stocky man stood and bowed slightly. "And our fair-skinned friend here is Michael." Furcho shrugged when Michael briefly dipped his chin but did not smile or stand like the other men.

"I'm honored to meet each of you," Alyssa said. She was at a loss for what to do next but was rescued by Second flinging the door open, her boots loud on the wood floor.

"Michael, Diego, and Raven. Firerocks are in the back of the transport. Let's get them unloaded and stored," she said without preamble. "I'll bring in the groceries. Furcho, you've got kitchen duty."

Although Second's tone was casual, the reaction was instant motion.

"I'll help," Alyssa said, gathering dishes and following him into the prep.

"Thank you, but you don't need to clean up after us."

"Please, I want to help." She began to fill the sink with soapy water and wash the dishes she'd brought into the prep.

Furcho cleared the rest of the table, then flipped on the blower and passed each clean dish under it to dry it before he put it away. The loud hum prevented any further conversation, and when they were done, Second was putting fresh vegetables away in the storage.

"Is Jael still upstairs?" she asked.

Furcho shrugged, but Alyssa shook her head. "She said she was going to meet whoever isn't here yet."

"Good. Jael was pretty grumpy this morning. Hopefully she'll let Tan take some of her edge off before they show up," Second said.

Furcho coughed and glanced at Alyssa. She hadn't thought much about the remark, but his reaction gave her a pretty good idea of what Second was insinuating.

"I wasn't raised in the temple because of some pious vow to The Collective. It was because—" She stopped, feeling irrationally irritated. She glared at them. "I'm not that kind of Advocate." She snatched the plug out to drain the sink and stomped out onto the deck.

She stared out over the mountains, not really seeing them. She would always be grateful that Advocate Han had saved her, but she hated that the tattoo on her face caused people to make certain assumptions about her. She stopped short of explaining that she was an empath because that always triggered a different round of assumptions. Even here among other talents—if they were like Jael, they must have some special powers—she didn't fit in.

Furcho surely didn't mean to offend her, but stars above, it still prickled at her. At least something was prickling at her. She rubbed her temple. Maybe it was her headache from last night returning. She propped her forearms on the railing and looked down. A wave of dizziness swamped her and she gripped the rail. She started to shake and almost dropped to her knees to wrap her arms around the railing. If she closed her eyes to stop the vertigo or let go of the banister to move back, she had an overwhelming fear that she would lose her balance and tumble off the deck. She was trapped. She was working up the courage to drop to the floor and crawl back to the door when warm arms closed around her.

"I've gotcha." The voice in her ear—or maybe in her head—was low and rich, and she latched onto it.

"I…I can't let go of the railing."

Long fingers closed around her hands and gently pried them from the wood to fold her arms against her chest. The arms tightened around her, and she pressed back against the solid body behind her.

"Let's take a step back. Right foot. Ready?"

She nodded wordlessly and tentatively stepped back.

"Other foot."

They stepped back again, and she sagged in relief when the boards of the floor appeared in her vision and the world stopped spinning. Her eyes slammed shut when the vertigo was instantly replaced by a pounding headache that made her stomach lurch. "I don't feel so good." Stars, please don't throw up. She'd already made an idiot of herself.

"She okay?"

She recognized Second's voice, but she didn't have to open her eyes to know her rescuer was Jael. Her very presence was an anchor in what felt like a churning sea. An arm behind her knees lifted her, and she pressed her face into the shoulder that cradled her. Pain, sharp and stabbing, tore at her temples, and she unsuccessfully choked back a whimper.

"She had an attack of vertigo. She hit her head pretty hard yesterday. It may be related to that. Hold the door for me and tell Tan to get the medical case and meet me in the bedroom."

"On the left," Second said. "I moved her into our...into my room."

She knew she wasn't a feather, but Jael carried her like she weighed nothing. She felt them climbing the stairs, but she didn't open her eyes, afraid another stab of pain would empty her stomach for sure. The bed was soft and blissfully cool.

"Darken the windows," Jael said.

"I've got it." Second again.

Gentle hands slid a cold pack behind her neck, and after a minute she tentatively opened her eyes. Just a crack. The light was thankfully dim and defused. She opened them a little more. The ice was already numbing sharp edges of her headache. So she looked up...and screamed.

Pain seared through her, and she gave herself to the hands that were guiding her to hang over the edge of the bed. Tears filled her eyes as she retched, but she was relieved at the watery image of the bucket someone had the foresight to put there.

"Balls, Tan. Go wash that paint off your face," Second said. "You scared her half to death."

The bed dipped as Jael sat next to her and stroked her back. When she'd finally stopped heaving, she realized two pairs of legs stood within her vision. Was everybody watching her throw up? She spit into the bucket. "This really isn't a spectator sport," she mumbled weakly. A bottle of water appeared in her view.

"Rinse and spit, eh? Sorry about the scare."

She complied and rolled back to lie on the bed. She closed her eyes for a minute, and when she felt the ice pack slide behind her neck again, she tentatively cracked one eyelid…then the other when concerned blue eyes filled her vision. Relief flooded her. Was it hers or Jael's?

"Better?" Jael said softly.

"Yes." She realized she was clutching Jael's hand. She was sure that was what kept the room from spinning.

"Fresh bucket," Second said. "I'll empty this one." The door closed with a soft click.

Jael's smile was reassuring. "That wasn't a nightmare. It was just Tan. She only looks like one."

"To each her own, eh."

Alyssa dragged her eyes from the mesmerizing blue gaze and blinked at the tall, brown woman with a Mohawk and a freshly scrubbed face. Small silver hoops, each holding several small turquoise beads, hung from her earlobes.

"Despite her unique choice of face paint and hairstyle, she's a licensed physician," Jael said.

"A physician who needs you to move if I'm going to examine the patient."

But Alyssa clung to her hand. "Don't let go. The room will start spinning again."

Jael's brow furrowed, and then she crawled over Alyssa without releasing her hand.

Tan sat where Jael had been and held up a pressure cuff. "Do you think you could let her hold the other hand? I need this arm."

She let go when she felt Jael grasp her other hand, and Tan slipped the cuff around her bicep. While it read her pressure, Tan took her pulse, then produced a small light. "Bear with me. I'll be quick."

She'd forgotten about the pressure point in her wrist until Jael's thumb pressed hard against it as Tan flicked the light across her eyes to test her pupil reaction. Tan sat back and removed the cuff after reading it, then began to type some notes into her IC. Alyssa closed her eyes and realized Jael had let up the pressure, her thumb absently stroking her wrist. Alyssa tried to focus on the warm hand and gentle stroking instead of the pounding in her head. Then a scene appeared in her head of a mountainside in the autumn. Leaves, splashes of yellow, red, and gold waved in a refreshingly cold breeze she could almost feel on her face, and she realized it was Jael in her head.

"You talk in pictures," she murmured, giving herself over to the serenity of the scene. It was like an ice pack inside her head, dulling the pain. "Thank you for not thinking of the ocean. I don't think my stomach could take that."

She heard Tan chuckle, then something cold pressed against the vein in the crook of her elbow, followed by the hiss of a hypospray.

"I think the vertigo is an aftereffect from yesterday's blow to your head," Tan said. Her low, rich alto burred in Alyssa's ears as whatever was in the hypospray began to work. "I don't have a scanner with me, but your reflexes are fine. I've given you something for the pain and nausea. It will make you sleep, but rest is what you really need."

Her eyes were heavy and she struggled to stay awake. Was Jael still there? If she could just move her lips. She couldn't get her tongue to work right.

"What is it?"

The voice was close to her ear. She sucked in a breath, and the scent of woods and pine and sunlight flooded her dulled senses. "Portal." She said that out loud, didn't she?

"We'll talk after you rest. I promise."

She wanted to nod, but her body was too relaxed. The last sensation before she sank into a thankfully painless sleep was of unusually warm fingers stroking her cheek.

Chapter Seven

T he Calling has been issued."

They stared at Jael. She didn't have to read their thoughts; their faces were enough. Second was already ticking off a mental list of what had to be done. Tan's eyes burned bright at the promise of battle. Raven's expression was sharp, but she would hear this council before reacting. Michael's nod affirmed his commitment to duty. Diego was incredulous.

Furcho, his body young but his soul almost as old as hers, was solemn and resigned. "Then let us sit," he said. "If it's done, then there is nothing for us to do but answer it."

They took their seats around the strategy table with Jael at the head. Although the tabletop was a paper world map protected by a thick plate of glass, it was purely decorative. Jael entered a series of codes in an embedded keyboard at the end of the table, and a hologram of the same map projected upright along the table's length.

The Calling has been issued for the Third and Fourth Continents. The threat is not yet detected on the others."

"How has this happened?" Diego looked around the table. "We have guarded our sectors for more than a hundred years without fail." He glared at Michael, the youngest soul among them. "Have you lost track of your badly born already, sparkler?"

Michael flushed a deep red, his mismatched eyes hard and defiant. He opened his mouth to respond to the insinuation he was not as skilled as the others, but Tan intervened.

"Maybe it was me who wasn't paying attention." She stared Diego down. "You got something to say about that, you old chunk of charcoal?"

Jael slammed her hand on the table and roared. "Enough." They were a unit. If they were attacking each other from the onset, they'd never succeed in leading an army. "It doesn't matter—"

"I am responsible." Furcho's calm voice sliced through the rising tension. He looked to Jael, and she gave a slight nod to confirm what she knew he suspected. "We've had several natural disasters in my sector. The last was at my base. The rain had been persistent since the first of the year, and the mountain gave way. Half the city was buried, and we spent weeks digging out the dead so their souls could be properly released. A badly born on my watch lost his son. His mate came to me later with news that he had disappeared." He looked around the room before meeting Jael's eyes again. "If I'd broken off to give chase to this one man, many more would be badly born."

"Protocol mandates that you request assistance." Second's tone was a question rather than reprimand.

Furcho nodded once in agreement with her words. "I sent an urgent d-message to Jael."

Jael closed her eyes and took a deep breath. There it was. The blame ultimately rested on her shoulders. She opened her eyes and met theirs. "I never received it. I knew sunspots had been interrupting the network. I should have been checking in with each of you telepathically at consistent intervals."

"It is what it will be." Raven rarely spoke out among their group. When she did, her words were chosen carefully and full of wisdom. Everyone listened. "There is no blame in things that are destined, and we have all known for many lifetimes that this Calling is our destiny."

"Agreed. We are wasting time asking why, when we should be asking 'what now?'" Second had effectively called the council to order, and all eyes turned back to Jael.

"Furcho, tell us what you can about this badly born. Then I will add what I have learned from The Collective."

"His name is Cyrus, and, until he disappeared, he was teaching at the university where I work. He's very dangerous because he's always been fascinated by the ancient religions and is well versed in their doctrine and the tactics they used to generate followers."

Jael picked up the thread of information. "He apparently recruited several followers at the disaster Furcho spoke of, and then they showed up at the scene of a later disaster and tripled their number. That group divided up and visited disaster scenes in multiple locations."

Diego frowned. "Which doctrine is he espousing?"

"He's drawing from the basic theme that ran through the most widespread and enduring religions—one deity that judges all and punishes those who don't pay homage to him."

Raven shook her head. "A patriarchy? This is very dangerous."

"Life springs from the womb," Michael said. "The Collective has understood this for more than a century. How could people be convinced to return to a patriarchy that is based on power and judgment rather than rebirth and renewal?"

It was a needless observation. Each of them had lived as male and female, had seen life from both sides. And all had lived through the Great War of Religions—the end to a long era of dissonance and a bloody beginning to a century of reconstruction before this past century of world peace. It also was the first calling of their covert Guard, three units of which existed in different parts of the world.

"Discontent, as always, is born from need." Furcho shook his head. "This recent cycle of severe weather has lasted longer than any that history has recorded. World food supplies are drastically decreased. He is promising that, if they adopt his beliefs, they will be among those who deserve to eat while others go hungry. He is telling them that the world is nearing the end and only those souls who follow his teachings will remain immortal."

"And so, The Calling was issued, and I was summoned by The Collective Council," Jael said.

"You have seen them?" Michael leaned forward eagerly. "You actually spoke with them?"

"Yes." Jael was aware of Second next to her, stiffening at her words. "There is a portal nearby."

"Which ones?" Second's voice was but a whisper. "Which of The Collective Council appeared to you?" Her voice was stronger but held a faint tremble.

"All." Jael clasped her cousin's forearm and squeezed. "I saw all of them."

"Our orders?" Tan voiced the question on every mind except Second's.

"Our immediate mission is to gather and train an army."

Because long peace had diminished the need for their skills, only twenty-one of The Guard remained active. They were the ones solely responsible for watching all who were badly born and making sure their souls were properly released by cremation at the end of their current lifetime. The time for watching had ended.

"This won't be easy," Raven pointed out. "Very few purebloods remain in the world, and even fewer true descendants like the ones around this table."

"The Calling will draw about a thousand, if the vision shared with me by The Collective Council is accurate. We will have to screen their DNA, and the close matches will have the option to partake of an elixir to enhance their genetic potential and to train for a bonding. The others will be offered auxiliary jobs in support of the army."

Diego threw his hands up. "This is doomed from the beginning. They'll never be able to bond if their blood isn't pure." He pointed at Furcho. "This is precisely why I said over and over that we should require that our kind only mate others of the same blood."

"That goes against the very premise of The Collective—strength through diversity," Raven said.

"And once we have our army?" Tan ignored the philosophical debate.

Jael again met the eyes of each before she spoke. "We will hunt and immediately destroy the badly born called Cyrus, as well as any who refuse to renounce his convictions and return to The Collective." She stood and squared her shoulders. "If any of you feel you cannot fulfill this mission or follow my command without question, speak now. If you feel you cannot work with, even give your own life for, any of the others in this Guard unit, speak now. You will be relieved without prejudice. I will not be kind if you swear allegiance now and fall short later."

They stood one by one, raising their right fist to their left shoulder. "I am sworn," they chorused.

She returned their salute. "And, to you I swear the same loyalty and trust." She motioned for them to sit again.

"The Calling will gather on a secluded plateau in the Sierra Madre." She canted her chin toward Furcho. "Not far from you since the nest is in your quadrant."

He nodded. "I've kept monitor on the nest, and they've grown larger in number than I've ever witnessed."

Jael nodded. "Good. We'll need every mount possible, I suspect."

"What about the pretty Advocate upstairs? Where does she fit into all this?"

She stared hard at Tan. "Hands off." She swept her gaze over the others. "She is a first-life and knows nothing of war and who we are. So, watch what you reveal around her. I'll decide how much she needs to know and when to tell her."

"There must be a reason she's here." Raven was always the perceptive one.

"She brought the message that summoned me to The Collective, but even the Council cannot foresee her purpose in this. They said only that her life path is entwined with ours." That wasn't entirely true. They said her life path was entwined with Jael's. "You know as well as I do that every aspect of our lives is not predestined. Our paths are determined by each choice we make along the way. Because they can't foresee our choices, even the Council cannot know exactly what the future has in store for us."

The answer didn't satisfy Raven. "Still, it's difficult to see what role a first-life could play as part of our unit, even if she is an Advocate of The Collective."

"She's an extremely powerful empath."

"So what? She's going to tell us how they feel when we incinerate them alive?" In twenty lifetimes, Diego still hadn't learned to filter his thoughts before they became words.

"She can project as well as read."

They stilled, each considering the implication of this gift. This talent was so rare that most thought it was as fanciful as dragons living in mountain caves. The fact that someone could make another person feel something was more intimidating than a telepath reading your thoughts. At least they were still your thoughts, not what someone else wanted you to think.

Second huffed. "Don't be idiots around her, either. She's very nice."

"Maybe you didn't really like her," Tan offered. "Maybe she was making you feel as though you like her."

"Why would that concern you?" Diego asked Tan. "You like anything breathing and of legal age. Is there anybody you haven't jumped?"

"Jealous?" Tan shot back.

"She hasn't jumped me," Michael said, grinning. "But I think I'm the lone holdout."

Jael slapped her hand on the table to silence them. Dragon balls, whatever happened to the strong, silent warrior types? If one of them said the sky was blue, the rest would argue over the specific shade of blue. "I've been deep into her thoughts. She has no ulterior motives, and she's trained to shield what she absorbs and what she projects. Han was her teacher."

The group relaxed back into their chairs. They all knew Han. Most had trained under him. If he trusted her, Jael knew they would, too.

"I'm going to check on the mounts." Jael stood. "I want each of you to prepare a quick status on your sectors and transmit them to Second. She'll leave tonight for the training site. Furcho and Diego will go with her. Since it is near their sectors, they'll have the contacts to help equip the camp. Michael and Raven, you'll leave tomorrow night with the rest of the mounts. I don't want them traveling in a single group. Tan and I will travel by land with the Advocate."

They stood as she left the room. Before she stepped through the doorway, she turned back to them and arched an eyebrow. They simultaneously snapped a belated salute, fists sounding dull thumps against shoulders. They were preparing for war, and it was time to act like soldiers, not a bunch of sleepy watchers.

Jael whistled softly and Specter jerked his head up from the clover he was munching. He flicked his ears in irritation, grabbed another mouthful, then began ambling toward her. She chuckled at the picture that formed in her head of the other horses finishing off the patch of clover he was eating. He wasn't accustomed to sharing and was a bit off temper at the onslaught of other horses visiting their mountain.

"Brat," she said, even though he didn't understand most words. She sent a picture back of a mountainside covered in clover. Plenty to go around.

A mental picture formed in her head of the training camp shared with them by The Collective Council, the mountains around them covered first with rock and shale, then changing so they were covered with hay and clover. It was a question and she shrugged her answer. He did understand body language.

He stepped closer and lowered his head so she could touch her forehead to his. Contact made their pictorial conversation easier. She conveyed to him that he and Phyrrhos, Tan's mount, would travel with Raven and Michael and their mounts. He pictured her with him, and she supplanted that image with her and Tan riding a solar train with Alyssa. He sent back an image that was a close-up of Alyssa. She replied with a confusing array of glimpses—Alyssa hitting her head on the door, her reading Alyssa's thoughts, Alyssa performing the tai chi movements. She wasn't sure how to explain the Advocate to him yet. He jerked back and shook his head, then pressed against her again.

He projected an image of dragon-horse travel without humans. This time, she shook her head. Blazing balls, did everybody have to argue with her? She showed him Raven and Michael guarding the group as they slept during the daytime hours. He swished his tail in irritation but dipped his head in acceptance. She understood his reluctance. Their bond made it difficult to be separated, even for a few days. She projected an image of them reuniting in the Sierra Madre to soothe him.

When she released him to go back to his clover, she knelt in the long grass that waved in the wind like a gentle sea. She turned her face up to the waning but still warm sun and spoke to the person she had heard walk up behind her during her conversation with Specter. "Go ahead and ask."

"You...you saw her? You saw Saran?"

Jael sighed at the break in Second's voice. It was a good thing she'd never found a soul mate, because if her heart could ache this badly for her cousin's pain, she didn't think she would survive if the loss had been her own. "Saran-Sung-Josh is well, but even in the eternal comfort of The Collective Council, I could feel her longing for you." She wasn't sure if that would ease or aggravate Second's pain, but they'd always been truthful with each other.

Tears ran down Second's sculpted cheeks. Jael and Second had once been nearly identical except for their eyes, but Second had lost weight since the mountain-climbing vacation that abruptly ended with Saran's fatal fall. "They say that our kind never fully bond with a soul mate because of our bond with our mounts, but it isn't true." Second's voice was tight but steady. "Every fiber of me aches to be with her."

Jael stood and wrapped an arm around Second's shoulders. "Seeing your pain makes me glad I never found a soul mate."

Second turned and grabbed her by the shoulders. "Don't say that. Don't ever say that." She shook her gently. "The soul bond is so exquisite that it's worth any amount of pain from separation. Would you deny the bond with your mount to spare yourself possible separation?"

"No, of course not."

"Think about what the bond means to you and multiply it a hundredfold. That's what a soul mate feels like. You still have time, cousin. That special soul may be out there looking for you at this very minute." She brushed the tears from her cheeks and wiggled her eyebrows, lightening the tension between them. "The Advocate is certainly attractive, and you seem to like her well enough."

Relieved to see Second smile again, she pushed her away with an affectionate shove. "I've got a war to run. I've got no time for mooning over some woman."

But Second was suddenly serious again. "When they taught you to shield your thoughts, Jael, I'm sure they didn't mean for you to shield your heart, too."

Dusk was falling, and she could see Diego and Furcho standing at the edge of the pasture, waiting for Second, waiting for the transition so they could be on their way.

"This war is my destiny, Danielle." It was rare for anyone to speak Second's birth name, but she wanted her to understand the commitment in her decision. "I feel in my heart that this mission is the fulfillment of my soul's purpose. Would you have me bond to some poor woman and leave her to grieve like you? I can't do that to anyone, especially not for my own selfish reasons."

Chapter Eight

Alyssa's first conscious minute was a sudden gasp for breath. She often woke that way. Sleeping in the temple dormitory had been torturous when she arrived because she would absorb the emotional leakage from her dorm mates' dreams and nightmares. Advocate Han had taught her how to sleep deeply enough to shut out those emotions, but it slowed her breathing to the point that waking required a sudden intake of oxygen.

The second gasp was from the surprise at opening her eyes to see a face only inches from hers.

Tan sat back. "Bloody. I thought I'd killed you. No one's ever recorded an allergy to the drug I gave you, but there's always the first time."

Alyssa's mouth felt like a desert again, but her headache was gone and she was hungry. "I'm not allergic to anything that I'm aware of. I just sleep deeply."

"How do you feel today?" Tan held out a cup of water with one hand while she moved a med scanner over Alyssa's head and chest.

She carefully scooted up to rest her back against the pillows and headboard of the bed and took the cup. No vertigo either. Still, she drank cautiously. "I feel a hundred percent," she said, marveling at that truth. She didn't even have a residual hangover from the drug.

"Good. We have to leave later today, so it's good to know you're up to traveling."

"Where are you going?" She shook her head. Maybe she was a little fuzzy. "I'm sorry. That's none of my business."

"Not me…we."

She scrunched her brow. She must not be focusing clearly. "Huh?"

"We all are going—you, Jael, and me. To the Sierra Madre, eh?"

"I don't understand."

"Michael has breakfast ready downstairs." Jael stood in the doorway, tall and lean in her tight olive-drab T-shirt and loose cargo pants. Did the woman sleep in those clothes?

Alyssa flushed when she realized she was the one who had slept in her clothes. Breakfast? "What time is it?"

"Oh-eight hundred," Tan said.

She blinked at them.

"You slept through the night." Jael's eyes were unreadable but impossibly blue in the sunlight that streamed in the windows. "We have a lot to do today, so I hope you're feeling better."

"She checks out fine." Tan held up the scanner. "I got the rest of my things from town so I could be sure. Head injuries can be tricky."

Jael nodded but didn't take her eyes from Alyssa. "You've got time to shower, if you want. I'll catch you up after you've had a chance to eat."

With that, she was gone. Tan stood up from her seat on the bed. "Don't take long. Michael is vegetarian so we won't have any bacon, but don't miss his waffles."

Alyssa was already scrambling out of bed. She was starving. Food first, information later.

The hum of the solar train normally would lull Alyssa into an instant, restful sleep, but even after two days of travel her mind was still moving faster than the train's glide of three hundred and fifty kilometers an hour.

She cast a sideways look at Tan. Even without the tribal paint she wore when Alyssa had first met her, she was intimidating. When they boarded the train, Tan had led the way to a nearly empty six-seat compartment and basically glared at the lone man occupying it until he left to find a seat in another compartment. Even now, she sat stoically in one seat by the door with her feet in the other, blocking anyone from joining them. Tan reminded her of a guard dog. Jael sat next to the window, perusing news bulletins on her d-tablet.

"Don't you think it's time you let me in on where we're going?"

Jael looked up at her, then glanced at Tan, who slid the compartment door shut. She tapped a few things on her tablet and handed it to Alyssa. She scanned the article on a new group called The Natural Order gaining momentum and members.

"I don't understand."

"Several centuries ago, before the Great War of Religions, people grouped themselves together by things like race, religion, sexual orientation, and income."

Alyssa frowned. "That's what history tells us, but I have trouble imagining such a thing."

"It's true. Races and ethnic groups were encouraged to marry within their own groups. There were many purebloods then, unlike now."

"I know that. I studied about it just like every other schoolchild. Except for some of the very ancient religions, few understood reincarnation." She shuddered. "I can't imagine people killing each other over these misguided beliefs and the world divided into countries that cared only about their citizenship. We know better than that now."

"People are hungry, eh?"

Alyssa stared at Tan. "Hungry?"

"Crop yields are down for the third year, even in the most productive quadrants," Jael said. "The World Council is concerned that, should the weather conditions continue, they'll have to impose food rationing."

"Two types of people you don't want to deal with are the hungry and the self-righteous," Tan said.

"This group is reviving some of the tenets of several old religions, playing on the guilt of survivors. They're threatening the cohesion of our peaceful society. We have information that they're confiscating and hoarding food," Jael said. "We're going to the Sierra Madre where people are gathering to defend and preserve The Collective."

Alyssa couldn't imagine it. Sure, their world wasn't perfect. There would still be crimes of passion and mischief as long as humans were involved, but the world government had rid society of divisive beliefs and political power plays. Women and children were no longer victims of patriarchal societies. The penalty for possessing a projectile weapon was death. People no longer hunted for sport, and animals used for meat were humanely euthanized. Peacekeepers carried only stunners for unruly citizens. "How am I to help?"

Jael shook her head. "I'm not sure. But The Collective Council feels you have a role to play. I guess we'll wing it and see."

"How many are gathering and what will we do?"

"That's all I can tell you right now." Jael's tone was dismissive, but Alyssa wasn't that easily dissuaded.

"You don't know, or you won't tell me?"

Jael frowned at her impudence. "I don't know some things yet, and it isn't the right time to tell you some others."

Alyssa didn't like being dismissed, but she had plenty to mull over until she did find out more. More than a century of peace and now *she* had been chosen to help preserve that peace for maybe another century? It didn't matter that Jael wasn't sure what role she was to play, just that The Collective Council had called them both. Well, summoned all of them.

She hadn't had a chance to really get to know any of the rest of The Guard before they left, but Tan had mentioned they would all be meeting again at the rendezvous site.

Who else would be gathering there? Defend and preserve? What exactly did that mean? If their purpose was to help disaster victims, they should be traveling to the southeast sector of the Third Continent, where an earthquake just last week had dropped several cities into the ocean and cracked open a sealed underground cache of spent nuclear waste.

But Jael said they were to stop the spread of The Natural Order. They must be headed to a massive convening to reaffirm The Collective's tenets of diversity and peace. Their destination was probably some sacred place. They would spend several days, maybe several weeks, in meditation and song, then disperse to spread the renewal and redistribute the hoarded food. She didn't know why it should be a big secret, except that word of it might cause those hoarding the food to hide their supplies. Okay. That made sense. Stars, she hoped they didn't expect her to lead the meditations. She wasn't that kind of Advocate.

She eyed Tan, who now sat cross-legged in her seat, her hands resting on her knees as though she was meditating. She could feel Tan's emotions, sharp and tense like harp strings twanging so loudly with bravado and anticipation that Alyssa had to throw up a shield to keep from being overwhelmed. Even at rest, Tan gave off an aura so fierce that Alyssa couldn't picture her joining hands with strangers and chanting affirmations, the things people did when they gathered at a temple to refresh their souls.

Alyssa flushed with embarrassment when she glanced up to find herself pinned by Jael's laser-blue gaze. She hadn't even felt Jael watching her. Never had anyone been able to so completely block her from reading their feelings. It put her off balance. Jael's mouth lifted in a slight smile, and Alyssa's body heated with a different kind of warmth. That was even more flustering. Sure, the woman was physically a goddess, but she'd been around attractive women before. She'd even had a few lovers, but Jael was an incredibly enticing mix of raw beauty, mystery, talent, and...power. Yes, power. She could feel the way the others deferred to her.

She smiled back, then turned to stare at the blur of landscape outside their window. Jael was as unreadable as ever, but Alyssa didn't think she'd been listening in on her thoughts. She'd felt Jael's probe before, like a polite knock before entering her mind. Still, it was a good thing Jael could read only thoughts, not emotions. She would have been laid bare if she thought Jael could detect the lust that wet her thighs every time she was near her. Souls above! She needed to get past this attraction.

Jael shaded her eyes from the sun's glare as she surveyed the boarding platform. When she spotted Diego, he was standing with a man and woman, both who wore tattoos that identified them as Advocates of The Collective. Diego waved them over.

"I have transport arranged for myself and three others," he said without greeting. He indicated Alyssa, then the man and woman who stood next to him. "I'll apologize in advance, however, because all I could manage was a ride aboard a freight carrier."

"How's the response?" Jael wasn't concerned about the travel accommodations. Her agitation at traveling separately from Specter over the past few days was like a thousand prickling needles, and she wouldn't settle until she could see him and center herself again with their bond. She knew Tan's separation from Phyrrhos had caused her grumpy mood, too.

Diego waved his hands at the crowded train station. "Last count was nearly eight hundred, and most of the people you see around you are here for the same reason. It's becoming difficult to house and feed so many. That's why I was having trouble securing transport."

Jael nodded. By her estimation, she would need a thousand candidates to put together an army of maybe a hundred.

The man with Diego offered his hand to Alyssa. "I'm Uri, and this is Nicole. We've been sent to accompany and assist you."

Alyssa's expression went from surprise to irritation. She turned to Jael. "I thought I was going with you. Diego said he only had transport for three."

Jael would have laughed at the hands-on-hips glare directed her way, but she didn't have time for this today. "Tan and I have a side trip. We'll meet you at our destination." She turned to Diego. "Raven and Michael have arrived with no problem?"

"Smooth journey. They're at the camp with Second. Furcho will meet you on the mountain." He pointed to a transport pulling three long narrow hover barges that were heavily loaded with boxes, buckets, and crates of live chickens. "There's our ride." He tugged on Alyssa's sleeve, trusting the other two to follow. "We should hurry. I don't think these guys will wait for us."

Alyssa looked back one last time, her eyes searching Jael's. Dung. She looked like a puppy some hard soul had just dumped out on the street.

Soon. I'll find you tomorrow. For now, I need you to trust me.

Jael was used to giving orders and having people follow them, so she didn't know why she felt compelled to offer this assurance. It was a good thing they were preparing for a battle. She'd obviously grown soft during this lifetime of peace. She watched them climb aboard the barges and find suitable perches for the last leg of their trip. Tan shifted restlessly but didn't question why they lingered until the transport and its passengers disappeared.

It was well past dusk when they broke free of the tree line. They'd traveled by transport past the sugarcane fields and coffee farms, riding as far up the mountain as possible. Then they traveled by mule for another three hours through more rugged terrain before dismissing their puzzled guide to return the mules back down the mountain.

"But it will be night in a few hours. There are many things you do not want to meet in the dark up here." The guide implored them. "Come back to my home. My mate will make dinner for us. We will get an earlier start tomorrow, and I will take you to the top in daylight." *Fire-breathing bats bigger than men live here.*

Jael didn't normally listen in on someone's thoughts, but this man was thinking very loudly. She shook her head. Bats. With so many species of bats in the surrounding forests, it was a reasonable assumption. But hadn't anyone ever heard of dragons? People just didn't read classic literature anymore. All they did was watch vids, especially now that the free world-digital network made access available in even the most remote places. She'd seen a lot in her lifetimes, but she still found it odd for a family living in a one-room hut made of mud and straw to be gathered around one of the digital tablets distributed by the world learning council, watching the latest vid.

"What sort of things?" Tan asked.

Jael shot her a warning look. She wanted to keep a low profile and didn't need Tan inciting the native residents with her teasing. Her Mohawk and fierce features had already earned them more attention than Jael found comfortable.

The man shrank from Tan and turned to Jael. "I will bring you back tomorrow, no extra charge."

Jael smiled and activated the IC on her wrist to type in a sequence of numbers. "Thank you, but we'll be fine. I've transferred the promised luxury credits to your account, with a generous tip." She showed the screen to the guide. Medical care was free, and credits for food, essential clothing, and other necessities of life were distributed monthly to every citizen of the world, but people still worked for extra credits to purchase anything beyond those basics.

The guide nodded his appreciation and shrugged. "As you wish." He unclipped the reins from the bridles of each of their mules and stored them in the saddlebags, then mounted the lead animal. "Should I come back tomorrow with the mules?"

"That won't be necessary," she said. "We'll be hiking back down a different route."

He shrugged again and turned his mule down the trail. The others followed in single file, tied together only by habit and the promise of a bucket of feed at the end of the trail.

Jael breathed a sigh of relief. Her need to see Specter had grown in intensity as they neared where their mounts were grazing and drowsing away the daylight hours. They were close now. Tan felt it, too. Her eyes were unfocused as the bond called to her. Wordlessly, Jael shouldered her duffle like a backpack and dove into the thick jungle, instinctively finding a narrow animal path. Breaking into a jog, she didn't need to look back to know that Tan was silently following.

They ran for almost an hour, jumping over jungle debris and ducking low-hanging vines. An occasional snake slithered overhead or underfoot, but the raucous chatter of the colorful avian denizens grew quiet, and the part of Jael that was bonded to Specter swelled with elation. If the jungle's silence in the presence of a strange new creature hadn't signaled their imminent reunion, the irritated picture that suddenly appeared in her head of monster-sized, biting mosquitoes would have. She burst from the thick foliage into a grassy clearing and slowed only when she was within a few feet. He stepped toward her and they immediately pressed their foreheads together, both relaxing at the touch.

She finally pulled her face away when he began to twitch and stomp again to shoo the biting insects from his sensitive hide. She shrugged out of her duffle straps and dug in it to retrieve two thumbnail-sized insect-repellent discs. She chuckled as Specter's suggestion of a plate-sized repellent disc formed in her head. "These will be sufficient," she said as she telepathed an image of mosquitoes fleeing the clearing. She clipped one in his mane and the other at the base of his tail, and he audibly sighed.

"We'll be above them soon, Spec," she said.

"How was your trip?" Furcho had waited for her to reconnect with Specter before approaching.

"Long." She pressed against Specter's side, grounding herself in his physical presence as she rubbed her cheek against his silky shoulder. She glanced over at Tan, whose forehead was still pressed to Phyrrhos'. "Restless." Specter shifted and pushed at her with his head, begging an ear rub and closing his eyes when she complied.

Furcho smiled. "I think that if you hadn't arrived today, he would have begun terrorizing villages to find you."

"Fire-breathing bats? Really?"

He glared at Specter. "You can blame your bonded for that. We've got more personal repellent discs on the way, but not enough to give every person one, much less livestock."

Specter opened his eyes, gripped Furcho's pant leg in his teeth, and tugged so hard he almost upended him. He did understand a few words, and livestock wasn't one of his favorites.

Jael laughed but slapped Specter on the shoulder. "Behave, brat."

Furcho took a step back and his horse, Azar, ambled over, pinning his ears at Specter in warning. "Anyway, when the mosquito hordes descended at sunset, Specter decided that incinerating them was a good idea, and the others joined in. I could see them from the next mountain, so I'm sure the native population noticed."

Jael shook her head. "Well, there's nothing we can do about it now, but we probably should find a different meadow for them in case some brave soul decides to hike up here to investigate."

Azar's silver dappled hide twitched against the biting insects, and Jael dug the bag of repellent discs from her duffle. She handed the bag to Furcho, who talked as he attached discs to Azar's mane and tail.

"Raven found a long-dead volcano that has formed a fairly flat and well-grassed field inside. The mouth isn't deep, but enough to hide the meadow unless you're above it, and it's a fairly easy hike down to the camp we've established for those who responded to The Calling."

"Good. How far is the nest?"

"A day if you're marching a hundred strong. You can fly it in about an hour."

It would take a lot of planning to infiltrate the nest, but they had plenty of time. She needed warriors first.

CHAPTER NINE

Jael should have been tired, but her night with Specter had refreshed her in a way sleep could not. The hike down into the sprawling valley was an easy one. The climb up was steep, which she hoped would work in their favor to conceal the small herd, but it didn't bother the members of The Guard, because several clearings where they could rendezvous with their steeds were located near the encampment.

She stood on an outcrop that provided a natural reviewing platform for the valley below. The problem of concealing their remarkable herd was solved, but nearly a thousand more puzzles were busily erecting temporary quarters, a medical clinic, and a headquarters building.

She'd been watching Second ascend but didn't turn when she stepped onto the outcrop behind her. "Report."

"One thousand and three have answered The Calling. Some are young, Jael, but Diego and I have culled thirty who are old enough to recall their past military lives. I designated sergeants and lieutenants among them to divide and organize. As you can see, they have our initial task of housing and sustenance well in hand."

"Good." She could always count on Second's organizational skills. She rubbed at her left shoulder absently. Although she'd been wounded there during several lifetimes, it was still whole in this life. The gesture was an old habit triggered by the too-familiar scene before her. She turned to face Second. "The Advocate and her assistants arrived okay?"

Second smiled. "She's organizing the medical clinic because she has training in natural healing. She's already assembled a group of medical workers for the hospital from among those who answered The Calling. First-life or not, she's a natural leader. People respond to her."

"Very good." This pleased Jael, but she sensed the happiness that infused her wasn't all her own. She scanned the valley, instantly finding the slender figure with fiery spiked hair staring up at her. Her smile wide, Alyssa raised her hand in a small wave. Jael self-consciously tucked her hand into her pocket when she realized she was returning the smile and wave.

Second didn't comment on the exchange but continued her report. "We'll be ready to begin genetic testing tomorrow, but it's not likely there's a pureblood in the whole lot."

"That's where the elixir will come in. Hopefully, a few hundred have enough genetic material that we can develop the warriors we need from them."

Alyssa watched Jael and Second climb down from the outcrop and disappear into the forest. When she could no longer see them, she returned her attention to the people around her and realized they were unusually happy about unpacking medical equipment, even though the humidity had them all perspiring and the insects buzzed incessantly about their heads.

"What are we so happy about?" Nicole's smile was blazing. Stars, she needed to get a better grip on herself. She was broadcasting to everyone around her, even though Nicole was the only one nearby who recognized her sudden joy was coming from Alyssa. She had shared her empathetic capability with Nicole and Uri. They were empaths, too, but couldn't project like Alyssa.

"Uh, the boss of this whole operation has arrived, and she's promised me some answers about what we're doing here."

Nicole's smile faltered. "She? I thought mucho hottie was in charge. What's his name?"

Alyssa chuckled. "Furcho." It hadn't been hard to read Nicole's interest when Furcho had checked in with them last night to make sure they had adequate quarters and assistance to set up the clinic. She wanted to tell Nicole that the striking man with dusky skin and soft brown eyes returned her interest, but it wasn't her job to play matchmaker. They could sort that out between themselves.

"Jael's in charge. She's the tall blonde who was ordering people around at the train station."

"Ah, blue eyes."

"Pardon?"

"That's the first thing I noticed about her. Her eyes are so blue, they're like lasers."

Alyssa felt a pang of jealousy, even though Nicole was definitely opposite-sex oriented and interested in Furcho. "Have you ever seen a laser?"

"Of course not, but I'm sure it'd be the color of her eyes…like a blue flame, you know?"

Oh, she knew. Thinking about Jael lit her flame in a very unsettling but pleasant way. She was so imposing and unapproachable one minute, then probing her mind with a touch as gentle as a caress or cradling her in those impossibly strong arms to carry her upstairs the next. She shook the thoughts from her head. They had no time for foolish sky-gazing. They had at least a hundred boxes to unpack, and medical equipment to assemble, and examination rooms to set up. "Really, Nicole, laser eyes? I love your imagination, but we need to focus here. We don't even have one examination room set up, and we're already treating cuts and smashed thumbs and strained backs—"

"Alyssa, uh, maybe—"

"So, let's save the talk about how handsome he is and how blue her eyes are for some other time."

Nicole glanced up and immediately began shuffling small boxes around. "Uh, sure. I'll just, uh…oh, look! It's the scissors we've been searching for." Nicole held them up as evidence. "I'll go distribute these among the exam rooms right now." She hurried off, leaving Alyssa shaking her head. They were nearly the same age, but those opposite-sex oriented girls just seemed a bit silly to her.

"Settling in okay?"

She froze and flushed at the familiar husky voice. Well, that explained what had sent Nicole packing. She stood and wiped her brow with her sleeve as though it was the humidity turning her face red. "Hello again. Your mysterious side trip was successful?" As attractive as she found Jael, she still found her secrecy extremely irritating.

"No mystery. We had to pick up some…livestock." The corner of Jael's mouth twitched upward.

"Ah, I walked the length of the valley early this morning and noticed the chickens and dairy cows in the pens at the other end."

The twitch turned into a smile. "Chickens, yes. Big ones."

Alyssa shook her head. Another inside joke, apparently, but she'd allow it if it transformed Jael's face into a smile. Stars, she was beautiful. "So, ready to let me in on what we're doing here?" She gestured at the swirl of activity around them.

Jael surveyed the people going purposefully about their assigned tasks. "I have a few meetings and need a brief nap because we were traveling all night, but I'd like you to come to the headquarters building for your evening meal so we can discuss some plans."

She noticed now that Jael's eyes were shadowed with fatigue. "That'd be fine. What time?"

"Seventeen hundred?"

"I'm sorry?"

"Five o'clock."

"Oh. That doesn't give you much time for meetings and a nap. We can make it later."

"I don't need much sleep, and I have things to do after night falls."

What could she possibly need to do after dark? "I'll be prompt, then." She wasn't about to miss her chance to learn more.

Jael nodded but didn't turn to leave. For the first time Alyssa could recall, she seemed uncertain about something. "Is there more?"

Jael quirked another small smile. "You have a big streak of dirt—" She gestured toward her own cheek.

Alyssa wiped at her cheek with her sleeve, but Jael shook her head and reached tentatively for Alyssa's other cheek. She held very still and watched Jael's face as she smoothed away the grime. Her fingers were callused but her touch gentle, and she fought the urge to lean into it. When Jael lowered her hand, Alyssa smiled at her. "Thank you," she said quietly. "Nicole would have let me go all day with that dirt on my face and never told me."

Jael blinked at her. "See you for dinner, then?" Her voice was low and soft.

"I'll be there."

Jael straightened and nodded before striding off toward the two-story headquarters building. It was amazing how fast they could erect these prefab buildings, Alyssa thought absently. Instant building. But not nearly as lightning fast and sharp as the attraction that was drawing her to Jael.

❖

Jael stared at the table set for two and the skewers of grilled meat and vegetables. "Where are the others' plates?"

Second looked up from the small galley. "You don't need them here, do you? I thought you'd want to talk to the Advocate alone."

Did she? She should, but it wasn't what she wanted to do. Just like she didn't want to remember the dream that woke her hot and aroused after a short ninety minutes of restless sleep. She rubbed her eyes. Her own hand and an occasional jump with Tan had happily sated her libido for a number of years now. So why were her ovaries obsessing now over a first-life Advocate half her age? This couldn't come at a more inconvenient time. She needed to focus.

"Bananas Foster for dessert."

"What?" This was a meeting, not a date. She glared at her cousin. "Second."

Second appeared unfazed by Jael's warning growl. "You need some fruit in your diet. You live off pro-chow way too much because you're too lazy to cook."

"I don't know how to cook very much."

"Okay. You eat pro-chow because you're too lazy to learn to cook."

Jael waved her arm over the table. "Where did all this food come from? You must have spent a month's worth of luxury credits."

Second shrugged. "It's no problem. I took the credits from your account."

"What? Maybe I should check to see what else you've been buying with my credits."

"Oh, please, you have enough credits built up for me to serve this meal to the entire valley out there, even though I've been diligently donating the percentage you specified back to the world-need account every month. You have no idea how many credits your books generate, do you?"

Actually, she didn't. Her needs were meager, and financial stuff was just a bother. Second, however, loved buying, selling, and trading on the digital network and was very successful at it. Since she trusted no one more than her cousin, she'd just turned her finances over to Second. "Why would a society based on peace want to buy books about war?"

Second made a disgusted sound. "Because they want to read a story about brave heroes and good overcoming evil. They've never heard the screams of the dying or seen children with missing arms and legs. They have a very romantic view of war."

"Then perhaps I should be more graphic in my stories."

Second shook her head. "If you do write more graphically to discourage them, then you'll make fewer credits for the world need account. It's a dilemma, isn't it?"

"What's a dilemma?" Alyssa stood in the doorway. She had obviously taken time to clean up and change into fresh clothes. She made loose khaki pants and a white cotton T-shirt look like high fashion.

Jael looked away quickly. She didn't want to linger over those forest-green eyes and cheeks colored by natural splotches of sunrise pink. She waved her hand dismissively. "Second is my personal banker. We were just discussing my charitable donations."

"Oh, I see." She surveyed the table and smiled at Second. "Thank you for cooking. It looks fabulous."

Jael cocked a brow. "Maybe I cooked."

Alyssa and Second both smiled indulgently at her but didn't comment.

"Everything is ready," Second said. "You two enjoy."

"You've prepared this great meal and aren't going to share it with us?"

"I've already heard what Jael wants to discuss with you, and I need to check in with our quartermasters." Second touched her fist to her own shoulder in a brief salute to Jael. "By your leave."

Jael nodded and ignored the wink Second threw Alyssa's way. As soon as they were alone, she pulled out a chair for Alyssa. "Please sit. We should eat before the food grows cold."

When they were seated, Jael filled their cups with water, ignoring the bottle of wine Second had chilled and placed on the table. "How soon will the medical clinic be up and running?"

Alyssa swallowed the bit of the grilled vegetable she was chewing and stifled a moan at its exquisite flavor. They apparently weren't going to take the time to savor Second's culinary artistry. "There's no shortage of hands to help, and we're already treating patients—minor injuries from all the construction work—but the lab and surgery rooms still have equipment that must be assembled and calibrated. I'm sure we could have it fully operational sometime next week."

Jael looked up from her food. "We'll need it sooner than that. I'll turn the clinic supervision over to someone else tomorrow."

Alyssa bristled. She'd been in camp only a day and had the clinic already treating patients. Sure, she was young, but a day was hardly time enough to decide she needed to be replaced. "I know the progress may seem slow, but I think—"

"You've done an amazing job getting things underway, but several other people can finish up. I need your specific talents elsewhere."

"Oh." That wasn't what she expected. "How can I help?"

Jael chewed slowly, then swallowed and sighed. "I'm not sure how to explain any of this."

"Why don't we start with why all these people are here? Are they refugees from disaster areas? Why in the world would you bring them to this remote place? What do you plan to do with them?"

Jael smiled as she sat back and held up her hands, palms out. "Whoa. One question at a time, okay?"

"Okay, sorry." Her cheeks warmed with the pleasure that stirred her blood every time Jael's stern features relaxed into a smile. "Why are all these people gathering in such a remote area?"

Jael considered carefully what she should say. She wasn't ready to reveal everything about The Guard, and she didn't think this advocate of peace was ready to hear the harsh reality of their mission. "We've chosen this area for two reasons. I'm only prepared to reveal one of them to you tonight."

"I don't like being kept in the dark, Jael, but I'll hear what you feel you can say before I judge you for not trusting me with all of it."

Jael dipped her head in acceptance of the concession. "The Natural Order sect is spreading their propaganda exponentially, branching out through digital media and the people they have recruited…disciples, so to speak. They call themselves believers. We need numbers to hunt out branched pockets of them, as well as a main contingent to go after the core of the movement."

"How can this happen? People being swept up in this movement must feel their separation from The Collective when they deny what we know to be true."

Jael regarded her. "How do *you* know our beliefs to be true? I mean, you're a first-life. You have no past-life memories yet. How do you know there is a Collective?"

"You doubt my commitment?"

"Not at all. The people joining this movement are young souls, too young to recall past lives. You're a first-life, so I'm trying to discern what makes them susceptible, but not you."

Alyssa measured her words carefully. "I trust the people who have instructed me. I know what they tell me to be true because I can feel their absolute sincerity."

"The rest of the population doesn't have your talent for discerning honesty. The sect that is disrupting The Collective preys on the distraught, people who are vulnerable in their grief. They claim to know why this is happening and say they have the answers to make it stop."

"But it's no secret that the severe storms are a natural phenomenon. Turning away from The Collective won't stop that. It's exactly times like this when we should draw strength from each other, not break apart."

Jael smiled at the conviction in Alyssa's words. She was young enough to still feel complete certainty. After many lives, Jael knew there could be no real certainty, only perception. No pure good versus pure evil, no black and white existed—only many shades of gray. She had learned to accept that fact, but she regretted now that she would be the one to ultimately steal that sureness from Alyssa. "People are complicated beings and often don't react as they should. They need to believe the problem is something they can fix."

"But—"

The sun had dropped closer to the horizon, so they didn't have time for a philosophical debate on the nature of mankind. Jael plowed ahead. "I suspect that you've used your ability to project feelings in many situations to help people."

Alyssa looked startled by the apparent change in subject. "Well, yes. I have."

"Can you give me a few examples?"

"I decided to learn natural healing arts because I'm constantly asked to soothe patients as well as their loved ones who are anxious or upset. Anxiety is an impediment to healing. Sometimes it's as simple as calming a crying child." She stared down at her plate, but her action didn't hide the sadness that flashed across her delicate features. "I've spent a lot of time in hospice units." She raised her eyes slowly to meet Jael's. "I helped patients and their families weather the end of life. Even when you know there'll be another, they grieve...like your cousin."

Jael's breath caught in her chest. Gazing into those knowing green eyes was like standing on a mountaintop and looking down into a valley feathered with thick, green spruce—eyes that had seen into Second and touched her private pain.

"Why do you ask?"

"What?" She needed to focus.

"Do you have some reason to think I'd misuse my gift?"

"No." Jael rubbed at her eyes and groped for her lost train of thought. "I just need to know the scope of what you can do."

"What do you need for me to do?"

Jael sucked in a deep breath. She needed Alyssa to be a little less earnest and a lot less enticing. She uncorked the wine and poured them each a glass. "This is difficult to explain, but let's sit outside and I'll give it a shot."

The evening was beginning to cool, and a faint breeze carried the clean scent of earth and fauna. She could think more clearly out here on the building's porch without the confining walls. The open sky and the first hint of stars called to her. Soon. For now, they both sat on a rough wood bench placed against the wall. "Everyone here has answered a spiritual calling. They don't know why, just that they feel compelled to be here."

"Why only certain people?"

How to explain this without revealing everything? "Are any other members of your family empathic?"

Alyssa frowned and shrugged. "A great aunt and a third cousin. My mother is mildly empathic but would die before she'd admit it."

Jael winced at the bitterness in Alyssa's admission. She couldn't imagine. Her own family was proud of the DNA they carried. "They have varying degrees of your gift because you all share some common genetic material." She swept her arm toward the rows of tents pitched between unfinished barracks. "They all have felt the call because they share some bit of common DNA that manifests as a talent. In the coming weeks, we must evaluate which ones have the greatest amount of that DNA and, therefore, potential to fulfill this mission."

Alyssa sipped her wine and appeared to think about that explanation. "So, you're saying they all have a common gift." She looked up, her eyes searching Jael's. "They share your talent?"

"Not telepathy. Another that I can't reveal to you yet." She took Alyssa's hand in hers and drew it into her lap, inviting a connection. It was a risky move that tempted her to revel in the cool of Alyssa's fingers and the soft skin of her palm. She allowed a small crack in her mental shield, hoping only her sincerity would filter through for Alyssa to detect. "I want to tell you everything, but I'm protecting sacred knowledge. It's critical to our mission and will be revealed to everyone at once. When that's done, anyone who feels they cannot fulfill the mission will have everything—our mission and their time here—wiped from their memory."

She searched Alyssa's face, realizing that she didn't want to be erased from her memory. She needed more time to make her understand. "I'm just now beginning to decipher your role in what we have to do here." She tightened her hand around Alyssa's. "I'm afraid that if I tell you everything now, you might leave." She was startled by her confession because she realized her concern extended beyond their mission. An unfamiliar, but undeniable, bond was forming between them, and she was curious about the Council's foresight that their lives would intertwine.

Alyssa's fingers curled around hers, and a firm loyalty rolled through her as clear as Second's salute. "I'll do whatever I need to earn your confidence, Jael, and serve The Collective to the best of my ability."

"Thank you." Jael released her hand. It was too enticing, the temptation to fling away her shields too inviting. "Each recruit will come to the clinic to be swabbed for DNA. When they do, I'll also ask them to submit to a very brief telepathic examination of their thoughts.

We need to know they are true-born and that they're mentally sound. I need you to evaluate their emotional stability."

"You want me to spy on people's feelings?"

"I want you to protect our mission."

Alyssa frowned, and her withdrawal was as tangible as the absence of her hand wrapped around Jael's. Never before had she deviated from a decided strategy unless she was on the battlefield, where she'd learned to trust her reflexes without question, and those reflexes were screaming at her right now. She stood, grasped Alyssa's hand, and led her back into the building. Once inside, she flipped off the lights and darkened the windows to give them privacy.

"Jael?"

She placed her hands on Alyssa's shoulders. "Stand here." Alyssa's pulse tripped against the back of her thumb where it rested against her throat, and Jael touched her cheek to reassure her before she stepped back. "I actually have three talents."

"Is one of them the ability to see in the dark?"

Jael chuckled, despite her serious intent. "No, I don't need night vision." She brushed her index finger against her thumb as one would strike a match, and a small flame shot from the end of her finger. She held Alyssa's gaze as they stood together in the pool of illumination. "I'm telepathic and a pyro." She cupped her hand, and the flame rolled into a small fiery sphere.

"Are you telling me that this valley is filled with pyros? Wouldn't we be safer meeting in a desert with no forest to burn?"

She smiled at Alyssa's response. Sarcasm was apparently her fallback when she was surprised or nervous. "You're probably right, but the third thing I can't reveal to you yet decided our location."

"Why are you showing this to me now?"

"You don't seem surprised. People are usually shocked when flames shoot from my fingers."

"I went with Advocate Han to treat a man who was in a mental hospital because he tried to cut off his hands after accidentally starting a fire that killed his child."

"Then you know how dangerous the ability can be."

"Yes. Back to my question: Why are you showing me now?"

"Three reasons."

"You like to make lists, don't you?"

Jael laughed. This woman challenged her, got under her serious façade like no one had before. She extinguished the flame and switched on the lights. "I guess I do make lists in my head. Lists are organized and succinct."

"Like your life."

Surprised at the insight, Jael faltered in her train of thought. Had she become too rigid and thus forgotten to relax and enjoy life? She refilled their glasses and swigged hers like a sailor to cool the heat that began building low in her belly as she watched Alyssa sip and swipe her tongue along her lips to savor the essence of the wine. "I've lived many lives as a wa—uh, in military and emergency work settings, so it's a hard habit to break. Not that I'd want to." She forced her gaze from Alyssa's enticing mouth and took another gulp of wine. "What was I saying?"

"Three reasons you revealed your pyro ability to me now."

"Right." She frowned at her muddled thoughts. "Many of the recruits have undeveloped pyro talents, and, as a healer, I want you to be prepared for some burn injuries. Second, if you detect someone whose emotions seem unstable, we need to cull them from the training groups. Pyros can be very dangerous if they aren't emotionally and mentally stable."

Alyssa sipped her wine, never taking her eyes from Jael's. "That's only two reasons."

Jael set her glass down and held her hands out, palms up, in an open gesture. "I need you to trust me, and I thought revealing as much as I can now would help." She dropped her hands. "I wish I could tell you the rest, too, but it has to wait."

Alyssa turned and stared out the darkened window. Silence stretched out between them, while Jael patiently waited for her to work through her thoughts. "Thank you." She turned back to Jael. "For trusting me with what you can." She reached for Jael's hand and squeezed it gently. "When do we start?"

"Tomorrow morning. Come here for breakfast at six. Bring your assistants, too, so they don't get stuck in the lines at the chow hall. We open the clinic doors at seven."

Alyssa smiled but shook her head. "I have to warn you that I'm not much of a morning person."

"Second's coffee is strong enough to wake the dead. But it wouldn't hurt to turn in early. It will be a long day with few breaks."

Alyssa finished the wine and set her glass on the table. "It'll need to be strong to get me going that early." She went to the door but turned back when she opened it. "See you tomorrow."

"Tomorrow," Jael said softly as she watched her go.

❖

Specter glided like a swirling white mist in a wide circle before alighting so adeptly his hooves could have been eggshells and not suffered a crack. Jael grinned at the gleeful picture forming in her mind of buoyant wind streams between the peaks. Specter was enjoying the high air currents crisscrossing the mountain range from the not-too-distant Pacific and Gulf coasts. She pressed her forehead to his and sent a picture of the two of them sailing toward a nest of dragon horses. He stomped a front hoof restlessly. "Soon enough," she told him.

"How'd it go with the Advocate?" Furcho landed next to them, Azar's silver dappled hide glinting in the moonlight.

"She stands with us still."

"How much did you tell her?"

Jael shifted, watching the rest of The Guard descend from the sky one by one to join them. "I told her about the DNA testing and asked for her help in evaluating the emotional state of each recruit."

"She was satisfied with that?"

Jael chuckled. "Of course not. So I demonstrated my pyro ability and warned her that, as a healer, she should expect to treat burns in the near future."

"She didn't freak out when your finger ignited?"

"She's met a pyro before. One who was at his worst after he accidentally injured his own child. So, no, she didn't freak out."

"Her life hasn't been all meditation and temples. She has seen a little of the uglier side of life."

"Yes. But I'm not sure it's enough to prepare her for the task ahead. She has the soul of a healer, not a warrior."

"She may be stronger than you think."

"I'm hoping she is."

Specter pawed at the ground impatiently, and she shook the image of a determined Alyssa from her thoughts. She was a distracting mix of forest and fire and sunset-colored cheeks, and Jael needed to concentrate on their mission. "Tell me about the nest," she said to Furcho.

"It's on a remote peak that the locals avoid, especially since the last team of curious scientists who ventured there never returned. They're an aggressive bunch. The surrounding peaks are scarred with burned clearings. The locals take it as a warning, but it's probably just them clearing forest to form new pastures as the herd grows."

"What do the locals say about them?"

"They call them fire demons and describe them as great bats, so I don't think anyone has actually seen one. They only see the fires at night on the mountainside or in the sky."

Jael nodded. When her dragon-horse army surfaced to quell the uprising, they would need to strike fear in the hearts of the enemy, but not in the minds of people they were sworn to protect. The dragon horses were a stunning breed, actual ancestors of the Akhal-Teke. Tall and lean like racing Thoroughbreds, the Akhal-Teke were valued for the unusual glittering, metallic quality of their coats. "What else?"

"A black, very formidable stallion guards the herd. You should be careful because Specter will want to challenge him."

"That's exactly what we need. Specter will challenge him to draw his attention while Second and the others recon the herd. I don't want to damage him unless we have to, so I want you and Azar at my flank to distract him before the challenge grows too serious."

Furcho's dark eyes gleamed in the moonlight at the prospect of battle. "As you command," he said, touching his fist to his shoulder in salute.

"Aloft!" Jael called out to the group as she leapt onto Specter's long back and slid up to tuck her thighs securely behind his wings. Seasoned dragon-horse warriors, The Guard wore no safety harnesses, but Jael made a mental note to have some designed for the new warriors. Staying aboard a dipping, plunging, twirling dragon horse required reflexive balance, very strong legs, and lots of practice.

Once they were in the air, the list of tasks forming in her head vanished. Nothing but the night, the stars, and the swoosh of Specter's great wings slicing through the chill air existed. The exhilaration and freedom was unmatched in all of Jael's experiences, all of her lifetimes.

Furcho signaled toward the dark peak ahead, where Jael could see the occasional flash of light, probably the younger animals testing their flame. She telepathed instructions to the group, and Second broke their formation to lead all but Jael and Furcho in a wide arc around the plateau of the nest.

Specter screamed into the night before spewing a spectacular stream of flame to draw the other stallion from his herd. Immediately a large shadow, darker than the night sky, rose from the hillside overlooking the plateau where the herd gathered. An answering scream bounced off the mountains around them, and Specter quivered as his bond to Jael kept him from plunging downward to engage his opponent. "Easy," Jael crooned, telepathing her intent to draw the stallion from the herd rather than attack. Specter's wings fluttered in irritation as they hovered in the airstream, but he obeyed and waited for the Black to come to him.

The stallion was the biggest she'd seen, his wingspan several feet longer than Specter's. His red-orange flame had an impressive reach, but it was no match for the superior heat of Specter's blue-white flame—the difference in the Black's mountain diet of phosphorus-rich rocks and the pure phosphorus fire rocks The Guard provided for their dragon horses to gnaw.

Furcho and Azar circled as the stallions flew darting runs at each other, meeting flame with flame in their aerial dance. It was an impressive show that Jael hoped would be mistaken for flashes of lightning by anyone who might be watching from the ground. The Black's aggressive charges were escalating, and Jael was relieved when Second and the others pulled back from the herd, their headcount finished. She signaled Furcho, and each of them flung spinning fireballs that met and exploded near the Black's flank. The distraction gave Specter the chance to withdraw, and with a final defiant scream, the Black returned to his herd.

Jael would have liked to stay aloft where the air was cold and clear and the weight of her responsibilities rode light on her shoulders. But it was already after midnight, and she needed at least a few hours' sleep if she was going to probe minds all day. They returned to the hillside clearing near camp, all alighting except Michael, aboard his glittering palomino Apollo, and Raven, astride her palomino pinto Potawatomi. They circled until the others dismounted, then escorted the released steeds back to their temporary nest where the horses would sleep and graze in their wingless form the next day.

Second jogged over to Jael, breathless and eyes dancing with excitement. "Furcho was right. We could cull a hundred mounts from that herd and reduce it by less than half. I've never seen a nest so large."

"Few places in the world are isolated enough for them to thrive like they do here," Furcho said. "But they threaten to outgrow this area. It's good that we're here to thin their numbers."

"I agree," Jael said. "We have the horses. Now we need riders." She turned down the trail that led back to the camp. "We'll have three extra for breakfast, Second."

"Three?"

"Alyssa and her two assistants."

"Need some help with the preparations?" Furcho asked.

"If you plan to actually help and not just stare at Nicole," Second said, giving Furcho a playful shove.

"I don't know what you mean," he said, his grin contradicting his words.

"Minds on the mission," Jael said sternly, even though her own thoughts were already filled with forest and fire and sunset-colored cheeks.

CHAPTER TEN

Encroaching twilight was at last pushing back the day's heat when Alyssa climbed the stairs to the headquarters. It had become her habit over the past couple of weeks, along with Uri and Nicole, to take her meals with The Guard. Their work was too important for them to waste time standing in the long chow lines at the dining facility.

She and Jael had worked side by side every day, with Alyssa discreetly evaluating each person's emotional state while she swabbed his or her cheek for DNA testing, then standing by while Jael explored the applicant's thoughts.

They'd spent more time together than apart during the past three weeks. Still, she automatically scanned the open layout of the headquarters for Jael.

"Where is she?"

Second gestured with her chin toward the closed door of the adjacent office. "In there again, claiming she's too tired to eat."

"She can't keep up this pace if she doesn't take care of herself."

The work was taking its toll on Jael as she delved into the thoughts of at least thirty each day.

"I've made the same argument with her, but she isn't listening. She just shuts herself in that office until the camp is quiet. Then she wanders from one end of the valley to the other. I don't think she sleeps at all some nights." She handed a tray that held a thick stew and a mug of steaming tea to Alyssa. "Maybe you can get her to eat."

"She'll eat if I have to stuff it in her mouth." She rapped on the door, then pushed her way in without waiting for an invitation. Jael sat at her desk, her eyes closed and her head resting against the tall back of her chair. "I'm not hungry," she said without opening her eyes. Tension furrowed her brow and tensed her jaw into a frown.

"I don't care. You need to eat."

Jael's eyes snapped open and she straightened in her chair. "I thought you were Second." She stared at the tray. "But my answer's the same."

Alyssa set the tray in front of Jael, pulled a small pouch from her pocket, and poured a measure of the powder it held into Jael's tea. "Let me guess. The thoughts you've had to sift through all day are still voices in your head that even a master like you can't quiet."

Jael put her hand out to stop her. "And you're just adding to the noise."

But Alyssa could see the fine tremor in her hand, and, instead of falling silent as bidden, she took that hand and clasped it in her smaller ones. The skin of Jael's fingertips and palm was thick, and she wondered if that was protection against the flame she produced. "I can help if you let me." She projected a feeling of complete calm. "Close your eyes again and feel my thoughts."

Jael hesitated, then relaxed back into her chair and closed her eyes.

Alyssa closed her eyes, too, and pictured the field of wildflowers blooming in the meadow outside Jael's home. The flowers were warmed by the sun and swayed gently by the breeze, and she imagined the wind carrying away the myriad of voices sounding around them until all was quiet. She felt Jael's hand relax and slowly opened her eyes. Jael was staring at her. Her eyes were still weary, but the lines of tension in her face had softened and she smiled. "Thank you."

They both had skipped lunch and the stew smelled delicious. She projected the hunger that was gnawing at her own stomach, and Jael's gaze flicked to the tray.

"I'm hungry, but I'm not going to eat until I see you empty that bowl," Alyssa said. "So, you eat while I talk."

"I didn't know an Advocate could be so bossy," Jael grumbled, but she picked up the bowl and began to eat.

"We should change our process. This is too taxing on you."

Jael, her mouth full of stew, shook her head.

"Hear me out. We have a high number that are proving to have more than 25 percent of the DNA profile you're testing for. If we screen their DNA first, then that should weed out the ones that match less than 25 percent of the profile you're seeking. That should reduce the number you have to probe by several hundred."

Jael appeared to consider this suggestion as she chewed.

"You could take a day off and rest while we screen for DNA. You'll be no good to us worn out from digging around in the thoughts of every person in this camp. And this process will go a lot quicker. We have a lab full of technicians to handle multiple tests at once. A single person probing each and every person is slowing us down."

"I do have some other things I need to do." Jael offered a spoonful of stew to Alyssa, and she held Jael's gaze as she took it in her mouth. The spicy broth filled her senses and she moaned with pleasure. "If your cousin wasn't already bonded, I'd have to marry her for her cooking."

Jael scowled and went back to eating. Was she jealous? Alyssa warmed at the thought and then immediately dismissed it as fanciful wishing. She'd finally admitted to herself that she was incredibly attracted to their tall, stoic leader. But she figured half the women and a number of the men in camp felt the same way.

She watched Jael scrape the last of the stew into her spoon, avoiding Alyssa's gaze.

"Drink your tea, too, please."

"What did you put in it?"

"Just some nutrients you need because you aren't eating regularly."

Jael sniffed the tea that had cooled, then downed it in a few swallows.

"And something mild to help you sleep."

Blue lasers bored into her. "You drugged me?"

"Yes. I did." Alyssa straightened to take advantage of the fact that Jael was sitting and she was standing over her. She put her hands on her hips and met Jael's glare. "If you won't take care of yourself, then, as your healer, I'll do it for you. You need to rest."

Jael angrily pushed her chair back and stood. Her extra six inches of height might have been intimidating if she hadn't immediately swayed from the effects of the tea and grabbed Alyssa's shoulders to steady herself. Alyssa slid next to Jael and wrapped an arm round her waist as Jael sagged against her.

"I thought you said it was mild." She slurred her words.

"I might have overestimated your weight." Alyssa didn't pretend remorse. She guided Jael to the leather lounger on the other side of the office where a pillow and blanket were evidence someone had slept there at least once.

"I'm sensitive to medicines…try to avoid them."

She gently pushed Jael's shoulders to make her lie down, but Jael struggled to sit up again. "Don't fight it," Alyssa said softly. "You'll only give yourself a headache."

Jael acquiesced and relaxed against the pillow. When she closed her eyes, Alyssa perched on the edge of the wide lounger and clasped Jael's unnaturally warm hands, her thumbs moving against the roughened knuckles in an automatic caress. She closed her eyes and projected a soothing calm as she filled her thoughts again with Jael's meadow. Unbidden, images of Jael and herself appeared among the wildflowers.

Jael turned, her hand gently cupping Alyssa's cheek as she bent to her. Jael's lips were as soft as her hands were callused, but her tongue was a flame that ignited a fireball burning through Alyssa's belly and down her legs.

Breathless, she withdrew her hands to break the connection. She blinked at Jael, but her breathing was deep and even, her features totally relaxed in sleep except—was that a faint smile? Had her subconscious imagined the kiss, or had Jael projected the image? Her stomach jumped nervously and her face warmed at the thought. If it was Jael's doing, was it intentional or an unguarded thought that slipped out because Alyssa had drugged her? It didn't really matter which, because both made her heart race.

She indulged herself with the rare opportunity to study a small crescent-shaped scar on Jael's cheekbone and another that bisected her upper lip. Her breasts were well shaped and small enough that Alyssa suspected she never wore a support band. At least she couldn't detect one now. She stared at the faint outline of nipples against the soft cotton of Jael's T-shirt, and her hands twitched with the impulse to stroke them into hard peaks. She jerked her gaze back to Jael's face, suddenly afraid those blue eyes would be open and Jael would be listening in on her very lascivious thoughts. But she slept on, her eyes moving in deep REM sleep under lids rimmed with thick lashes. Alyssa wanted so badly to cup her sculpted cheek and feel Jael's mouth against her for real, not just in an imagined scene.

Jael's hands rested on her flat belly, and Alyssa ached to hold them in hers again. But she was afraid of waking her. Her nails were short and neat, but her knuckles were crisscrossed with small white scars. She stared at Jael's long fingers and wondered how those hands would feel on her skin, against her sensitive nipples, pushing inside her. Stars, she needed to get out of here, go somewhere else, think of something other than Jael's long body, naked and touching her everywhere.

She reluctantly stood, gathered the empty dishes, and left Jael to sleep.

Jael stood in the shower and let the water pour over her. When she woke, her head and thoughts were remarkably clear. She would have never expected to get a remedial lesson in meditation from a first-life, but the legion of voices that had been lingering in her head was finally gone.

She was refreshed but not relaxed. Tension sang through her body like the twang of a bowstring. Her deep, restorative sleep had been followed by a series of tantalizing dreams that took her back to that field of flowers and Alyssa. She closed her eyes and allowed herself one last indulgent memory of spruce-colored eyes, fiery spikes, and snowy skin. Dung, she needed a tumble. She slid her hand down her belly. She was slick and hard and swollen. She rested her back against the shower wall and widened her stance. She conjured an image of Tan kneeling, that talented mouth working her sensitive flesh as she massaged the turgid nerves. Tan was probably downstairs. One quick mental message would easily bring that mouth upstairs to replace her fingers for real. But the image that made her swell to bursting, throb to the edge, and explode in a wave of pleasure wasn't Tan's dark eyes and smooth brown skin. Instead, emeralds and fire burned through her and left her legs trembling, her chest heaving, and her belly with a pleasant ache.

"Let this flow as it will, First Warrior. This is not a river you need to dam and control."

Maybe she'd never soul-bonded, but she'd had crushes and lovers in many of her lifetimes. They were always affectionate relationships but ones she knew she would move past if circumstances sent them along separate paths. She didn't understand this sudden infatuation at a time when she should be focused on her mission. But fate paid no heed to human logic. She'd learned that many lifetimes past.

So, maybe she should just let go and kiss her. Jael flushed with the thought, and she rinsed quickly to step out of the shower before the pulse building again in her crotch needed a second round of relief. First, she had to be completely honest. If who Jael had been, who she still was, didn't scare the Advocate away, then she'd kiss her.

The chatter around the dining-room table fell silent when Jael descended the stairs to join them. She hadn't taken a meal with the group most of the past week, and, judging from their expressions, they were surprised at her appearance now.

"I'm starving," she announced without ceremony and settled into the seat at the end of the table. The smiles and chatter instantly resumed as they passed platters of spicy scrambled eggs, chorizo, tortillas, refried beans, and sweet fried plantains to her.

Nicole went back to entertaining everyone with a story about hiking and stumbling onto an amorous threesome skinny-dipping in a crystal-clear pool at the base of a waterfall. Jael watched Furcho spoon plantains onto Nicole's plate, his eyes never leaving her as she waved her hands about to punctuate her tale. Apparently, Jael wasn't the only one interested in a little physical awakening.

While Nicole was gregarious and animated, Alyssa's other assistant was serious and quiet. She'd only heard Uri say more than a few words once when he struck up a debate with Diego on the merit of luxury credits as incentive for invention. Uri argued that necessity is incentive for invention. Diego argued that luxury credits stimulated enterprise before necessity dictated it.

But she wasn't interested in Nicole or Uri. Her gaze followed Alyssa as she rounded the table with a fresh carafe of coffee, refilling everyone's mugs. Second picked up her plate and motioned for Alyssa to take her seat. It just happened to be the chair next to Jael's.

"Good morning," Jael said.

"Good morning," Alyssa cocked her head as she studied her. "You look rested for the first time this week." She glanced down and smiled at Jael's plate heaped with food. "And hungry."

"I am, thanks to you. But don't think you can get away with drugging me again. I won't be so trusting next time you dump something in my tea." She softened her admonishment with a smile.

Second returned from the kitchen and set a plate of food and a steaming cup of tea in front of Alyssa.

"Sorry, but the hordes have already consumed the plantains. I know they're your favorite," Second said. "Next time, I'll put some aside for you."

"Thanks, but we've got to get over to the clinic. I'll just take a tortilla with me," Alyssa said, stuffing a couple with eggs and beans.

"Eat your breakfast," Jael said, transferring some of her plantains to Alyssa's plate. "I think you and your assistants could use a day off, too. Let somebody else take DNA swabs today."

"Really?" Nicole was listening, and her eyes lit up at the prospect. "I'd love to find a way into town for a little shopping."

"I have an order placed at the local market that Furcho can pick up for me, and then he can accompany you to whatever shops you want to visit," Second said.

Diego frowned. "You already asked me to go."

"Let Furcho," Jael said. "We'll start training in another week, two, tops, and I need you to check the preparations for that."

"Fine. I didn't want to tag along after a woman shopping anyway," he said.

Furcho patted his shoulder. "How about I bring back a keg of your favorite beer?"

Diego stopped frowning. "Deal. The cargo transport is parked out front. I'd planned to leave right after breakfast."

Nicole turned to Alyssa. "Want to go? We could hit a few shops while Furcho picks up the order."

Alyssa hesitated. "I am running low on a few teas."

Jael cleared her throat. "If you could give Nicole a list, I thought you might like to hike up the mountain with me today. I want to show you something."

"I'm not low on anything urgent, and I love to hike."

She laughed, remembering Alyssa's incessant complaining as she'd walked the four klicks up Jael's mountain. She gestured to Alyssa's feet. "Well, it will be much more pleasant if you wear the proper shoes, rather than those sandals."

"I have some hiking boots and thick socks you can borrow," Nicole said. "I'm pretty sure we wear the same size."

"Are you sure you don't mind?"

"Not at all. Do I have time to run back to my quarters for my credit disc?" Nicole asked Furcho. "I can grab the boots and socks for Alyssa, too."

"Go. I won't leave without you," Furcho said, smiling as she jumped up and raced out the door.

"Wait," Alyssa called. She turned back, her face flushed with excitement. "I'd better change, too, into something more appropriate for hiking. I'll be right back"

"Take your time. There's no rush," Jael said, smiling. "You should eat your breakfast first."

Alyssa snatched up a stuffed tortilla to take with her and pointed at her plate. "Don't eat my plantains. I'll be right back."

Jael eyed the sweet treat she'd put on Alyssa's plate and moved to steal a bite.

"I wouldn't do it if I were you," Second said.

Jael looked up and winked at her cousin, then shoveled the remaining plantains from her plate onto Alyssa's. "She's going to need the energy for the hike up the mountain."

Second regarded her. "You're taking her to the nest?"

"Yes. Ours, not the wild one." She waved off Second's offer to refill her coffee. She was edgy enough about the task ahead without the added caffeine of the strong, dark coffee. She nodded her thanks when Second poured her a glass of juice instead. "It's time to be honest with her. We'll have everyone screened in another week or ten days. When that's done, we'll be telling the rest of them anyway." She looked at Second. "Are you worried about her discretion?"

"Not at all."

"What then? I can see it on your face. If you want to say something, say it. We've never kept anything from each other."

"You like her, don't you?"

Jael had finally admitted that to herself, but she wasn't sure she was ready to admit it to anyone else. Not even Second. "What's your point, Second?"

"I can see she's special. I just don't want you to screw things up."

"Are you saying I don't know how to handle women?"

Second barked a laugh. "I've seen you handle plenty." Then she grew serious. "But this one could be different."

Jael stared at her empty plate. "I was reminded last night, when I fell into her trap and was drugged to sleep, that I have no control over what happens with her." She looked up into Second's affectionate gaze. "The Collective Council warned me to just let things happen. Their words, I believe, were something to the effect that our destiny is a river that shouldn't be dammed."

Second gave her a crooked smile. "Just watch out for the rapids, because I'm betting that red hair comes with a few rough spots."

CHAPTER ELEVEN

P rophet! Prophet! Prophet!"
The lights blinked and people hurried to fill the few seats left in the coliseum, while others stood shoulder to shoulder on the ground floor in front of the stage. The lights dimmed and they chanted louder.

"Prophet! Prophet! Prophet!" The rafters reverberated with the thunderous sound as a lone man walked onto the stage. A spotlight followed Cyrus to the center, and he stopped to face the chorus of voices. He held up his hand and they immediately fell silent.

"I've just received news that tornadoes have leveled almost an entire city in Region Three-North Sector." The coliseum filled with the rich quality of his amplified baritone, laced with undertones of sadness and regret. "Thousands are missing or confirmed dead, and this town, which is the center of egg production for the North Sector, has been put out of business for the foreseeable future."

A murmur rippled through the facility.

"The World Council, of course, has sent disaster teams armed with nourishment and temporary shelters until the town can be rebuilt." Cyrus searched the thousands of faces as if working out his next words, then held his hands out, palms up, in a beseeching gesture. "But who will nourish their misguided souls? Who will deliver the message they need to hear?"

The crowd shifted restlessly. "Who will be a messenger of truth?" Cyrus pointed his finger and swept it from one side of the coliseum to the other, as if searching for a button to push. A man among the standers shot his arm up, and Cyrus zeroed in on him. "Come up and speak, brother."

The man shuffled through the press of bodies. An usher clipped a small amp to his shirt and helped him onto the stage, where Cyrus shook his hand.

"What message do you have for us, brother?" Cyrus asked.

"Uh, I was gonna say, uh, that my mate's family are chicken farmers just outside that town." His voice broke with the next sentence. "We haven't been able to contact them since yesterday when the storms hit."

Cyrus put a comforting hand on his shoulder, and the man nodded his thanks. When he spoke again, his voice was stronger. "I'm headed that way tomorrow to find them. And when I do, I'm going to tell them about, uh, The One. I'm going to help them see that we've been wrong and now we're being punished."

"And why do you feel compelled to do that, my friend?"

"Because it's the natural order of things. And, in departing from the natural order, we have brought this plague of hunger and death upon us. The only way to right things is to return to The One and the way he intended our world." It was the practiced response of the cult and he recited it well.

"Very good, brother." Cyrus steered the man toward the side of the stage where someone had placed a folding chair. "I want you to sit right over there, and before we all go home, we'll ask for volunteers to accompany you on your mission." He waited until the man was seated, then turned back to the crowd. He let their anticipation build during a prolonged dramatic silence before he spoke.

"I have spent a lifetime studying the ancient religions. Each had its own faults. Each let the carnal nature of mankind subvert its system of beliefs. So, it's no surprise the two great religions that survived as others died off—the Muslims and the Christians—became extinct when their struggle for dominance culminated with the Great War of Religions." He paced the stage to let that message sink in.

"But as I read the ancient texts, I realized that both were built upon the same basic truths—one creator, one power, our compulsion to sin and the judgment that will surely follow. Both texts tell us The One called disasters upon mankind as a warning when we were disloyal and deserted the natural order of things. You might ask, what is the natural order set forth in those texts?"

He held up one finger. "Man was created first to be protector and guide to woman, the giver of life. It is the natural order. As men, we are born with the physical strength and level emotions needed to keep order. Women are the incubator from which life springs, and it is our job to keep them safe from harm, whether it is harm others would do to them or harm they would do to themselves by trying to fill a man's role in life."

He held up a second finger. "The natural order is for man to join only with a woman and a woman to join only with a man. The diversity The Collective preaches is merely justification for departing from The One's natural order and giving yourself over to carnal lusts. It has led to chaos, men lying with men, women lying with women, and many women refusing to bear children at all."

His voice, indignant, rose with each sentence.

He held up a third finger and shouted at them. "We began to burn our dead. The ancient texts tell us that when the day of final judgment comes, we will rise up from our graves to rejoice in heaven or burn in the eternal purgatory of our wrongdoings. The Collective thought is that we must burn our earthly bodies to reincarnate into another life. I'm here to tell you that reincarnation—if it truly exists—is nothing more than souls struggling to be born again and again, hoping their next life will finally end in the peaceful grave where they can rest until the great judgment."

He wiped spittle from his lips and nodded as male voices murmured affirmations to his rant.

He lowered his voice to normal, soothing tones. "But The One has been patient, waiting patiently before stepping in and laying down a warning. Unrelenting rain has brought mountains down on our heads. Violent storms have leveled entire cities with tornadoes in the midlands and hurricanes on the coasts. Drought in some sectors and floods in others have destroyed crops, and for the first time in more than a hundred years, we don't have enough to feed the entire world. So, who will eat and who will go hungry?"

Cyrus took out a handkerchief and mopped his sweating brow. He had them on the edge of their seats, and he loved it. This was so much better than a classroom of bored students. "I'm here to tell you that members of The Natural Order will be fed. The One will smile upon us, while those who ignore his warnings will go hungry."

He motioned for the man seated on the stage to join him. "Now, who will go with this brother to spread the word? We have volunteers down here at the front with information about where and when to meet so that you can travel together to deliver our message and feed those victims who respond. We need men for certain, but we need a few women, too, to talk to their sister women who are surely lost and grieving the loss of loved ones. While people are signing up, I am going to turn you over to Brother Donald."

Another man, blond and fit, jumped onto the stage and tapped his IC to activate the amp application. "If you'll look on the back of your program, you'll see the words to an anthem I wrote. I'll sing the first verse, and then you join in when you catch on to the tune." He took a deep breath and began singing in an energetic tenor. "We are soldiers of The One marching to The Natural Order. We've turned from the path of chaos and disorder—"

Cyrus hopped off the stage, and several beefy men escorted him to the tunnels under the seating that led to dressing rooms, offices, and equipment storage areas. He was constantly on the move these days, going from one location to another, but he wasn't tired. These appearances energized him.

"Cyrus, I need to speak with you." Simon was his right hand and the keeper of his schedule. While Cyrus preached his message, Simon did a stellar job organizing the movement. He claimed past lives as both a political and religious organizer, and was honest when he claimed loyalty to neither The Collective nor The Natural Order. But that didn't bother Cyrus, because he could count on Simon's addiction to organizing success. And The Natural Order was proving to be very successful.

"Let's step in here." Cyrus ducked into an empty office and Simon closed the door behind them.

"Two things."

Cyrus also appreciated Simon's brevity.

"Rumors are circulating that The Collective is gathering an army to deal with The Natural Order."

Cyrus snorted. "To do what? Arrange a mass meditation, then hold hands for a chant-a-thon?"

"A real army."

"Impossible. It goes against everything they stand for. Besides, what will they use for weapons? Do they plan to smoke us out with incense? You've been listening to the rantings of my daughter again."

"That's the second thing. Since she got a taste of what it would be like to live outside your protection, she's asking to see you."

"Where is she?"

"I thought you'd want to speak to her, so I sent a believer to bring her here."

At the sound of a knock, they both turned to the door.

"Enter," Cyrus said.

A pudgy man with an acne-scarred face stepped into the room, tightly gripping the arm of a pale twenty-one-year-old woman who stumbled in behind him, eyes downcast. Cyrus grimaced. That girl was unnaturally tall and boyish for a female, just like her mother. At least her mannish defiance had disappeared. She was pale, waif-thin, and, judging from her smell, in need of a bath. Still, her blue eyes and dark hair were the same striking features that had attracted him to Laine. The weight she'd lost over the past weeks made her cheekbones even more striking. He'd easily find a mate for her once they'd cleaned her up and dressed her in clothes more appropriate for a woman.

"You wanted to see me, Kylie?"

"Yes," she whispered.

"Pardon?"

"Yes, sir." She spoke louder, but she didn't look up.

"Have you enjoyed the past weeks, living as you would outside The Natural Order—without sufficient food or shelter?"

"No, sir."

"It's a hard life, Kylie. It's a life those who subscribe to pagan beliefs are destined to live. The One has been patient, but he will not be appeased until his people return to The Natural Order. Do you understand that now?"

"Yes, sir."

"Good. What did you want to see me about?"

She looked up for the first time, and he flinched. Her face held no expression, and her eyes that once burned with fiery intellect were dead and unreadable. "I want to come in…to join The Natural Order," she said.

He was silent until she began to shift restlessly under his scrutiny. At last, he spoke. "No talk of running off to find your mother and brother? You finally believe me that they are dead?"

"No, sir. I mean, yes, sir. I believe you. I won't run away again." She stared at the floor.

"Good. Because you and your sister are all I have left. I need you at my side. As part of The Natural Order, you will have plenty to eat and warm shelter, and I will find you a suitable mate."

"Thank you, sir, but I don't need…deserve a mate. I only want to serve the cause."

"You are strong enough to bear many children. You will serve the cause by serving your husband. That is The Natural Order."

She stared at the floor and didn't answer.

"Simon, please arrange some food and a bath for my daughter. Then, I want her put under Ruth's direct supervision. She can teach her how to dress and act more feminine. I'm afraid her mother wasn't such a good example."

"Father, please, if I may speak."

"Yes?"

"I understand that a contingent is traveling to the latest disaster site. I would like to go with them, to help them spread the word." She fidgeted when he didn't immediately answer. "I mean, after the past weeks, I think I understand better than most what they face if they don't join us. I think I'll know what to say to persuade some who may be reluctant."

He was struck by the change in her. The defiant stance and belligerent eyes were gone. She met his eyes only in darting glances now. Her slumped posture and hand-wringing showed that he'd finally broken her. Good. "Very well. I'll ask Ruth to help you prepare and assign you to a group of women."

"Thank you, Father."

He found a sheet of paper and pen on the office's desk and scribbled a note that he handed to the believer who had brought her. "Take her and this note to Ruth. Don't turn her over to anyone else."

Cyrus watched them leave.

"I wouldn't trust her," Simon said. "Starving her with only water and a half cup of chow a day may have worked for the short term, but what happens after she's had a month of full rations and a warm bed? I don't believe she has been that easily reformed."

"Do you think me a fool? My note instructs Ruth to have her watched every minute. Granting her request is a small reward that will bond her to me and our cause."

"When are you going to listen to me? I've helped many men reach positions of power—politicians, generals, religious leaders. Fear is the only bond that never breaks. Her defiance will return when she regains her strength."

Cyrus spun on him. "I want her to love me, not fear me. Laine took my son from me. He idolized her, and that killed him. Her daughters will be mine, and Laine will feel the ache of loss just as I do."

"Kylie is unnatural. You know it as well as I. She'll never let you mate her to a man. She'll need one who can force her into submission."

"I won't beat my child. That's wrong. If she refuses The Natural Order, then I'll give her a reminder of the past few weeks. When she gets hungry enough, she'll accept the young man I've picked for her to marry." He was growing impatient with this subject. "Speaking of food, we need a truck of supplies to accompany the group to the North Sector."

"No problem. We've just acquired a warehouse of food that was to be shipped to the Second Continent."

"Good. We've been feeding those grass-hut people for decades. It's time they quit being a burden on us."

Chapter Twelve

Jael was careful to keep her pace slow, because Alyssa had to take two steps for every one of her long strides. But, dragon's teeth, she was happy to be stretching her muscles rather than standing in a clinic probing the thoughts of every person with a trace of warrior DNA. Surprisingly, she really didn't mind the leisurely pace or the half-hour breather they spent at the rock ledge that overlooked the valley, sharing a snack from the food Second had packed for them.

She was enjoying the clear summer day and Alyssa's chatter—the conversation occurring in her head rather than what she was voicing. She wondered if Alyssa even realized she'd dropped her shields so that her thoughts were broadcasting. She chuckled. It was interesting to learn that her eyes rivaled the blue of the sky and Alyssa preferred the narrow parts of the trail because it meant she could watch Jael's "killer sexy" butt unobserved. Just to be fair, she dropped her shields a small bit, too, and let Alyssa feel how much she was enjoying their outing and her company.

"What's so funny?"

"Uh, nothing." Jael stepped into a sun-filled clearing where a creek pooled briefly and the low banks were littered with the track of area wildlife. "We've got about a klick to go. Want to take a breather?" She dipped her bandanna into the cool water and soaked her wrists and neck to cool her body. Although she could consciously raise her body temperature and withstand superheat temperatures, she relished anything cool against her skin. She dipped it again and handed it to Alyssa to do the same. "Keeps you from overheating," she said.

"Thank you."

Jael watched as Alyssa bathed her delicate wrists, then her neck and face. The splashes of pink on her cheeks had spread and darkened with her exertion, and Jael thought an artist couldn't have conceived a more lovely face.

"Since I don't have the advantage of being able to read your thoughts, maybe you can tell me what you're thinking right now."

Jael jerked her eyes away and shrugged. She'd made a private vow to be completely honest today, but it was harder than she'd anticipated.

"Jael." Part admonishment, part gentle plea.

Still, the confession of her intimate thoughts stuck in her throat. She took the bandanna from Alyssa and dipped it in the water again and handed it back. "Tie this around your neck. The last klick is the steepest section."

The silence was sudden and deafening. She realized that Alyssa had intentionally lowered her shields to let Jael hear her thoughts. The raising of that shield again was as abrupt as a door slamming shut and left an aching emptiness in its wake.

"Don't," she said softly. She raised her eyes to Alyssa's. "I was thinking that you are very beautiful."

The shield lowered again and Alyssa stepped closer. *Kiss me.* She shouldn't. Not until Alyssa knew everything. But eyes as green as the forest captured hers. *Don't be a coward. Kiss me.* The challenge wasn't necessary. She'd already decided on surrender.

She cupped Alyssa's chin, cursing the thick skin on her hands, then bent to brush her cheek against Alyssa's. Her skin was even softer than she'd imagined. She smelled of honeysuckle and summer rain. And, when Jael pulled back and lowered her head again, Alyssa's mouth tasted of pineapple and sweet fried plantains, her tongue like satin against Jael's. A delicious wave of passion and longing washed over her. Her emotions or Alyssa's projection? It didn't matter. She savored it, wallowed in it, deepened her kiss to prolong it. She was nearly lost to it when she realized Alyssa's hands were tantalizing against her stiff nipples and Alyssa's butt fit perfectly in her hands. So, she gently disengaged. Honesty was imperative before this went any further.

Alyssa stared up at her. "Fireballs and ice cream," she breathed.

"What?"

"Hot and sweet and everything between."

"Yeah?" This woman was like none she'd ever encountered.

"Yeah."

Jael grinned, her heart soaring higher than Specter's wings had ever taken her. She impulsively swept Alyssa into her arms and jumped the creek as she shrieked. She set Alyssa on her feet again and waved her toward the trail. "Go ahead. We're almost there."

"I kind of like bringing up the rear."

"You like looking at *my* rear."

"Have you been listening in on my thoughts?"

"Hard to shut them out when you're shouting them. You need to go first because the trail is steep and I might need to catch you if you start to slide back down."

"Admit it. You just want to look at *my* butt."

"There has to be some reward for playing backstop if you start to tumble down."

Alyssa's grin outshone the sun, and the deliberate sway of her hips warmed Jael more than the late-afternoon heat. But the arduous climb curtailed any further banter until they crested the lip of their destination. The wide crater sheltered a meadow dotted with glittering jewels.

"Stars above, they're beautiful, Jael."

She stepped around Alyssa and offered a hand to steady her as they descended the brief slope. She liked the feel of Alyssa's hand in hers, so she didn't release it when the ground leveled off at the meadow. "Come meet Specter."

Alyssa saw a pale stallion, greyhound lean, raise his head and study them. He shook himself and ambled toward them. One by one the other horses followed. The stallion stopped in front of Jael, and, when he lowered his head, she closed her eyes and pressed her forehead to his. They remained like this for several minutes before Jael straightened and turned back to her.

"Remember how you said that I think in pictures?"

Alyssa nodded, recalling the picture Jael had projected into her thoughts when she was dizzy from the vertigo. "Yes. It was like a movie in my head."

"I don't naturally think in pictures. I learned how to do it because that's how he communicates. He understands only a few words and, of course, body language."

Wow. This was amazing. More amazing than fire springing from Jael's fingertips. "You were talking to him, just now…when you touched your forehead to his?"

"Yes. It's not necessary, but it makes communicating effortless and clearer."

"Can he talk to anybody?"

"Just me. We're bonded."

"He has blue eyes like yours. Is that because of your bond?"

"No. He's a perlino. It refers to his color. It's a rather rare gene, but the blue eyes usually come with the pale-gold coat color."

"Can I pet him?"

"Sure. His favorite scratching spot is at the peak of his withers… right there where his mane stops on his shoulder."

Alyssa scratched gently in the spot Jael indicated. "Hello, Specter. I'm Alyssa."

She stepped back to let the huge blue eyes study her. After a minute he turned back to Jael, and she pressed her forehead to his again. His ears worked back and forth, and then he turned back to Alyssa. She held out her hand, but he gave it only a bare sniff before pushing his nose within an inch of hers. His breath was warm as he scented along her cheek; his whiskers tickled as he smelled her neck. Then he raised his nose skyward and comically curled his lip.

"Hey, is he saying I stink?"

Jael laughed. "No. He's opening his olfactory receptors to fully experience your scent. It's how he'll identify you in the future."

"Just now, what'd he say, uh, picture for you?" She stood very still while he gently lipped at the Advocate tattoo that ran from her left temple to her throat, as if testing to see if he could pull it off.

"He wanted to know who you were."

"What did you tell…I mean, what did you show him?"

"I showed you working to heal people in the clinic. Then I showed, well, you know. I showed us…at the creek."

She glanced over at Jael and smiled. "You're shy."

Jael scoffed. "Hardly."

"You are. I don't mean in the I-don't-want-to-be-seen-naked traditional sense. You're shy about expressing your feelings." She laughed at Jael's scowl until she finally smiled back.

"I'll admit to being reticent."

His inspection done, Specter stepped closer, the skin at the top of his shoulder twitching away an invisible insect, and Jael laughed. "You suck-up," she said to the horse. "He wants you to scratch him again. Your nails are longer than mine and he likes them."

Alyssa scratched the stallion's shoulder. His color reminded her of champagne. "Why are they so skinny and what makes them glitter in the sun? I've seen plenty of horses before, but never any that glitter like jewels."

"They're all descended from the Akhal-Teke breed. The Akhal-Teke gene is what gives racing Thoroughbreds their long, lean bodies. The Akhal-Teke had the speed of a Thoroughbred and the endurance of an Arabian, but they were mainly bred for the unusual metallic-like glitter in their coats."

"Are all of them yours?"

"No. Each belongs and is bonded to a member of The Guard." Jael pointed to a shimmering buckskin, his mane and tail black like the lower half of his legs. "Titan is bonded to Second, and the silver-dappled mare next to him is Azar, who is bonded to Furcho. The black is Bero, bonded to Diego. The palomino is Michael's Apollo, and the gold-and-white pinto is Raven's Potawatomi."

"That's sort of a mouthful to say. Pot-taw…"

"Raven calls her Tomi for short."

"Much better. And the one that looks like copper? Let me guess— Tan's?"

"Yes. That's Phyrrhos. It means flame."

"Sort of stands out in the group, like Tan does."

Jael laughed. "Her coat is only a few shades lighter than your hair."

Alyssa self-consciously ran her fingers through her rakish spikes. "I hate the color of my hair. Kids always teased me about it when I was growing up. They called me things like flare head."

Jael grabbed her hand and pulled it away. "I love it. It was the first thing I noticed about you." She brushed the more sensitive backside of her hand against Alyssa's hair. "But then I've always liked to play with fire." She smiled, and Alyssa felt as if the sun had suddenly changed direction to rise higher and shine brighter even though the night beckoned. And, when Jael's fingers brushed against her neck as she lowered her hand, they left trails of heat that burned all the way to her belly.

She wanted Jael to kiss her again. She wanted to wrap herself in Jael's heat, her strong body. She wanted them both naked so Jael could feel with her skin what the thick pads of her fingers couldn't.

But Jael stepped back and dropped to sit cross-legged in the grass. "Sit. I need to tell you more about why we're here."

❖

Kyle pulled the towel around her body tighter and stared at the clothes Ruth laid on the bed for her. "I've never worn a skirt. I think I'd be more comfortable in pants."

"All of the women in The Natural Order wear skirts, Kylie. It's more feminine and preserves their modesty around the male members."

"My name isn't Kylie."

Ruth looked surprised. "Your father calls you Kylie."

"The name my mother wrote on my birth certificate is Kyle. I prefer it."

"Well, Kylie is much prettier." She gave Kyle a pointed look. "And your father prefers it."

She picked up the skirt and held it against Kyle. "My, but you're tall. This will barely reach past your knees, so we certainly don't need to hem it any shorter. I think Angela could sew you a few more a bit longer before we leave tomorrow. Skirts aren't difficult to make." She smiled. "When we return and have more time, I'll teach you how so you can sew your own."

"I have pants that are long enough now. No need for Angela to go to any trouble."

Ruth frowned. "Pants are not appropriate for women, young lady. Now, get changed and then join me in the kitchen to help prepare dinner for your father." Her face was stern as she eyed her. "Will I need to tell him that you won't be eating because you refused to dress properly? I'd hate to do that because you look like you can't afford to miss another meal."

The threat was thinly veiled, and the very thought of real food made her mouth water. Even more important, she needed nourishment to get her pyro ability back. She was so debilitated after weeks of starving that she could barely produce a matchstick flame. But she must be careful. Her father didn't know about her gift, and she was afraid of what he'd do to her if he found out. Kyle lowered her eyes. "No," she said quietly. "I'll only be a minute."

Ruth nodded. "Good, because your father is very busy and likes to eat exactly at six o'clock."

Kyle waited a heartbeat after Ruth closed the door, then dropped down to lie across the bed. She'd tried twice to escape and return home, but that Simon jerk just kept dragging her back. She couldn't, wouldn't believe that her mother and brother were dead until she saw their ashes. No. Their bodies. Her father had said he'd buried them on the back part of their residential cooperative's homestead. Buried! She didn't know how she'd find them, but she would. And she'd build funeral pyres for both. Nobody in her family would be badly born into the next life if she had anything to do with it.

Her stomach growled and she sat up. She looked at the skirt and sighed. She'd better get dressed. Her hunger compelled her. She also needed to earn her father's trust. The next time she left, she wouldn't be a hotheaded kid running away from her parent. She wasn't a child any longer. She'd reached legal age more than a year ago and he no longer had the authority to confine her, even if he was her father. She had to form a strategy and squirrel away a stockpile of supplies. She didn't know how she'd travel, since the credits system used to buy everything was easily traceable. But she'd find a way. Only her immediate destination wouldn't be the valley that had been her home. Another chain of mountains, somewhere much farther south, was drawing her. She didn't understand why, only that time was running out.

Alyssa sat, stretching her legs in front of her and bracing with her arms behind her to lean back. "I'd rather you show me than tell me." She wondered if the flush rising up Jael's neck was from arousal or embarrassment.

"I meant that I'll explain why the valley below us is filled with people."

She sat up to mirror Jael's pose. Despite her disappointment that Jael had obviously switched gears, she was eager to finally learn more about their mission. "You said you couldn't reveal everything until you could tell everyone at once."

"I want to tell you now." Jael's gaze bore into her. "But you can't breathe a word to anyone else."

Alyssa touched her right fist to her left shoulder as she'd seen Second do. "You have my word."

Jael smiled briefly at the gesture. She stretched her legs out, then bent them to rest her forearms on her knees and stare at the horses that had wandered off to graze. Alyssa waited patiently for her to finally speak.

"I've lived many, many incarnations—lives you would likely find completely foreign and appalling."

"Were you a criminal? A slaver? A prostitute or a politician?" She was a little disappointed when Jael ignored her attempt to lighten the mood by pairing prostitute and politician in the same sentence.

"You could say I was a serial killer of sorts. I was…have always been a warrior."

Did Jael really think her past made a difference to her? True, she'd known Jael only a few weeks, but she'd sensed no malevolence in her or any of The Guard. All she felt was an intense commitment to duty and honor. "That's not the same as a murderer. Warriors don't go after innocents. They battle adversaries."

Jael's inviting lips flattened into a tight, bitter line, and her warm blue eyes turned winter cold. "What do you know of war?"

"Obviously, I have no personal experience to recall, but I've been reading your books in the evenings." Alyssa celebrated a small, silent victory when the hard lines of Jael's handsome face eased and surprise flickered in her eyes. "Besides, you're not a warrior now. But if you didn't write about war, people would forget its violence. So, no matter what destruction you may have wrought in past lives, you write about it now so society won't repeat that bloody part of our history."

Jael's sigh was resigned. "I write about it because it's what I know. It's who I am." She shifted to face Alyssa. "Give me your hands and close your eyes."

Alyssa didn't hesitate to close her eyes and slide her hands into Jael's. She smiled when she felt a smooth forehead press against hers and Jael's warm breath caress her cheek.

Then the images came. Furiously fast, awful glimpses so real she could hear and smell and taste them.

A sword thrust through a man's chest and then twisted with a chilling crunch of bone and sucking squish of mutilated organs. A choking river of blood gushed forth as a dagger sliced a bearded throat. Cutting, slashing through a field of chaos, men shoulder to shoulder. Screams and yells filling air permeated with the stench of blood and bowel and fear. Soldiers transferring a pile of arms and legs onto a wagon behind a surgeon's tent. The *rat-a-tat* of gunfire and a deafening explosion. Limbs and torsos scattered about like puzzle pieces. The pop of a sniper rifle in the distance, followed by a spray of brains and skull from a soldier standing two feet away. Silver predators streaking the sky, spewing napalm on jungle, bunkers, and villages alike. Human torches—some child-sized—staggering down a rutted road, trying to outrun the flames eating them. White-suited figures wandering down a street littered with bodies, a city's entire population murdered instantly by a smart bomb that had left the buildings intact except for shattered windows.

Alyssa jerked away, heart pounding, lungs starving for breath the horrible images had stolen. She gulped great sobbing gasps and struggled to crawl away as Jael drew her onto her lap and wrapped her in a tight hug, stroking her hair and back to calm her.

"I'm sorry, I'm sorry." Her kisses were gentle on Alyssa's wet cheeks. "I can take them back. I can erase them so you won't remember. I just needed you to see."

Alyssa stopped her struggle and buried her face in Jael's neck. She felt safe in Jael's embrace, even though the images still scorched her. She'd briefly lived Jael's memories, wielded Jael's sword, fired Jael's weapon. But it was the last image that disturbed her most. "You killed her." Jael's booted foot had rolled a body onto its back. The woman's eyes were bloody and unseeing, her mouth working until the barrel of Jael's laser rifle pressed against the woman's forehead and buzzed. Then her mouth was still.

"The smart bombs in 2180 were a mixture of percussion bomb and biological weapon. They'd plant them in heavily populated areas. The impact would scramble the brains of everyone in a one-mile radius, killing them instantly. Anyone who, for whatever reason, wasn't impacted enough to die was infected with an incurable virus that liquefied their insides within twenty-four hours. It was very painful, and we could do nothing but end it quickly for them."

The sun dipped lower and still they clung to each other in silence, Alyssa trembling and Jael stroking. Finally, Alyssa spoke.

"Why?"

"That's a broad question."

"Why did you need for me to see it?"

"I want to be honest with you. I need you to see who I am, how different we are. As a warrior, I've done terrible things. I'll take them back now so that you won't remember specific images that can show up in your dreams, only that they were awful." Jael's hands stilled. "I…I hadn't meant to kiss you until you knew everything. I'm sorry. I can erase that, too, if you want."

Jael's pain sliced through her and Alyssa opened to it, absorbed it. When rough fingers closed around hers, she jerked her hand away. "No."

Jael blinked at her. "I was just going to—"

"Don't take them from me." She cupped Jael's face in her hands. "They're horrible memories and I can feel how they hurt you, so I want to carry them for you, with you." She brushed her lips against Jael's. "And, even if you can take away the memory of our kiss, you can't erase my need to kiss you again." She moved her mouth over Jael's, tracing her tongue over Jael's lips until she opened and Alyssa sucked her inside. She quivered at the way Jael's tongue filled her mouth, how Jael flooded her senses, and she ached to cradle her bare breast in Jael's rough palm, to hold Jael's long fingers inside.

Alyssa slowly disengaged. "That's what'll fill my dreams tonight."

"I have more to show you."

"Can't it wait?" She smoothed her hands down Jael's strong arms. She didn't want to see more death and destruction. She didn't want to dwell on their differences. Fate obviously was drawing them together. They should concentrate on what they shared—this mission, this attraction, this field, this minute. She altered the path of her hands, and Jael caught them in hers just as she was about to explore the taut nipples under Jael's T-shirt.

"No, it can't wait. Twilight is seconds away. I have to tell you a story before night reaches us."

"A story."

"Yes." Jael was serious again.

"Okay." Resigned, she slid off Jael's lap but sat close enough that their shoulders still touched and her hand rested on Jael's hard thigh. She couldn't bring herself to break their physical connection. Not yet. "I'm listening."

"We've been testing DNA for the past weeks so we can identify the people who carry a portion of the DNA sequence shared by the members of The Guard. It's the genetic element that allows us to bond with them," she said, gesturing toward the horses.

"You're just confusing me more. I thought this whole mission thing was about the weather disasters and a cult that is preying on the victims. What do horses have to do with it?" She'd waited weeks for Jael to open up, and now that she had, all Alyssa could think about was getting past this discussion and back to kissing.

"So impatient. It's a story that spans hundreds of years, but I'll try to summarize and get to the point quickly."

"Please do, before we move on to our next lives."

Jael didn't acknowledge Alyssa's sarcasm. "Even before my first life, there were legends of great dragons on what was once known as the Asian continent. The Welsh recorded tales of winged dragons that breathed fire and guarded castles. The Greeks wrote about a mythical winged horse, Pegasus. They also wrote about Centaurs who were half human, half horse. Throughout history there have been legends of shape-shifters, skin-walkers, and other things we scoff away because we can't explain them with logic or science."

Alyssa struggled to concentrate on what Jael was saying rather than the movement of her lips. "Those are rather otherworldly."

"Like reading the thoughts or feelings of other people? Or like shooting fire from your fingertips?" Jael snapped her fingers to ignite, then extinguish a small flame.

She frowned. "People are quick to dismiss things they can't immediately understand." She shook her head. "But fire-breathing dragons and flying horses?"

The horses moved restlessly in the fading light, their hooves dull thumps against the turf, and Jael stood, holding out her hand to help Alyssa to her feet, too.

"Behind every legend is usually some grain of truth." Jael's fingers closed around hers as she ignited a bright, blue-white fireball in the palm of her other hand and held it aloft to push back the gathering darkness. Jael's tight grip was the only thing that kept Alyssa from a screaming, headlong sprint down the mountain when the hide on Specter's shoulders began to move like something was trying to get out.

CHAPTER THIRTEEN

Two bony protrusions sprouted and punched through bloodless skin as Specter's shrill whinny turned to a predatory scream that chilled every cell in Alyssa's body. The protrusions grew to at least a meter each and snapped open to form three-meter leathery wings. He shook his great wings and reared, baring sharp teeth and huffing his own blue-white fireball into the dark sky.

"Stars above," Alyssa breathed. "Great stars above!"

One by one, the other horses transformed and lunged skyward to disappear into the darkness. Only Specter remained, breath escaping in a plume of white smoke.

"Where are they going? We have to warn people." Her thoughts ricocheted wildly in her head. Giant bats, indeed. Would they descend on neighboring farms or the camp in the valley to carry off cattle or people to roast for a meal?

Specter snorted, shooting small spurts of flame from his wide nostrils.

She sucked in a breath, her eyes still fixed on him. "We have to stop them." She blinked in the darkness when Jael extinguished the fireball in her hand, but a full moon was rising and her eyes began to adjust.

Jael slid an arm around her shoulders. "They're flying off to meet their warriors. The bond is strong and drives them to reaffirm the connection each time they transform."

"They're not going to terrorize the countryside and steal cattle?"

Jael smiled and shook her head. "They're horses—herbivores. The only things they eat that regular horses don't are rocks made from the minerals that enhance their fire-breathing ability."

Okay. The wing-sprouting was pretty weird, but fire-breathing wasn't much different from Jael's pyrotechnic ability. Who was she kidding? This fire-breathing, flying horse thing *was* big. Bigger than realizing she was an empath. More incredible than having a message implanted in your brain by your mentor, then extracted by tall and sexy. More fantastic than…well, not more fantastic than the kiss…or any of Jael's kisses. But, stars, her mind was spinning like a wind turbine. She pressed against Jael's side and wrapped her arm around Jael's waist. She was solid. The fit of her length against Alyssa was real in a world that was becoming too surreal. She took a deep breath. It was just a horse with wings—okay, a horse that glittered even in the moonlight and breathed fire. Another deep breath and curiosity began to replace her initial panic. This winged horse was incredibly beautiful. "Can I touch them?"

"Touch them?"

"His wings. Will he mind if I touch his wings?"

Specter stepped forward. The bones in his face were sawtooth ridges now. His round, dark pupils had transformed into bloodred vertical slits. Jael released her and she hesitated, but he dropped his head and slowly spread his wings low enough that she could touch them. The thin membrane of skin that stretched between the framework of bone was actually covered with thin, silky hair that glittered like the rest of Specter. "It's like someone sprinkled him with fairy dust," she said softly. She touched the hard, jagged ridge that ran the length of his face. "A very scary fairy."

"I hope you're over the vertigo, because he's our ride down the mountain."

Her heart leapt with both fear and exhilaration. "We…we're going to fly down?"

"I don't recommend stumbling down in the dark."

She tentatively touched his lips. Huge spiked teeth had replaced the blunt molars used for tearing off and chewing grass. "If he doesn't eat flesh, why does he have these wicked teeth?"

"At night, after they've transformed, they need the teeth to split rock into small-enough pieces that they can grind them into powder with their back teeth."

"They actually eat rocks?"

"Yeah. The herd managed to find an old coal mine once, and it took weeks of brushing to get their teeth white again."

Alyssa laughed at the ridiculous image in her mind of Jael brushing Specter's teeth, and Jael grinned at her. She was beginning to love that smile and the surprising flashes of Jael's playful side.

"Because of their natural grazing nature, they still forage for minerals some, but we feed them hard cubes of phosphorus that meets their metabolic needs and their desire to chew hard stuff."

She had so many questions. "So, they're regular horses during the day and flying horses at night?" She jumped when Specter lifted his head and screamed.

"He doesn't like to be called a flying horse."

Alyssa massaged her ringing ears. "Stars. I thought he didn't understand language."

"He recognizes some words."

"Okay, what should I call him?"

"He's a dragon horse. The members of The Guard are dragon-horse warriors."

"How do you get to be a dragon-horse warrior?"

"You must be born to it. Bonding with a dragon horse is dangerous, even impossible if your DNA doesn't contain the correct strand to bond with the animal's. Acceptance of diversity has brought peace and unity to the world, but it's diluted any pure ethnic or racial bloodlines so that purebloods are rare today. The dragon-horse bloodline—at least enough to maintain The Guard—has been preserved through strict protocols."

"Protocols? We're not talking about arranged marriages, are we? We learned about those in history instruction. It was a barbaric, primitive tradition."

"Marriages were arranged in the early days. Once science developed better methods, every generation has used in-vitro fertilization to ensure at least two purebloods from their lineage in each generation."

"So you're a pureblood?"

"European Caucasian, as are Second and Michael. Raven is descended from the First People. Diego and Furcho have Spanish origins. Tan came from African bloodlines, even though she talks like she's from a north region of the Third Continent. I would guess from your physical characteristics that you're nearly pure…or at least a collection of recessive pure genes, which is what we're looking for in the DNA testing we're doing in the valley."

The puzzle pieces were starting to fall together. "So, their dragon gene lured them here, and you're filtering them for the most pure?"

"We're looking for people with enough of the dragon-horse DNA sequence to possibly establish a bond."

Alyssa pondered this information while she absently stroked Specter's wings. He was quiet, resting his head against Jael's shoulder, and she wondered if he was talking to her or just reaffirming their bond, like Jael had said before. "If Furcho and Diego are both from the same line, why don't they look alike, the way you and Second are nearly identical?"

"Ah, well, because we're different." Jael left off stroking Specter and absently rubbed her shoulder. "An accident prematurely claimed our line's male pureblood several generations ago, but we were able to continue through cloning. People think clones are identical, but it depends on how the procedure is done. Also, two different surrogates gestated us, and a number of things can cause genes to mutate as the fetus grows in the womb. Second's brown eyes are a mutation. And, like identical twins, we don't share some other less obvious traits.

"She cooks, and you don't."

Jael returned her smile. "I'm right-handed and she's left-handed."

"But wouldn't that make you…I don't know…sisters?"

"The mothers who gestated and reared us were sisters, so we identify as cousins rather than sisters or twins."

"You said two from each bloodline, but there's only one from the First People and one of African descent."

"There are two more Guard units in other parts of the world. Twenty-one of us in all."

"And you're simply sleeper cells, so to speak?"

"No. Our job in peacetime is to watch and…well, burn."

"Burn?"

Jael rubbed at her shoulder again—a gesture Alyssa realized meant she was struggling with what she needed to say. She abandoned her wing-stroking to take Jael's other hand in hers. A tactile connection wasn't necessary for her to project her complete trust and respect, but touch apparently enhanced Jael's talent for reading. And, honestly, she was just giving in to the constant, overwhelming desire to touch her. She needed to hold Jael's rough hand, snuggle into her embrace as much as she wanted to tear her clothes off and explore, lay claim to every inch of her skin.

"Stop," Jael said softly. "You're projecting, and it's making it hard for me to focus."

"Sorry." What were they talking about? Burn. Stars, she was burning in her belly with need she'd never experienced. Jael's hand briefly tightened around hers, and she worked to redirect her thoughts. "What did you mean by burn?"

"More people than you'd imagine die alone in remote places. The Guard tracks the ones we know about to make sure they're cremated upon death so their souls can pass properly to the next life. The ones we miss—someone who's buried in a landslide or lost at sea for example— are badly born into their next life, and it's our duty to make sure they don't disrupt The Collective before they can be put back on track."

"Like this Prophet guy has done."

"Yes. His cult is a twofold threat. Its teachings are disrupting the unity of The Collective, and, even more dangerous, they're preaching burial rather than cremation. Their numbers already are increasing exponentially. Unchecked, we soon will be overrun with badly born, and the world will sink back into the chaos. They must be stopped."

Alyssa was beginning to connect the stars. The thousands who were drowning in despair after losing their homes and loved ones needed something to buoy them. This cult leader was claiming to have answers, however misguided, and a solution to stop the carnage. The Collective could gather an army of workers to confiscate the bodies and deliver them to crematories, but wouldn't it be better to capture the imaginations of the public with something fantastic like dragon horses? It was genius. People would drag in every dead relative they could find for the honor of being cremated by the mythical creatures. "What can I do to help?"

"We should be able to finish the screening next week, and then I'll reveal our mission to everyone. Judging from your initial reaction to Specter, we're going to need some crowd control. Your ability to project soothing vibes could be critical."

"There'll be hundreds. The most I've ever tried to calm before was a nursery with a dozen screaming babies." She pulled away, turned from Jael. She wasn't just asking her to control a huge crowd; she was asking her to drop her shields among them. She'd be inundated with their fright. Jael's arms slid around her, and her length, pressed firm against her back, absorbed Alyssa's trembling.

"I won't let you be hurt." Jael's voice was low and soft. Her cheek was warm against Alyssa's ear. "I can throw up shields if their noise overcomes you."

She turned in Jael's arms. "You need to prepare them better than you did me."

Jael nodded. "I will. I promise."

Alyssa regarded her. "You haven't been kissing up to me, so to speak, just to get my help, have you?"

Jael's kiss was hard, bright-hot cinders searing through Alyssa like flash fire, taking her breath, scorching her body. She was panting on the very edge of orgasm when Jael abruptly withdrew and pinned her with a diamond-sharp gaze. "Do I need to swear it? Or do you trust what you feel, empath?"

"I don't know." She sucked in a breath and cleared her throat to restart her brain. "I might need more proof like that to decide."

Jael's eyes darkened, and Alyssa had lifted her face for another kiss when a head-butt from Specter nearly knocked the two of them off their feet. Jael growled as she caught and steadied them.

"He's hungry and thinks the other dragon horses are going to eat his ration of phosphorus before we fly down the mountain."

"We're really going to fly?"

"Are you up to it?"

"I guess I'll have to be if the alternative is stumbling down the mountain in the dark or spending the night in the open with no bedroll."

"Okay. I'll help you on first, and then I'll hop on behind you."

"Are you sure he can carry both of us?"

Specter stamped his front foot and unfurled his wings so that Alyssa had to duck or be knocked away like an irritating fly. "I don't think he likes me."

"You insulted him."

"You said he didn't understand words."

"Sorry. I've been translating what you say in my head for him. I guess I should have toned that one down a bit."

Specter shook his head but canted his wings forward so Jael could lift Alyssa onto his back, then hop up behind her. She groped for some purchase on his slick hide, and Jael silently guided her hands to clutch his thick mane, then wrapped an arm around her waist to anchor her. "Trust that I won't let you fall and just enjoy the ride."

The press of Jael against her back and the powerful sweeps of Specter's wings lifting them from the meadow wiped any reply from her conscious thoughts. She buried one hand in Specter's silky mane while she held onto Jael's forearm with the other, clinging as tightly as possible.

Specter's shoulder muscles worked under her legs, and the flapping as they ascended was like a great sail snapping in the wind. But once they were aloft among the warm summer crosswinds, they glided through the dark in near silence.

Surprisingly, she wasn't scared. The moonlight likely distorted her depth perception, but the ground didn't look all that far away and the air currents that buoyed them felt as thick and strong as ocean tides. It was exhilarating.

Less than half an hour later, Specter executed a perfect four-hoof landing in a clearing not far from the camp's edge.

The rest of The Guard was waiting, and Second greeted them with a bucket that Specter plunged his nose into without preamble. Alyssa grimaced at the cracking and grinding as he chewed the rocks.

"He has no table manners," Jael said, helping her dismount.

Second grinned at Alyssa. "So, how did you like your trip down the mountain?"

"Amazing." The solid ground under her feet again was a bit disorienting, and she grabbed Jael's hand to steady her wobbly legs. "But I expect to wake up from this dream at any time and realize it's just too fantastic to be true." She turned to Jael, holding her gaze. "Everything is too incredible, too amazing to believe."

Second cleared her throat. "Yes, well." She glanced at their joined hands and raised an eyebrow at Jael. "I have a few loose ends to tie up when my incredibly amazing cousin can make some time for business, but tomorrow will be soon enough."

Jael ignored Second's teasing and led Alyssa to a trail that took them back to camp. But when they reached the edge of the forest, she stopped. "I have to say good night here. You should check the cold storage. I'm sure Second saved something from dinner for you."

"What? Where are you going?" She caught herself. They'd shared a few kisses, and she was already sounding like she had some claim to Jael. Still, she didn't want their time to end. She'd imagined…well, never mind because she wasn't ready to think those thoughts with Jael close enough to read them. Not when she obviously was being dismissed. "You have to eat, too. Second said she didn't need you until tomorrow."

"I'll eat. I'll have a full day tomorrow examining candidates. Duty calls now and it will be very late when I'm done. Remember, you can't tell anyone what you saw today. Not yet." Her eyes were silver in the moonlight and her breath a caress on Alyssa's lips. "I've enjoyed the day…our time together…very much." The kiss was slow and languid, but much too short. "Get some rest. I'll see you at breakfast."

The night was balmy, but she shivered at the absence of Jael's heat while she watched her disappear into the forest. She touched her fingers to her lips. The entire day seemed like a dream, and she expected to awake any minute now in her bunk, throbbing and breathless. On the other hand, if it were a dream, she wouldn't be standing at the edge of the woods, alone and aching for more.

"So, the day went well, I gather?"

Jael nodded. When she'd returned to the clearing, The Guard had been ready, and they flew several mountains away for their nightly aerial drills and flame-throwing practice. Now, the dragon horses had been released to prowl the night on their own, and The Guard was headed to their bunks.

It was late, and, while she didn't want to sleep, she longed to be alone with her thoughts and memories of her day with Alyssa. It had been a very, very long time since she'd kissed a woman and felt something more than raw lust. Kissing Alyssa had fueled her fire rather than doused it. That wasn't something she was ready to share with Second, even if her cousin was her closest confidante.

"She freaked at first when Specter's transition began, but that was helpful because I know now that I'll need to better prepare the prospects before we let them witness it. Giving her a preview was a good strategy."

"Is that all it was?"

"What do you mean?"

"I might not be an empath or telepath, but it sure felt like there was a little more than just strategy going on between you two."

Jael shrugged. She'd never hesitated to admit a physical liaison before. Dung, it was just biology. "I kissed her and she didn't slap me, if that's what you mean." She shifted under Second's gentle scrutiny. "The problem is, I don't know if I'm endangering or fulfilling our fate. I don't know if she's here to test me or help me with our mission."

"Your instincts have always been good, Jael. What does your gut say?"

Jael glanced away, then returned her gaze to hold Second's, unable to stop a small smile. "My gut wants to kiss her again."

"So, what's stopping you?"

"This is going to be a bumpy ride for her," Jael admitted. "I haven't explained the elixir or the bonding that will follow. I don't think she actually realizes that we're gearing up for a battle, not a rescue. She's never experienced physical suffering or violence."

"Didn't she tell you that she's worked with hospice patients before?"

"Yes, but hospice is about accepting death that can't be prevented. This will be about intentionally inflicting suffering. I think she'll find that very different."

"She knows death is but a gateway to rebirth."

"She accepts it because she believes in The Collective. But she's a first-life. She has no memory of previous lives as proof. Suffering can shatter belief with no foundation of proof. That's exactly why this uprising has gained a foothold."

"Don't underestimate her, Jael. She's stronger than you think. And, if she wavers, you must be her foundation, her proof that everything— no matter how brutal—is as it must be."

"I've never been good at taking things on faith myself," Jael admitted. "How can I ask her to do what I can't?"

"How can you not? The unity of The Collective is at stake."

CHAPTER FOURTEEN

The azure sky faded to gray as the punishing sun cooled to a dying ember that licked at the surrounding peaks and streaked the horizon.

The week had been endless. Despite pre-screening, they'd spent exhausting hours examining the last several hundred prospects. At the end of each long day, Jael had retreated to her study, her shields firmly in place to block the mental noise. More than anyone, Alyssa understood her need for seclusion. But the shields shut her out, too, and the barrier was jarring after the unguarded day they'd spent together, sharing kisses and fantastic secrets. The hollow ache grew in her chest every minute she spent working at Jael's side yet separated by a great chasm of emotional silence.

After five days of silence, yesterday had been the breach in the dam. Summer had reached the broiling point, but thinking about last night made Alyssa shiver despite the sweat that trickled between her shoulder blades.

Jael had eaten dinner with the rest of them for the first time that week rather than alone in her study. Afterward, she wordlessly took Alyssa's hand and led her upstairs. Her heart skittered when she realized the second floor held only sleeping quarters and personal facilities, but it sank at the sight of the twin bunks. Jael had a roommate. But Jael guided her past the bunks to a balcony that overlooked the valley.

Like tonight, dusk had been imminent.

"*Specter will be expecting you.*"

"*I told him that this evening was for you.*" Her lips were soft against Alyssa's, her hand rough and hot against her cheek. Jael's weariness flooded Alyssa, and she met it with all the tenderness that was in her heart. Jael sighed and guided them to a single lounge—the lone furniture on the balcony—and settled Alyssa between her legs, her chest a firm backrest. The camp below them teemed with people hurrying to complete tasks or line up for their dinner shift. "*Drop your shields. No filtering either,*" Jael said softly.

She was hesitant but lowered them to the din of emotions below her. Frustration, exhilaration, grumpiness, arousal, apprehension, happiness, boredom. It all slammed into her from the hundreds of souls radiating their emotions. Then it slowly quieted to a dull hum before it was gone and there was nothing again but the cocoon that was Jael.

"*How did you do that?*"

"*The same way you can fill me with peace so sweet it quiets the voices in my head.*"

She wanted to fill Jael with desire, but now wasn't the time. Jael was obviously exhausted. It was difficult to tamp her own yearning, especially with Jael's heart a strong, steady throb against her back and Jael's breath bathing her neck.

"*I'm sorry about this week,*" Jael murmured. "*Missed you.*"

Alyssa had started to turn in her arms and claim the mouth she'd dreamed about every night since their flight down the mountain. But she felt Jael relax and her breathing deepen. Not the hot, breathless coupling she'd let herself hope for when they were finally together again, but strangely satisfying nonetheless.

She had slept, too, and when she woke, it was morning and she was alone with a pillow under her head and a sheet covering her. None of The Guard was at breakfast, and she had few answers for Nicole's and Uri's questions as they ate the food she found warming in the oven, then headed to the clinic to begin their daily routine. The candidate screening finished, Alyssa felt Jael's absence like a missing limb as she bandaged cuts, treated strained muscles, and even helped set a broken arm. But a growing anticipation permeated the camp by late afternoon, and when Alyssa sensed the gathering, she led her assistants to the training field.

"Stay close," she told them. "We're about to finally learn what our secretive friends are up to."

"You're awfully calm," Nicole said, studying her. "Do you already know?"

"Jael has revealed some of it to me, but not everything, I think."

"I wondered," Uri said. He wasn't judging, just confirming that her growing closeness to their stoic leader hadn't gone unnoticed.

"She needs my help with crowd control." She should warn them, too. "What she's going to reveal is rather stunning, so be prepared to shield against the reaction."

Nicole and Uri traded a look of understanding and then took up positions to flank her as if they could physically shelter her from the crowd. Their loyalty overwhelmed her and she squeezed the hand of each. "Together, then."

Hundreds remained after weeks of evaluation, and those who had been appointed by The Guard as unit leaders grouped them into tense knots of men and women, young and mature, around colored flags that matched the armbands they wore. A raised platform had been erected at the edge of the field. When the milling about settled, all waited expectantly in the waning light.

Alyssa smiled to herself when she felt Jael's whisper in her mind. *"Ready, Advocate?"*

"Always."

The fatigue that had etched Jael's face the night before was gone as she strode to the command dais and activated the IC strapped to her forearm. She seemed impossibly tall and imposing in a flowing red cape that clasped at her neck and draped fully around her shoulders to reach just above black knee-length boots.

A hush fell over the crowd as Jael paced the long platform. Loose from the usual braid, her wheat-colored hair lifted in the wind and danced against her broad shoulders. When only the snapping of flags in the wind sounded, her low, rich tones flowed like warm silk from her communicator's amplifier.

"Each of you is here because you have blindly answered an ancient blood call. You honor The Collective with your presence and, more importantly, your patience." Her laser-blue gaze scanned their faces. "Now it is time for understanding. The things I will reveal to you tonight will test your loyalty and your concept of reality."

An uneasiness nibbled at Alyssa. What if they panicked? What if their fear overcame her?

The Guard, cloaked like Jael, discreetly moved to ring the field. Others began to notice, too, and the crowd shifted nervously. She looked to the dais and Jael's eyes held hers. She nodded at the unspoken request and focused to project feelings that would calm the rising restlessness.

Jael turned back to the crowd. "I will demonstrate, and then I will explain. Please sit so everyone can see."

When the crowd settled again, she swept the cloak behind her shoulders and every bit of breath was sucked from Alyssa's lungs. A silvery tunic and leggings hugged every muscle of her lean, strong body. The ruby-red tribal image of a winged horse was emblazoned across her chest. She licked her lips but her mouth was just as dry. Calm. Project calm. Stars, but Jael should have prepared her better. If she didn't block off the erotic images in her head, Jael's audience would be tearing their clothes off and storming the stage. Jael shot her an amused glance and paused to give Alyssa time to settle. Then, she held out her right hand, palm skyward. Only a sliver of sun still peeked over the mountains, and the flame that flickered and sprang from her palm burned bright in the twilight.

"Some, most of you, already know that you possess some pyrotechnic ability, but I'm going to show you much more than simple magic tricks."

The flame grew in volume and intensity, and when she cupped her hand, it spun into a turbulent ball. The crowd gasped as Jael flung the burning orb into the sky and it exploded like fireworks at a New Year celebration. An uncertain applause tittered across the field and then died when the fireball dissipated and they realized the sun was gone, too.

Huge solar panels positioned on the edges of the field flickered to life and pushed back the darkness to reveal that Jael was no longer on the platform, but standing on the ground with a glittering ghost-like horse. Murmurs of appreciation rippled through the ranks as Specter pranced in place under the lights.

"Do not be afraid of what you see next. There is absolutely no danger."

Jael's command was filled with authority rather than reassurance, and Alyssa fought the urge to roll her eyes. Warriors. You couldn't just command people to be calm.

"You've all read fairy tales of great lizards called dragons that breathed fire. And you know the Greek legend of a great winged horse. The truth is not far from those children's stories."

Specter's eyes glowed an eerie red and the crowd went completely silent.

"Get ready," Alyssa murmured to Uri and Nicole.

"Behold, a living, breathing dragon horse."

Specter reared as Jael's voice rang strong and loud across the field. His gleaming hide moved and shifted. Clouded breath escaped in great puffs from his wide nostrils. His deep neigh rose to a chilling shriek as great leathery wings sprouted forth from his withers and fanned the full length of his body.

Men and women sitting in the forefront crab-crawled backward, their faces white with disbelief. Some stood and stumbled backward. Alyssa felt their panic rise. Uri made a choking sound, and Nicole's fingernails dug into Alyssa's forearm.

She closed her eyes to conjure every serene picture she could imagine—a deserted beach, puppies and kittens, and her favorite field of wildflowers—then pushed her calm outward. Her head throbbed with the effort. There were too many. Their terror was too strong.

Then Uri's large hands settled on her shoulders, and Nicole's fingers curled around hers. Their energy braced her and she drew strength from them.

Alyssa!

No. We've got this. I'm okay.

The crowd steadied. Many of those wearing black armbands—marked for having the strongest DNA match—edged closer, their eyes bright with curiosity.

Specter lifted his bony head and, with a long sweep of his wings, spewed forth flames. Jael raised her hands, and flames shot forth to meet his in an explosion of blue sparks. The exclamations at the fiery display had turned from fear to wonderment.

Dragon horse and master extinguished their show, and Jael leapt onto Specter's back. She sat easily astride but held tight to his coarse mane as he reared to launch himself into the air and ascend with powerful sweeps of his great wings to fly past the solar lights and into the darkness.

The night went suddenly still, as if holding a collective breath. Then a distant whooshing grew closer and louder until the great noise filled the air. Conflicting winds rocked the solar panels and buffeted those standing. The Guard flung back their capes to reveal silvery uniforms the same as Jael's, except that their dragon-horse insignia was displayed in black.

Jael and Specter reappeared out of the inky night, and the dragon horse's hooves rapped sharply against the wood as he settled on the platform. Jael raised her hands, her amplified voice cutting through the lashing wind. "Guard. Call your mounts."

They raised their arms and a chorus of shouts and whistles rang out. Dragon horses swooped from the sky, first one, then more, until each had a prancing winged steed at their side. The wind and noise quieted as the animals settled.

"Behold, The Guard of Peace."

Their wings glittered under the lights like raindrops sprinkled on a gossamer web. They were so powerfully beautiful next to their silver-clad handlers that gooseflesh tingled down Alyssa's arms. Their stances spread and capes popping in the wind, each member of The Guard turned to Jael and saluted their leader, right fists thumping against left shoulders.

"Furcho," Nicole breathed out. "Oh my stars!"

Alyssa fell into Jael's vibrant gaze and was flooded with the dragon-horse master's pride, honor, commitment to duty, and…a wisp of sadness. But she had no chance to decipher that. Jael's attention returned to her prospective army.

"The Guard is as old as civilization. Dragon-horse warriors were here even before the dark centuries in which the population was filled with fear and fragmented by their misguided beliefs that only chosen souls could ascend to the highest plane. Then the Great War of Religions gave us a clean slate and the unity of The Collective was realized." She swept her arm toward The Guard. "Only a core of that Guardian army has been maintained as watchers during the long peace that followed." She strode to the edge of the platform, her expression fierce and her hands clenched into fists. "But a new, dangerous threat to our peace has risen, and The Guard must respond. Their numbers are growing and so must ours."

Murmurs rippled across the field as they anticipated her next words.

"I told you earlier that instinct drew you here. More specifically, you all possess some fragment of the DNA that produces pyro ability." She paused and looked into the faces of those wearing black bands. "Some of you have a significant amount of the ancient genetic material required to bond with a dragon horse."

The hard wall of fear abated, and Alyssa relaxed as the crowd stirred with a mix of excitement and caution. Jael paused, scanning the field as the din of noise rose. When her gaze settled on her, Alyssa felt her triumph. She nodded her encouragement, and Jael returned her attention to the crowd. She raised her hand, but as the crowd quieted a young man stood.

"Choose me! I can ride a dragon horse." He pulled off his black armband and held it aloft as he flicked his other hand to ignite his fingers in an unnecessary show.

A woman, nearing her fourth decade, stood and mimicked the fist-to-shoulder salute of the Guard. "I'll pledge to your service," she declared.

Others came to their feet, their shouts ringing out and overlapping each other in a groundswell. Jael raised both hands over her head and they fell silent.

"The Guard is honored. But before you pledge, you must consider some things. Sit and listen very carefully."

Jael glanced her way and Alyssa drew a sharp breath. For a sliver of a second, little more than a blink, she felt uncertainty. She must have imagined it. Jael was the most certain, absolutely sure person she'd ever encountered.

"Diversity is the very foundation of the peace and has brought many good things to pass. Today, no child is hungry or uneducated. Anyone who falls ill receives care. Women and men are treated equally. We are free to mate and bond with anyone of our choosing." She paused, as though searching for words. "And while The Collective celebrates this, it has diluted the strength of the dragon-horse warrior bloodlines. None of you are purebloods. Your DNA has mutated into forms that make your suitability for service uncertain. Your participation is fraught with danger before you ever take to the skies on a dragon horse."

She paced the platform, her cape swirling behind her, and gestured as she explained. "If you elect to serve, you will undergo thirty days of intense physical, pyro, and military training. You will receive a daily dose of an elixir to enhance your pyro abilities. It could make some of you slightly ill and some gravely ill. For a few, it can be potentially fatal. Unfortunately, we have no way to judge your reaction until you ingest it."

Alyssa drew back in surprise, her assignment forgotten. She felt Uri's hand on her back, steadying her.

"The physical and pyro training will be dangerous, as well. The elixir will increase your ability a thousandfold." She turned her hand up and palmed a fireball. Second wheeled over a handcart piled high with building debris from their camp construction and parked it at the end of the stage. Jael's fireball burned orange, then blue, then nearly white before she flung it. The cart ignited in a whoosh, and, a second later, nothing remained but ash and melted metal. "A misstep during training can seriously injure or incinerate you or your fellow trainees."

Some glanced about, checking the reaction of their peers, but the eyes of a core group never wavered from Jael's face.

"Finally, there is a nest of wild dragon horses a short travel from here. If you survive the elixir and the training, then you will have a chance to bond with your own dragon horse. That, in itself, holds great danger. A misstep and the animal you have chosen could incinerate you before you can bond." She paused, meeting the gaze of one volunteer, then another and another. "If you survive all of this and successfully bond, then you will face your greatest test. Ask yourself this: Can you prematurely end the life of another to defend and preserve The Collective?"

Alyssa stared at the pile of ash. Sure, she'd deduced that Jael's abilities would be used to cremate the dead, but she'd never considered the possibility that a live person could be intentionally incinerated.

"Many of you have other things you must consider—children, mates, elderly parents dependent on your support. There are potential bond animals for fewer than a hundred. So, you will have no shame in weighing your priorities and returning home. If you stay and fail to qualify at any point, many other support positions are available that are vital to forming and mobilizing this unit. You have twenty-four hours to consider it. No one will be permitted to leave the valley during this period. Those who choose to leave tomorrow will have this place and our mission wiped from their memory. Then each will be given a transport ticket home or to join one of The Collective's disaster-relief teams." She straightened to her full height, her hands on her hips. "Guard, take your posts."

Another salute and each of the six leapt onto the back of their steed and lifted upward in a great flapping of wings. The trainees shielded their eyes from the whirlwind of sand and grass created by the turbulent downdraft. When the echo of the dragon horses' chilling screams died, she held their attention for a silent minute, then issued the last command. "Dismissed."

Well done, my warriors. The Guard was no longer in sight, but Jael knew the members would receive her telepathed message. They must be vigilant, relentlessly patrolling the exits from the valley over the next twenty-four hours. One spy slipping away unnoticed could give away their location and their secret. No one could leave without having the past weeks wiped from their memory. She would join their patrol, too, after she checked on one fiery-haired matter. Although Alyssa physically remained on the field, her vibrant essence had vanished. She had shut down, shields firmly in place.

Alyssa hadn't taken her eyes from the pile of ashes and melted metal, and Jael approached her cautiously. A jerk of her head sent Nicole and Uri reluctantly on their way so she could talk to her alone. She laid her hand on the crest of her shoulder, a gesture that would be interpreted as friendly if one didn't notice the caress of her fingers against Alyssa's neck.

"Are you okay?"

Alyssa shook her head.

An unfamiliar fear nipped at her insides. "I…I'm sorry. When I tried to shield you, you waved me off. I should have sensed that you were in trouble." Had she been so buoyed by their initial success that she hadn't felt Alyssa being overcome?

Alyssa shrugged off her hand and whirled to face her. Her eyes were green sparks of fury. Despite being taller, stronger, and battle-trained, Jael took a step back.

"I wasn't overwhelmed. I was fine. But this—" She waved her hand at the dark lump that remained of the handcart. "This is not fine."

"I told you before we started screening people that you should expect to treat burn injuries in the clinic once we began pyro training."

Alyssa pointed to the ashes again. "How would I treat this if it were a person? Even the most advanced medicine can't regenerate muscle and skin on a pile of ashes."

"We'll take every precaution so something this severe won't happen."

Alyssa crossed her arms over her chest. "I almost got caught up in the romantic notion of dragon horses and guardian warriors, too, but this, Jael, is too much." She punctuated her words with her hands. "There's got to be a better way to deal with this problem. We don't have to turn people into human torches."

"Listen to me. We got word a few hours ago that this cult has taken over a central food-distribution center for the Fifth Sector. They've stopped all shipments except to their own followers."

"Let the peacemakers handle this."

"With what? These people have armed themselves with stunners they stole from the peacemakers' headquarters while the officers were assisting disaster victims. We've heard that they've even fashioned some projectile weapons—guns and rifles—using instructions hacked from encrypted digital archives. Sooner or later, they're going to figure out how to make weapons that have been banned for more than a hundred years, and I'm not talking about bullets that can be stopped with armor. Lasers, Alyssa. How will we deal with them then? How will we stop their food-hoarding to feed their followers while others starve?"

"I don't know. But you can't just fly in there on dragon horses and turn them into ashes."

Jael was silent.

As Alyssa's own words sank in, her expression turned from angry to horrified. "That's exactly what you've been planning all along. You're going to incinerate crowds of live people."

"Not crowds. Armies." Jael reached for her as Alyssa stumbled backward, but she batted her hands away.

"Don't. Don't touch me. I trusted you. I believed that you had evolved like the rest of the world beyond the violent mayhem of your past. How could I not have sensed that an animal still existed in you?"

Jael's insides, her heart went cold at Alyssa's bitter words. "My destiny is to serve The Collective. I am this animal because they need me and my warriors to protect their reign of peace."

Alyssa stared at her for a long minute, her face unreadable, then turned to walk away. She had gone only a few paces when she turned back, and Jael braced for another wave of vitriol.

"I will never find violence acceptable or those who wield it, especially not in the name of peace." Her eyes filled with tears and her voice cracked with disappointment. "I trusted you. I was—" The words that were lost in a choked sob twisted into Jael more cruelly than a long, jagged blade. *I was falling in love with you.*

CHAPTER FIFTEEN

"If they don't have at least second-degree burns, I don't have time to see them, no matter who it is." Alyssa regretted snapping at Nicole the minute the words had left her mouth. She sighed and finished wrapping a sterile bandage around the hand of another pyro-training casualty. When Nicole announced she had a visitor, she immediately thought of Jael. It had been ten long, excruciating days since their confrontation, and her nerves were raw to the point of tearing. But it couldn't be Jael. She wouldn't have asked Nicole to announce her visit. It must be someone else. "Please tell them I'm too busy treating patients."

Alyssa gently released her patient's hand. "It's looking much better and we need your bed, so I'm going to clear you to return to your quarters. Check in with the medic assigned to your building. They'll have your treatment plan d-messaged to them and will be responsible for changing your bandage and monitoring your progress." She made a series of notes on her digital tablet. "Which building are you assigned to?"

"The Dragon House." The young man squirmed under Alyssa's hard stare. "Uh, building D." He indicated the black band tied around his head. It had been around his arm marking him as a prime prospect when they brought him in, and when they'd had to cut off the sleeves of his tunic to treat his burns, he'd refused to part with it. "All the black bands live in that building. That's why we call it the Dragon House. When can I get back to training?"

Alyssa wanted to shake him. Was he that anxious to take another life? Ha. She shouldn't be too worried. Judging from his wounds, he was more likely to incinerate himself before he could hurt someone else.

"I can only heal your wounds. I have no idea if you'll be able to even handle fire again. That's up to—" What should she call her? Tanisha? Dr. Tanisha? She'd heard some use military rank, which she had no idea about.

"Captain Tan?"

"Yes. She'll have to clear you to resume training."

Nicole appeared in the doorway.

"Nicole, can you process Anwar's return to his quarters?"

"Sure. What about your visitor? He insists on waiting."

Alyssa closed her eyes and dropped her chin to her chest. She was physically and emotionally exhausted. The constant flow of training injuries barely left her time to sleep, so it hadn't been hard to avoid Jael, but not talking to her had created what felt like an empty crater in her chest where her heart used to beat. "I've got nine more patients to see on this ward alone. I don't have time."

"Not even for an old friend?"

The rush of confusing emotions nearly drowned her. She wanted to burst into tears, and she wanted to scream in anger. Her mentor, the man who had started her on this tumultuous journey, stood in the doorway, smiling. "Honored Advocate."

Han accepted her flat greeting with knowing eyes and a polite nod. "Perhaps if I could lighten your workload by seeing some of your patients, we would have time to talk."

To refuse would show disrespect, and she recognized this was not a request, but a gentle command. He did outrank her in the temple hierarchy. She nodded and indicated the beds lining the left side of the ward. "I'll work this side if you take the other. This is the burn ward, so almost all need bandages changed and wounds evaluated."

She figured he must be well over ninety years old, but he still moved with an easy grace. She'd never thought about it before, but she wondered fleetingly if he was a pureblood of Asian descent. The emphasis on DNA over the past weeks had made her see people differently. Was this how people in the previous century viewed each other? Grouping themselves by hair color, eye shape, and complexion? Was it different from the way she'd always grouped people by whether they possessed a talent or not? Did she view those who did not have a special talent as less then her? The questions were too hard to ponder in her depleted mental state. Or maybe the answers were too hard to accept.

She shook her head to clear her thoughts and picked up the next chart. "Bast, let's have a look at the burn on your leg."

The young woman, not more than eighteen years, was long-limbed and athletic. Her Mediterranean coloring and features hinted at an ancient lineage. She had a quiet manner but had proved to be a tireless worker when they were setting up the clinic. Although her only experience was lifting large boxes and hammering shelves together, her questions about the herbs and their uses had Alyssa considering her as an apprentice. Those plans were dashed the day Bast rushed into the clinic to show off the black band tied around her arm.

"Can you use the regenerator on it? I want to get back to training as soon as possible."

"This is a pretty deep burn. It'll be a lot less painful if we let the muscle heal slowly. Then I'll use the regenerator to repair the skin."

"How long will that take?"

"Several weeks for the muscle to heal."

"No! I can't miss that much training."

Alyssa frowned and sprayed the wound with a numbing solution. "How did this burn happen?"

"We were learning to refract."

"Refract?"

"Bounce our flame off metal or rock to hit a target." Bast's usually guarded expression was animated. "Different materials refract at various angles. You have to learn to take that into consideration when you bounce a flame off something. It's sort of like the angles in billiards. I'm pretty good at it. Top in the class, actually."

"If you're so good at it, how'd you manage to almost burn your leg off?" Her enthusiasm only irritated Alyssa more. She activated the debris scanner. She was becoming used to the stench of dissolving skin as the scanner evaporated dead tissue from the wound.

Bast grimaced. The numbing solution couldn't fully anesthetize the live flesh when it was still covered with dead tissue. "Got…careless. Won't…do that…again." She let out a breath when Alyssa switched off the scanner.

"Hurts, huh?"

Sweat beaded on Bast's upper lip. "I can handle it."

"If I use the regenerator on the muscle and force those nerves to repair quickly, it'll hurt even more. And the pain won't stop until the nerves have fully regenerated."

"How…how long?"

Alyssa studied her patient. "Three days minimum, maybe as long as a week."

"Then I'll be healed? I can get back to training?"

"A week of constant, shooting pain. Medication can dull it, but it's impossible to stop it. I don't recommend it."

"How long if I don't do it?"

"Four weeks for the muscle to heal enough for me to regenerate the skin and close the wound."

Bast shook her head firmly. "I'll miss the bonding." She sat up straighter, her eyes boring into Alyssa's. "I can't miss the bonding, ma'am. I have to be a dragon-horse warrior. First Warrior is counting on me."

"First Warrior?"

"Jael, ma'am. She's First Warrior to The Collective. She's the… the general over everybody."

"General?"

"That's a military rank—the highest you can be."

"Yes, I know."

"She's amazing."

Alyssa gritted her teeth. She wanted to roll her eyes at the reverence shining in Bast's eyes. She wanted to grab her and shake some sense into the young woman. But then she'd have to shake some sense into every other patient in the ward. They all idolized Jael and The Guard.

"Do you know what my name means?"

"No."

"It means born of the sun." Bast held out her hand and a small fireball appeared over her palm. "I was born for this."

"Bast, do you understand what they're training you to do?" Her question was gentle.

Bast looked away, but her expression was stoic. "Yes. I do."

"You may have to take another person's life. Do you think you can do that?"

When Bast looked up, her eyes were filled with certainty. "I haven't experienced a lot of things, seen a lot of places like you have. I'm just a girl who grew up on a farm cooperative. But I know about doing what has to be done. When my family was hungry and grain stores were low, I had to slaughter the animals I'd help birth and tended. If I didn't, my family would starve."

"Taking a human life isn't the same. You'll live the rest of your lifetime with your regret."

"If the First Warrior says it must be to protect The Collective, then I will not regret doing what must be done."

Alyssa sighed at the absolute conviction in Bast's quiet declaration. This was a battle she couldn't win. "Muscle regeneration must be done in a surgery room. I'll schedule you for tomorrow morning, if you're sure."

Bast nodded firmly. "Very sure. Thank you."

The rest of the burns were much like Bast's. As the warrior candidates drank their daily elixir, their pyro abilities intensified and the burn injuries coming into the clinic became more severe. Still, those candidates hoping to be dragon-horse warriors never faltered. Not even when four were severely burned over eighty percent of their bodies because they couldn't control their own flames. Not even when one of the four died.

To Jael's credit, she held very public funeral pyres for the unfortunate candidate and another who died almost instantly from a violent allergy to the elixir. She didn't try to hide the danger or consequences of their training and mission. But, apparently, the possibility that it could be just as easily one of them burning on that pyre to release their soul didn't dissuade the eager candidates. She remembered her reluctance to embrace her own talent and felt a bit ashamed in the face of their unflagging dedication. Maybe it was part of their warrior DNA.

She looked up from making notes on her final patient and found Han, his last patient resting peacefully, waiting patiently for her by the door. She was still mentally working through her warring emotions and wasn't ready to explain herself, to argue her case. But what was there to argue? Peace could not be won by violence. She believed that with her very core. A wide, roaring river separated her and Jael, no matter how much she wanted to bridge their differences.

"Walk with me," Han said when she approached.

She followed silently as he led her to the southern edge of the encampment, past the animal pens to a small grove of banana trees that were in various stages of ripening their fruit. They walked among the wide, tattered fronds of the plants, and he picked two of the ripe fruit for them to eat.

"Did you know that bananas are the number-one fruit consumed in the world?"

As bone weary as she was, she recognized Han's tone. A lesson was coming, and she was surprised to feel the weight of her internal conflict and responsibilities lighten a bit as they slipped into their familiar teacher-student roles. "More than strawberries?"

He smiled at his intelligent pupil's expected question. She never accepted a lesson without challenging him with questions.

"More than strawberries, because this fruit is a food staple in many tropical regions. It's not a dessert but essential to their diet."

They walked through the grove and Han pointed to different varieties of the fruit, all growing in the same stand of plants. He cited their names and uses: cooking bananas versus those typically eaten raw.

The sound of chopping grew louder as they neared the center of the grove, and they came upon a man wielding a machete to hack the large plant into sections and toss them onto a ragged blanket spread on the ground nearby. They watched until the shoots of the plant were gone and the man picked up a shovel to dig.

When he'd exposed the corm, the huge bulbous heart of the plant, he knelt and laid his hand on it. "Forgive me, old friend. You have borne fruit and fed my family for many years. You have multiplied, and now your children that surround us feed many families. I thank you for your service."

He stood and began to dig around the corm, cutting through the roots that nourished the plant.

"Sir, why are you killing your banana tree?" Han asked.

The man didn't look up. "A fungus has infected it," he said as he continued to dig. "If I don't remove the plant, I could lose them all."

"Is there no other way?"

"The fungus lives in the corm and spreads through the roots, so I must kill the heart of the plant to stop the disease. It must be done to save the rest."

Han nodded and they walked on until they reached a clearing bathed in warm sunlight and carpeted with thick grass, where he indicated for her to join him in sitting cross-legged, hands resting palm up on their knees. She closed her eyes and turned her face into the sun, absorbing its warmth and energy as they rested in companionable silence. She relaxed into their meditation and began to drift.

Jael's meadow was filled with an explosion of color—wildflowers dancing gently in the breeze. Children she recognized from the school at her old temple played around her, shrieking and laughing as they chased each other. She laughed, too, and tied daisies into necklaces for them to wear. She felt rested and happy for the first time in weeks.

A loud bellow from the edge of the woods startled her. The children froze in terror as a great bear lumbered out of the tree line and stood upright, its small, dark eyes finding the youngsters. It roared again and pawed at a wood shaft protruding from its ribs. It was wounded and angry.

The children's shrieks were filled with terror now, and they ran to her. She reached out to the bear, but a wall of delirious fury and pain met the soothing thoughts she projected. It charged and the children screamed. The house. They needed to run to the house. She turned, but it seemed impossibly far. She shouted to the children, but they only clung to her in their fear so she couldn't run either. The bear roared and gnashed its great teeth as it galloped toward them.

Suddenly, great balls of flame exploded in front of and around the bear. Jael! The silver uniform of the dragon-horse warrior glinted in the sun. She threw fireball after fireball, but the bear didn't alter his course. Alyssa's ears rang with his snarls. She could almost feel his foul breath and smell his fetid wound when a swirling ball of white-hot flame enveloped him in a huge whoosh. The force of it knocked her to the ground and seared her skin. She covered the children with her body to shelter them from it, and the bear vanished with a sharp yelp.

The yelp, she realized was her own as she jerked back to reality, panting against the terror that constricted her chest. Her heart thudded in her ears. There was no bear—only Han sitting across from her, watching.

"Stars." She scowled at him and started to rise.

"Sit." His command was gentle, but she sank back to the ground, her legs too weak to stand. The vision had been so real, it had sapped what little strength she had left after her long hours in the clinic.

"Why did you shelter the children with your body?"

The question wasn't what she'd expected him to ask. "It was a natural reflex."

"The natural reaction to fear is flight. But you did not run."

"I wanted to, but the children were too afraid to run with me."

"Perhaps if you'd let the bear eat just one child or maybe two, he would have been satisfied. You could have escaped with the others, and the First Warrior would not have killed him."

She stared at him. That was ludicrous. She stood again. "Look. I know where you're going with this. But taking a human life isn't the same. We have time and options other than incinerating people." This conversation was headed nowhere and she needed to return to the clinic. She turned to leave, but he stood and stopped her with a firm grasp on her forearm.

"Time? Do we? You've been sequestered by your duties in recent weeks and unaware of what's happening. This group that calls itself The Natural Order already has hijacked food distribution in the Third Continent. People are choosing sides for and against them. The cities are filled with bloody rioting. Do you need to hear the cries of the hungry children? Do you need to see the bloodied bodies of those who are fighting for control of the food supplies? The fungus is already spreading to the grove. The First Warrior and her army must destroy the root so the fungus will die."

In all the years she'd known Han, she'd never heard him speak so ardently. Was it fear or anger that hardened his eyes?

"Peace cannot be won with violence."

"Was the meadow again peaceful once the bear was gone?"

She stared stubbornly at the ground, refusing to concede the point. "You can tell Jael that sending for you was a waste of your time."

He cupped her chin to raise her eyes to his. "Jael didn't summon me. The Collective Council sent me. Even ones as evolved as they still grow in understanding. They have a message for you."

Her breath caught. "For me?" The Council was sending a message to a first-life?

Han nodded. "War and peace may seem like night and day. But without the dawn, day would not break. Without dusk, night would not come. The Collective can only be restored when the warrior finds peace and an Advocate takes up her mantle."

"My mantle? What does that mean?"

"The message is repeated as spoken, but I believe they are saying that it will take both the First Warrior and the First Advocate to make our world right again."

"First Advocate?"

Pride shone in Han's eyes, admiration for *her.* "The Council has declared it."

Alyssa wavered. "I can't."

"Compromise. Meet in the twilight and seek the dawn." His voice softened and he took her hand in his. "From the time your parents first brought you to the temple, I knew there was something great in your future. You must let it happen. You must go to her." He raised his hand to stop her protest. "Just as it was inherent in you to shelter the children, the First Warrior has been born many times over for one purpose—to protect The Collective. She is doing what she must, and your condemnation is a wound that has left her vulnerable before she ever reaches the battlefield."

She hung her head. She knew her words had been harsh, but she expected that they'd bounced right off Jael's stubborn sense of right. Had her anger actually wounded her? She couldn't bear the thought. Stars, she wanted to go to her. She wanted to massage Jael's temples and offer her respite from the voices, the pyres that weighed so heavy on those strong shoulders. She wanted to feel Jael's arms around her again. She wanted those callused hands on her breasts and her hands on Jael's naked body. She wanted Jael's mouth everywhere. She shuddered. "She probably doesn't want to see me. I said some mean things to her."

He smiled. "Then a twilight truce is in order. You will learn to apologize, and your warrior will learn to forgive."

CHAPTER SIXTEEN

Kyle crept softly down the hallway, glad they at least let her wear tennis shoes with the mid-calf skirt. Damn, she hated these clothes. But now wasn't the time to sulk over wearing dresses. She recognized the male voices at the end of the hall, and she needed to hear what her father and Simon were planning. She sidled close to the door, her back pressed to the wall to keep watch in both directions.

"You were right that the larger cities would be the easiest to win. They are hungry for The Natural Order."

"Didn't I tell you that without resources for growing their own food, the city dwellers would fall in line as meek as sheep?" Simon's gravelly voice was a sharp contrast to her father's smooth baritone. "Food is power. We control almost a third of the world's food distribution now. When we take the central warehouses in the Fourth Continent, we'll control another third. They can join us or starve."

"I take no pleasure in starving people, Simon, but The One has told me it is necessary to take care of our followers and recruit more. If others are hungry, it's because they refuse to recognize the imperative to return to The Natural Order. Society cannot survive without a hierarchy and natural selection."

Simon's laugh was cruel. "Yeah. Natural selection. I miss my old life of capitalism and cutthroat politics."

Cyrus growled. "This isn't a game, Simon. This belief in a collective conscious is nothing more than dressed-up socialism that rewards the weak and strong equally. It's unnatural. It steals drive and ambition. It's not what The One intended when he created this world."

"Game or not, you better have some strategy ready for when The World Council finally decides to fight back."

Kyle was convinced that her father was insane, but Simon was the more dangerous of the two. He seemed to have no conscience. How many times did a soul have to be badly born to be that damaged?

Cyrus scoffed. "I'm not worried. They have no army, no general. Leadership requires vision and they have none. They're just a bunch of quartermasters worrying over shipping schedules."

"I already have reports of gatherings in the First Continent, the Second Continent, and near us in the lower Sierra Madre."

"Stupid rumors."

"No. Reliable reports from spies I pay good credits."

There was a long silence, and Kyle heard footsteps behind her. Another minute and whoever was coming would round the corner and see her lurking outside the door. She had nowhere else to go, so she knocked softly on the wall and stepped into the doorway. "Oh, I'm sorry. I thought Father was alone. I'll come back later."

"Kylie." Cyrus frowned. He was sitting at his desk while Simon stood near a window. "Where's Ruth? You should be in the women's dormitory."

She stepped into the room. "I, uh, was going to the personal facilities to shower." She held up the towel and plastic bag of toiletries as evidence. Thank the stars she'd thought ahead. "I planned to speak to you tomorrow, but I was walking past and was hoping maybe I could see you tonight." She made a show of ducking her head and looking embarrassed. "I'm rather anxious to speak to you about a personal matter."

She had half listened as the footsteps grew closer and turned when Ruth appeared in the doorway. "Kylie. There you are. It's almost time for the evening teaching." She smiled at Cyrus and glanced nervously at Simon. Kyle wasn't the only one who was cautious around him. "I hope she didn't interrupt anything important."

"Kylie said she wanted to speak to me about something," he said.

"I can talk to you tomorrow," she said, making a show of glancing nervously about the room.

"I have a full day of meetings tomorrow. You can speak freely in front of Ruth and Simon."

Crap. She'd hoped she wouldn't have to pull out her only ace so soon, but she had no choice. She offered a small smile to Ruth but wouldn't even pretend to acknowledge Simon, no matter what the cost. "It's just that, um, I wanted to speak to you about a young man I met."

Ruth's face lit up with a broad smile. "Will! I knew you two had hit it off."

Kyle ducked her head again and nodded. She was getting good at this acting stuff. "He's nice and I...I like him."

Cyrus sat back in his chair, his eyes suspicious until Ruth spoke up.

"The young man joined the group at our last mission site. He was seeking help for his mother who was in very poor health and unfortunately passed away shortly after they arrived. I wasn't sure he would stay, but I think he did because he seems quite taken with our Kylie." She smiled again at Kyle. "He's very handsome and well-mannered."

Cyrus drummed his fingers lightly on the desk.

"I was hoping you could meet him and give us permission to sit together at services," Kyle said, twirling a lock of hair around one finger in what she hoped would appear as a girlish nervous gesture.

The finger-drumming stopped.

"I tell you what," Cyrus said. "I am arranging a trip to affirm our mission in the Fourth Continent." He glanced at Simon. "Simon had the brilliant idea of traveling by solar train so we can stop in the towns along the way to personally carry the message of The One to everyone." He looked back at Kyle. "Your young man may come along with the other men I've chosen so I can get to know him. You and Ruth, and two other women Ruth selects, will accompany us to take care of domestic chores for the group."

She didn't have to pretend this time. Her smile was genuine. "Father! Thank you. The Fourth Continent! I've never been there." He couldn't know that his trip would be taking her within hiking distance of her goal. "This is so exciting. I can't wait to tell Will. I need to pack."

Ruth laughed at Kyle's enthusiasm. "I'm sure you have plenty of time. Now, go shower quickly so you won't miss evening teaching."

Cyrus stood. "Do as Ruth says. We won't be leaving until day after tomorrow."

Kyle stepped forward tentatively, then gave her father a quick hug. He jerked in surprise before closing his arm around her. "Thank you, Father," she whispered against his chest.

She surprised Ruth, too, with a quick peck on the cheek before she fled the room and nearly floated to the showers. Meeting Will had been sheer luck. Or was it fate that had brought their paths together? He was tall and muscular, ruggedly handsome, intelligent, funny…and one hundred percent same-sex oriented.

❖

She fell to her knees, head bowed as the funeral pyres burned around her, their flames jagged against the night sky. Warriors' shields glowed red hot at the base of each pyre, identifying the dead. The shield in front of her was her own, but she was not the human torch at the top of the pyre, and the shield strapped to her own arm wasn't hers. Second. They were gone, all gone. She had failed.

The heat seared her skin. The absence of voices, the thoughts of her army was a maddening, hollow silence. Embers riding on the wind stung her skin like fiery needles. She deserved the pain and so much more. She welcomed it.

A scream tore at the quiet, and she staggered to her feet. Specter! She wasn't alone. Not yet. She ran, weaving through a hundred pyres, her lungs burning, her legs threatening to collapse. She could see him, his breath a blue-white flame as it ignited still another pyre. But there was no shield at the base of this pyre. A profound dread filled her as Specter fanned the flames with his great wings, and she raised her eyes to the shroud laid atop the frame of the traditional open pyre for a warrior.

The shroud moved and fell away as the figure sat up. Dark-red spikes contrasted against the blue-white flames, and forest-green eyes stared down at her. Jael. Jael.

"Jael. Jael. No, it's okay." Soft hands caressed her face, her neck, as a soothing blanket of calm wrapped around her terror. "It was just a dream."

She blinked to focus in the dim light, her rapid breaths harsh in the quiet. No, it wasn't quiet. She never thought she'd be happy about white noise of a hundred thoughts bouncing off her mental shields, but it was a million times better than that horrible silence. A halo of red spikes and concerned green eyes filled her vision, but these were real.

She surged upward and wrapped Alyssa in a desperate hug, burying her face against her cool neck. She smelled of coconut and vanilla.

"Honey. What is it? You're drenched and shaking."

She couldn't say it. If she shared her doubts, it would give them root…as if they weren't already growing in her subconscious. She'd never doubted before. Not like this. She'd second-guessed tactics, even retreated to regroup. But she'd never doubted success in the end. This was the most important battle of her many lives, and she was losing her nerve. It would mean sure disaster for those who followed her.

"I'm sorry." She let go, swinging her legs over the side of her bed and turning away from her embarrassing display. Dung. She was clinging like a baby to a first-life who had more confidence than she.

"No, I'm sorry." Alyssa's hand pressed against her sweaty back.

Jael sprang to her feet and moved across the room. She didn't deserve the connection, the comfort it gave her. But Alyssa followed, pressing against Jael's back and wrapping her arms around Jael's waist, preventing further escape.

"This is my fault. I'm responsible for your doubts. I planted the seed for that horrible dream."

Jael shivered at the light kisses peppering her bare shoulders. She'd been sleeping as usual, clad in only her low-cut briefs. "You could see my dream?" Nakedness never bothered her, but Alyssa's hands gently stroking along her stomach were making it hard to think. She felt Alyssa shudder.

"It was horrible. You were thrashing about and I only intended to calm you. But when I touched you, it was like when you showed me your past lives." She shuddered again. "I'm so, so sorry. I was angry and hurt, but I was wrong to say such awful things."

Jael turned in her arms and drew her against her chest. "You only said what you believe. Maybe you're right. Maybe I'm the one who's wrong. Things are different after a hundred years of peace. Maybe my time has passed."

"Neither of us is wrong, and neither is right," Alyssa murmured, her cheek rubbing against Jael's nipple.

She buried her face in Alyssa's soft spikes and stroked her hands down Alyssa's back.

"Jael?"

"Huh?" Sun and moon, she felt good. Cool against Jael's overheated skin. She felt like—

"Can we figure this out later? I don't think I can focus right now."

Dragon dung. What was she thinking? Alyssa had seen the same dream. She must be even more shaken than Jael. She tightened her arms around her. "Are you okay?"

"No. No, I'm not." Her breath skated across Jael's chest, tightening her nipples and groin. "You're kind of naked and making me crazy."

She looked up, desire burning in her eyes, a flame drawing Jael down and swallowing her in its heat as their tongues met and stroked and stoked their burning.

"Bed," Alyssa breathed. "Make love to me, Jael."

She wanted to. Stars, she needed to. "Second will be coming up for bed in just a minute."

"No. She's not. She's sleeping in your office tonight."

She swept Alyssa off her feet and into her arms in one swift move, then carried her back to the rumpled sheets. She'd think later about the conspiracy behind this rare privacy or the narrow bed designed for one. She wanted this woman with a need so deep, she could wait no longer.

She lowered her gently to the bed, holding Alyssa's gaze as she drew her pants and briefs down her legs and tossed them on the floor. Alyssa sat up to shed her tunic and Jael stepped out of her briefs. They stared at each other for a long minute, and then Alyssa held out her arms. Jael carefully lowered herself so that they were on their sides, facing each other.

This was about finding passion rather than relieving need, so she would go slowly.

She traced the curve of Alyssa's hip, smoothed her hand along the arch of her back. She claimed her mouth with a soft brush of her lips, then a slow, languid swirl of their tongues. She tasted the lobe of her ear and sucked gently at the throbbing pulse of her neck while she traced the firm slope of her shoulder.

"You're so beautiful." Her words were too ordinary for such an exquisite woman, but no words existed that would suffice.

She took a taut nipple in her mouth and turned her hand to brush the soft backs of her fingers against the other. Then Alyssa stopped her, turning Jael's hand and opening it to cover her swollen breast.

"I want all of you, even the calluses on your hands." Her hand covering Jael's, she rubbed it against her skin, across the hardened nipple, and moaned. "It feels good. So good."

Her moan was Jael's undoing. She could go slow next time. She slid down and shouldered her thighs apart. Alyssa's hips lifted with a jerk when Jael closed her hand around her breast again and nipped at the inside of her tender thigh.

"Please, Jael. I need you."

Jael growled when Alyssa reached down to open herself to her lover. She was hot and slick and heavy with desire. She breathed in her scent, musky and sweet, and tasted her in long strokes. She slid inside her, stretching and massaging the firm walls.

"Oh, stars, I can't, I'm going to—" Alyssa grabbed the pillow under her head and covered her face, screaming into it as Jael thrust deep, sucking her swollen clit against her teeth.

Her head was dizzy, her groin aching with Alyssa's muffled cry and the wave of pleasure she projected. She couldn't wait, didn't want to wait. She rose and opened herself to bring them together. She was throbbing and slid easily against her lover's sex.

Alyssa's heels dug into her thighs. "Yes, baby, like that. Sun! I'm going to come again."

She thrust wildly, bearing down to assuage the burning pain of unimaginable yearning. When Alyssa's fingers pinched hard on her nipple, the world exploded in light and color and passion that roared in her ears and screamed through her veins. And she knew she would never be the same.

The weak rays of dawn beckoned Jael from a dream so sweet she could feel the cool weight of a lover, the brush of silk tickling her breasts and the gentle exhalation of breath on her belly. She didn't want to open her eyes and leave this imagined bliss. She felt rested. No. She felt restored. The nightmare from the evening before was a faint memory, a tiger without teeth or claws.

But as the light grew stronger, her eyelids could no longer keep it at bay. Reluctantly, she blinked slowly at the ceiling. She was wet and aroused. She must not really be awake. She moved her legs, but a pleasant weight pinned her to the bed. She looked down and stilled. All she could see were wild red-gold spikes and a long bare back that begged to be stroked. It wasn't a dream.

They hadn't exactly sorted out their differences, but Alyssa had come to her. That had to mean something, didn't it? She closed her eyes and took a careful, deep breath. Their joining last night meant more than she was ready to admit.

They were dark and light. Ice and fire. A sharp blade and a slender reed. So different, yet a perfect fit. Alyssa was the melody to her percussion. She was a churning sea against Alyssa's calm, blue sky. Alyssa was the north star in Jael's velvet black night.

And it was wrong, too wrong. Her soul was so old and Alyssa's so young.

Sharp teeth tugged at the skin on her belly. "I can hear you thinking."

Jael opened her eyes again, this time to Alyssa's affectionate gaze. "When did you become telepathic?"

"It doesn't take a telepath to feel the tension in your body, and you're worrying loud enough for any amateur empath to sense."

"Alyssa—"

"If you're thinking that last night was a mistake, then think again, First Warrior."

Jael looked away, unable to say what she needed while she was drowning in those green eyes. "There's one thing you still don't know."

"Then tell me." Alyssa grasped her chin and gave her a small shake. "No more secrets, Jael." It was a soft plea.

Jael traced the rosy blush that colored Alyssa's creamy cheek. "What we shared last night...it was more than...I don't know. Just more." She stilled her finger and stared into those beautiful eyes. "This is my last incarnation, Alyssa. You are only in your first. If I...if we allow this between us, then you could spend the rest of many lives alone, like Second."

"Does Second regret her soul bond?"

"No. That's not what I'm saying."

"Are you a seer, too?"

"No, but—"

"Then how do you know this is your last incarnation? How do you know I must live many more?"

"I just know. You're not being reasonable."

"Oh, sweetie, there's nothing reasonable about this. The world has gone crazy. People are hoarding and fighting over food. In a society advanced enough for green energy, a worldwide digital network, and medical care that can cure almost any disease, we're preparing an army that will ride flying, fire-breathing horses."

Jael gently launched her last fireball. "My mission hasn't changed," she said quietly.

Alyssa sighed. "Neither has mine. But fate has paired us for a reason, and I'm done questioning it." She lowered her mouth to Jael's. "And I'm through talking."

Jael sucked in a breath when Alyssa's fingers dipped between her legs. She was full and ready and too weak to fight her any longer. Alyssa's kisses trailed down her belly. Her defenses were shattered. She closed her eyes as Alyssa's mouth claimed her flesh, her fingers filled her body, and her affection infused her soul.

She was out flanked by The Collective Council, by their mission, by this bewitching Advocate, and by her own need. She could do nothing but surrender.

CHAPTER SEVENTEEN

"Is there something on the back of my shirt?" Will turned his back to Kyle and looked expectantly at her over his shoulder.

She frowned against the glare of the sun. "Like what? I don't see anything."

"Like a target painted on my back or a hole burned between my shoulder blades where your father keeps staring at me."

She shoved him playfully. Will was the only part of this deception that was bearable. "At least you don't have to wear stupid dresses and wait on stupid-ass men every minute of the day. I swear, if that guy with a week's worth of food in his beard looks at me one more time like he can see through my clothes, I'm going to knock those bad teeth of his out of his head so he can go ahead and get dentures."

Will shuddered. "Ew. I'd hit him for you, but I don't think I could stand touching him. We've been on this train two weeks, and I don't think he's bathed the entire time."

Ruth's glare silenced them and they turned their attention back to where Cyrus stood on top of the solar train and stared out at the gathering crowd of villagers. His amplified voice boomed over them as he paced atop the train car.

"And in my bleakest hour—my mate and beloved son lost under the tons of mud that swallowed our home—He came to me. I was blinded by his light, and yet I was not afraid. 'Who are you?' I asked." Cyrus deepened his voice. "'I am The Creator of all that lives,' he replied. 'I breathed life into the sky and the earth and all that is between. I control the wind and the seas and the skies. You are nothing except what I made you to be.'"

Cyrus paused for dramatic effect. "My grief turned to anger." He raised his fists to shake them at his unseen deity. "'Then you are responsible for taking my family, for killing millions with wind and fire and flood,' I cried. 'No,' The One said. 'Your own actions have brought these consequences. I was silent while you appointed yourselves as a collective deity and denied your destiny of Elysium or eternal damnation. I did not interfere when you subverted The Natural Order I had created. But I have been patient long enough. And you, Cyrus, will warn the world. As my prophet, you will show your kind back to their true path.'"

He raised his eyes to the sky and opened his arms in an imploring gesture. "'What message am I to give them?' I asked." He returned his gaze to the crowd and deepened his voice again. "'Hear me speak and heed the truth or perish to an eternal void. All are not created equal, and *this* is the only life I have granted you.'"

A murmur ran through the crowd, and Cyrus waited for it to quiet.

"The ingenious will lead, and the strong will find their reward in hard labor. We have weakened our species with marriages that have diluted pure bloodlines. We have crippled our society by rewarding the productive and the non-productive equally. We have subverted The Natural Order by forcing our women from their intended purpose—to bear and nurture our children."

The crowd began to shift as people dismissed his message and moved to leave. They stilled when Cyrus's disciples slid open the doors of several train cars and began to unload food and medical supplies. He had their full attention now.

"The Advocates who pretend to represent a nonexistent collective conscious have filled you with lies, promising you other lives if you waste this one. For them, The One will show no mercy." He gestured to the crates being unloaded before the crowd. "But those who will join our mission to restore The Natural Order will reap the rewards of this earth. For its soil and everything it yields to us rightfully belongs to The One and his army of righteous soldiers. Swear your allegiance and you will share in our reward."

"You are the one who speaks lies." The man who made his way to the front of the crowd appeared to be just like the other brown-skinned, dark-haired villagers dressed in loose cotton clothing stained with sweat and dust. But there was something—

Kyle grabbed Will's arm. "That man." He appeared to be a villager, but some instinct told Kyle that he wasn't.

Will squinted in the sun. "Do you know him?"

"Yes. No. I don't know him." She closed her eyes. An image of fire and the sky filled with great birds appeared. No, not birds. Then it was gone. She opened her eyes. "I can't explain, but see if you can get close. We need to talk to him."

Will didn't hesitate. He slipped into the crowd.

Cyrus stared down at the man. "Who are you to let your defiance deprive your neighbors of their reward?" Below him, Simon signaled one of the believers, who also began to move through the crowd toward the dissident. Kyle tensed. Will already had disappeared into the crowd. It was too late to signal him to come back.

"I am Diego, and those crates bear the stamp of the central distribution. It would seem to me that you, sir, have already deprived them of the supplies intended for this and other villages." Diego gestured for several villagers to help him confiscate the crates. "I think we'll simply gather up what is already theirs, and you can take your misguided imagination elsewhere."

The people, angry now, shouted and pressed forward. Kyle stood, trying to keep her eyes on the stranger. Her hands heated and itched to hurl a fireball at her father's henchman. He was throwing people out of his way to get to Diego. But her poor position and the jostling mob made accuracy impossible. Will was edging his way through the throng, but the believer was a step ahead. Diego's hand was on the first crate when a sharp zap cut through the shouts and his body bowed with the surge of electricity that coursed through him. The rest of Cyrus's disciples drew stun sticks from their pockets and attacked men and women alike as they scrambled to break open the crates and gather up all the food and medicine they could carry.

Kyle was stunned. The mob seethed with violence. Zaps and screams sounded as stun sticks connected with flesh. Women wailed and babies cried. Stones flung by the villagers pelted the train and anyone standing near it. The sharp sting of a jagged rock piercing her brow shook her into action. She pushed Ruth toward the train car, using her body to shelter the older woman from a hail of rocks. Several more nailed her in the back, but she kept her head low.

They were barely inside when the train began to move slowly. Her father's men abandoned the unloaded crates and scrambled to jump aboard before the train picked up speed. The car filled with moans and curses, with the pungent odor of adrenaline-laced sweat and the stench of vomit as one man held his bloody head and retched.

She stumbled to the rear of the car, sank into a cushioned seat, and closed her eyes. Even the throbbing in her head couldn't stop the constant play of images swirling in her mind. She'd never witnessed violence before. Ever. It had dazed her. People attacking people. Yet every fiber of her being sang with it. She'd wanted to wade into the fray. She'd wanted to fight at Will's side. Dung. She hadn't been able to talk to that man. Who was he? Diego? More than a villager, she was sure.

Gentle hands pressed on the source of her pain and held her firmly when she tried to pull away.

"Hold still. I have to staunch the bleeding," Ruth said quietly. The cloth she held against Kyle's head smelled of antiseptic, and she swallowed against the impulse to gag. After a few minutes, Ruth let up the pressure. "I believe it's stopped." She patted the wound with a dry cloth, squeezed some medi-glue in the cut, and held the skin together for the few seconds it required to bond. "I'm afraid it's going to scar, though. Are you hurt anywhere else?"

Kyle paused to take stock of her aching body. "Maybe a few bruises on my back, but I think I'm okay."

"Turn around and let me see."

"I need to find Will. He was out there, trying to help. I don't know if he made it to the train." She started to stand, but a wave of dizziness stopped her.

"I'm sure he's fine, but I'll see what I can find out about your young man. Now, turn around."

Kyle was very tired and felt like the contents of her stomach were trying to crawl up her throat, so she dutifully turned in her seat.

Ruth hissed when she lifted Kyle's shirt. "No cuts, but a couple of very bad bruises." She plucked a four-by-four thermal cloth from the first-aid kit Kyle hadn't noticed before and twisted it to activate the cold crystals embedded in the fabric. Then she gently applied it just below Kyle's shoulder blade. "Recline that seat as much as you can and rest for a bit. I need to see to the men who are wounded." She activated a smaller thermal cloth and placed it on Kyle's injured brow, then taped a pain patch against the vein in her arm. "Thank you, Kylie."

"For what?" Kyle closed her eyes and covered them with her hand. The light was sharp shards striking her bruised brain.

"I was paralyzed by fear, just standing there." Ruth pushed the switch to darken the window against the sunlight. "If you hadn't pushed me toward the train—" Ruth shook her head as if she couldn't think of what might have happened. "If you hadn't sheltered me with your body, those bruises on your back would've been mine. You're very brave."

Drowsiness enveloped her as the pain medication seeped into her bloodstream. "I'm not brave. My mother was brave."

"Then she would be very proud of you today." Ruth patted Kyle's knee. "You rest. I'll check on you later."

Ruth was wrong. If her mother were alive, she'd have stood up to Cyrus no matter how long he starved her. She would have waded into that crowd and fought for the villagers. Blazes, Laine wouldn't even be on this train. And Kyle wouldn't be either as soon as they hit the next stop. They were close enough. She could sense it. That stranger in the crowd was part of whatever was calling her. And she would answer that call or die trying.

"Bero has returned without Diego."

Jael was instantly awake, fully cognizant with the first whispered word from Second. She slipped out from under Alyssa's cool body and couldn't help smiling down at her. Alyssa slept the comatose sleep of a child that doesn't wake even when picked up, moved, and resettled. She pulled a blanket up to cover her. Not because they were both nude. Shared showers and baths were the norm in this life to conserve water, a precious resource. Nakedness hadn't been taboo in decades. But Alyssa was cold-natured, and the one thing sure to wake her was the absence of Jael's unnaturally warm body. She pulled on a T-shirt and cargo pants, then motioned Second into the hallway.

"What were you able to learn from Bero?"

"Nothing useful. The best I could determine was that Diego left him in a wooded area at sunrise yesterday but didn't return at dusk as usual. Bero waited until it was nearly dawn, then flew back to rejoin the others."

While the dragon horses would only communicate with their bonded warrior, they did share rudimentary images between themselves, and a warrior could glean some secondary images via their bonded steed. The end result, however, could be jumbled. Dragon horses didn't think in the clear linear patterns of humans. Their minds often jumped to a totally unrelated image before the first was fully focused, like a butterfly flitting among a meadow full of inviting flowers. Information filtering through two of those brains was, well, often unreliable.

"Gather the Guard in my office a half hour from now."

Second's reply was a fist-to-shoulder salute, and then she was gone.

"What is it?"

Jael turned at the soft voice behind her. Her hair stuck up in spectacular disarray, and a tiny drop of mouth-cleaning foam still clung to Alyssa's lip, but the very sight of her filled Jael with something she couldn't put words to—an anchor to her restlessness, wings to her heart, flame to her passion. Since that first night they made love two weeks ago, Second had discreetly moved her things to bunk with Raven and Tan, and Jael's quarters were refurnished to accommodate her and Alyssa. She pulled her close and licked the foam from Alyssa's lip. "I haven't had a chance to clean up yet."

Alyssa's lips brushed against hers. "I think I used more than my share of mouth foam this morning, so I'm perfectly willing to share."

Mouth warm and minty, her body fit perfectly against Jael's. She sighed. The road ahead would be rife with pitfalls. She believed Alyssa's commitment to their mission, to the bond growing between them. She also knew that accepting the concept of battle was nothing like witnessing the reality. If only she could shield Alyssa from it. But she couldn't.

"Whatever it is, we'll face it together." Alyssa's arms tightened around her.

"Souls. You make me forget to shield because being with you drowns out thoughts from any others."

"You worry so loud, I doubt even your shields could keep it from me."

She released Alyssa and stepped back. "I need to finish dressing. I have a meeting in a few minutes."

Alyssa grabbed the front of Jael's shirt and raised an eyebrow.

"I mean, *we've* got a meeting."

Alyssa released her shirt and pushed her playfully. "Slow, but you're making progress."

❖

"We leave at dawn tomorrow." Jael drew three paths with her finger on the small screen projected by her IC, and it, in turn, displayed them for the others on a much-larger holomap that hovered over the conference table. "We have a hundred and twenty bond candidates, plus support troops. I don't want to draw attention by moving that many people in one group, so we'll split into three units."

A pair of peaks stood at the end of their valley and between them and the mountain where the nest of wild dragon horses was located. She traced a path around the outside of the mountain on the left. "Second and Raven will take one unit along this route." She drew a path outside the mountain on the right. "Furcho and Tan will take another unit along here." She indicated the shortest and most direct path between the mountains. "I will lead the third unit. We'll leave last since we have the most direct route."

She looked up from her IC. They were waiting for an explanation. "Diego is missing." She was stating the obvious. They all knew Bero had returned without his warrior.

"Are we sure he's not just gone off for a jump before we head for the nest?" Tan's tone was light, but her finger tapping lightly against the tabletop gave a clue to her very real concern.

"He was searching for supplies," Second said. "We've been avoiding the major distribution centers in the larger cities so we wouldn't draw attention to ourselves. Diego has instead been coordinating a large number of shipments from a series of smaller warehouses. Those warehouses have emptied in the past week because their shipments from the central supply stopped coming. He might have stumbled onto whoever is diverting those shipments."

Furcho stood. "I'll ride down to the nearest village and see if I can gather any information. Then I'll fly out tonight to find him."

"No. I need you and Second here today to oversee preparation for the mobilization." Jael turned to Michael. "Go to the village. Ask questions."

Furcho frowned. "He won't exactly blend with the general population. His pale skin, not to mention those mismatched eyes, wouldn't go without notice even in the cities, much less the villages."

"That's precisely why I'm sending him. I want people to remember him. We want them on our side." She turned back to Michael. "Tell them you're trying to find out why their shipments have stopped and that you think Diego is being held by the people who have hijacked the food they need to feed their families. Tell them The Collective is preparing to stop these misguided souls who are hoarding. We're ready for word to get back to Cyrus. I want him to know we're coming for him."

Michael gave a curt nod. "It will be my pleasure."

"Tonight, Bero will be drawn to find his bonded. Follow him and see if you can discover what's become of Diego." Jael stood. "One last thing. Alyssa will be with my unit. I want her two assistants to each accompany one of the other units. They'll be able to sense the reaction of anyone you might run across on the way to the nest."

"Nicole can go with my unit," Furcho said. "Uri with Second."

"No surprise there," Tan muttered. "I guess I'll have to play chaperone."

Jael would have smiled at Tan's tease, but there was work to be done.

"Guard." They stood in unison at Jael's stern call to attention. "You have your assignments. You're dismissed."

Michael, a word.

Michael hung back as the others filed out, and Jael touched Alyssa's shoulder in silent permission for her to also remain. He looked at her expectantly.

"If there is time, report back to me about what you hear in the village…before you follow Bero tonight."

"I will."

Jael eyed her young warrior with respect and true affection. The First People celebrated their homosexual members as one person having two spirits. But Michael was literally two genders in one person. Even in this enlightened age of acceptance, the rarity of his kind made most people uncomfortable. Diego was one of those who shied away from him, yet Michael didn't hesitate at his assignment to track him down. "I don't want to reveal our *special* abilities yet. If Diego is in a situation that you cannot remedy quietly, report back for further orders."

"Understood."

She clasped his lean shoulder, her voice gentle. "Take care. I need all of my Guard with me. Do not risk yourself unnecessarily."

The burn scar on his neck reddened at her unusual show of concern, and he straightened as he thumped his fist against his shoulder. "As you command, First Warrior."

She dismissed him with a nod, then sat on the edge of the conference table to stare at the doorway for a minute, remembering the very young teen Han had sent to her for training. He'd been shy and spoken only to answer her questions.

"How do you prefer to be referred to?"

He had submitted to her mandatory mind probe but had yet to meet her gaze. "My name is Michael."

"You know that's not what I'm asking." She had examined his thoughts, seen his memories. The wound she'd found was much too great for one so young.

Michael blushed furiously. "I'm neither, yet both. My parents just referred to me as it or the child. Call me what you wish."

Jael grasped his chin to force it up, but Michael still averted his eyes. "Those we select to become dragon-horse warriors hold their heads up and look people directly in the eyes. You will have to learn to do that." She knew Han had told him of the mythical warriors but left it to Jael to approve his chance to bond.

Those mismatched eyes, blue and green, locked on hers. "A...a dragon-horse warrior? Me?"

"You have the gene. Han tells me that despite your efforts to hide it, you are an accomplished pyro." She dropped her hand and suppressed a smile when he straightened his shoulders and thrust his chin out. "But the bonding is risky. You must train hard because you only get one chance. If you fail, you could be a pile of ashes in less than a minute."

Michael's eyes gleamed with a spark that hadn't been there before. "Please. I can do it. I know I can."

She shrugged. "I don't know. A dragon-horse warrior would know who they are. They wouldn't leave it to me to decide." Even though much had evolved in society, there still was no pronoun for the rare third-gendered person. And the third-gendered people who seemed to constantly pop up in her past lives usually leaned more toward one or the other of the common genders.

"He," Michael said quickly, then hesitated. "I'm unable to bear children and have no interest in frills or babies. So I'm more comfortable presenting as male."

"Good. Women already outnumber the men in this Guard. It will give us a little more balance."

The hand that cooled her cheek brought her back to the present.

"I can see why you're a good leader. Michael worships you. Hearing that you need him gives him a sense of belonging he finds nowhere else. He would lay down his life for you or any of The Guard."

Of course, Alyssa would be able to sense that. Jael nodded and brushed her lips against Alyssa's as she stood. She had much to do and no time to linger over deep thoughts. "I hope he won't have to."

Kyle lingered, clearing the dishes as quietly and unobtrusively as possible. Any bit of information that would help her escape would be worth the reprimand, even if her punishment was to clean the men's toilets again. She shuddered. Last time she'd drawn that duty, she'd had to clean urine splashes off the floor and walls and even the lavatory. She'd been tempted to ask for a hazard suit and pressure hose. Will said only a handful of them were nasty. He said some wouldn't even bother to flush their own dung. But if any of the other men complained, the messy ones ridiculed them, calling them "girly" for wanting clean facilities.

"How many men did we lose in that forsaken place?" Cyrus asked.

Kyle put the dishes she'd collected on the cart to be wheeled into the kitchen car, then grabbed the coffee carafe from the sideboard. The number didn't matter, but she wanted to hear if they said anything about Will. It had taken her several days to confirm that he didn't make it back on the train. That was one more person she needed to eventually look for—her mother, her brother, Will, and her baby sister who was still at The Natural Order camp they'd left several weeks ago.

"Only three. One was that boy your daughter fancied." The man providing the information glanced at Kyle.

She felt her father watching her, so she ducked her head and feigned brushing away a tear. She did, indeed, miss Will's company, but she had no doubt that he could take care of himself.

"But we lost the six crates we'd already unloaded from the cars."

Cyrus drummed his fingers on the table. "Kylie, tell Ruth we are ready for dessert," he said.

Kyle intercepted Ruth, who surprisingly appeared at that very minute with a huge cream fruit roll she'd baked. She entertained a fleeting thought that maybe Ruth was gifted with foresight since she always seemed to turn up at the right minute, then dismissed the idea and traded the dessert for the empty coffee carafe. "I'll serve if you can bring more coffee," she whispered.

Cyrus watched Ruth leave. She was doing a good job instructing Kylie in proper feminine behavior. He nodded his approval when Kylie served him first, and then he turned his attention back to the men. "Three believers? Their reward will be plentiful when their service is judged by The One."

Their train had at least thirty cars, and a second engine pulling fifty more trailed them. All had been filled at the central warehouse, and they'd probably emptied only a third along the way as they stopped to distribute supplies among those who swore allegiance to The One. Potrerillos was the only town or village that had offered any resistance or questioned the source of the supplies.

"We can make changes," another man offered. "No unloading crates. We can distribute supplies straight from the cars. If there's a disturbance, we can just close the doors and pull out."

"Good idea," he said, digging into Ruth's cream fruit roll. She was a great cook and would never serve him that tasteless prepackaged stuff Laine would leave for him while she was working.

"We're just wasting time," Simon growled. "When I suggested this train trip, I told you we should stop only at major cities."

Cyrus scowled at him. He'd spoken to Simon more than once about contradicting him in front of the men, and his patience was growing thin. He was The Prophet. The One spoke directly to him, not Simon. In fact, The One was in his head more often than not lately. It was as if they were merging. But he would keep that to himself for now, and The One was not finished using this irritating man. For now. "Perhaps you'd like to elaborate, Simon?"

"Every hour that we tarry, those dissidents are out there gathering forces against you. We're spending time and money stopping in every little mud hole between here and Brasilia, and you have no guarantee the people you're providing supplies are even giving you a second thought once you leave." He activated a holomap from his IC. "We need to take control of this area. We should hire men, lots of men, to guard the remote warehouses and resume shipments. We can start here, and here," he said, pointing out locations. "We'll sell the supplies and give a cut of the credits to the guards to keep them loyal. The rest will come back to us."

Cyrus frowned. "But these stops are spreading the message. These supplies are meant for believers, not just anyone with credits."

"Yes, yes." Simon drummed his fingers on the table. "How about this? We'll have the guards take control of those pagan temples where people go to meditate and whatever. You can staff them with your people and make services mandatory. If they aren't on the list as having attended the meetings, then they can't buy supplies no matter how many credits they have."

As much as Cyrus was beginning to dislike this man, the plan made sense. Still, he loved standing on the train car and delivering his wisdom to the wayward masses. He was The Prophet.

Simon seemed to read his thoughts. "You can save yourself for the large cities, the stadiums filled with thousands instead of a few hundred farmers standing next to a train. When we return to the Third Continent, we'll have gleaned enough credits from the warehouses to build a golden temple where we can broadcast your message to every IC on the digital network." Simon smiled. "You'll reach billions around the world."

Billions around the world. Cyrus sucked in a breath. Yes. He was The Prophet. He was the one who would bring salvation to the world.

❖

"I don't understand. There was always food for everybody when it was shared. Why would these men take our allotment when they surely have their own?" The woman shook her head in disbelief, a sentiment apparently held by the dozen or so citizens gathered under the trees of the small square. Michael sat at a table outside a small café, sipping a local ale he'd purchased and listening. The group cast surreptitious glances his way, recognizing him as an outsider, and he made no effort to hide his interest in their conversation.

"A man who calls himself The Prophet says the food is only for people who join his group. My mate's brother said they're taking our food shipments on a train to Brasilia, but they stop at villages and hand out some of it to people who swear their allegiance to their cause," one man said.

A second man frowned. "What is their cause?"

The first man shrugged. "This Prophet says we should turn away from The Collective. He says our sharing equally has subverted the natural order of nature to reward the strong and eliminate the weak."

Their faces flashed with surprise and disbelief. "It makes no sense," a woman said. "We are stronger together. Who is this Prophet?"

Michael saw his chance and left his table to join them. "This man is one of the badly born, a learned professor of ancient times, when it was greatly believed that each soul has only one life to live. He suffered the devastating loss of his son in a mud slide where his family lived on the Third Continent. The loss has driven him mad. He is convinced that the ancient society where only a few held power over many is what he refers to as the true path. His insanity, unfortunately, has been given wings by other badly born who crave to be one of those few with power."

One woman scoffed. "Who would listen to such drivel?"

"Anyone tired of listening to the cries of their hungry children. People who also have suffered and are desperate for answers for the recent weather disasters. If you would take the d-tablet from your children occasionally and watch the information broadcasts, you would know that." The tall woman who spoke pushed to the front of the group. She eyed Michael, her gaze challenging. "We're an agricultural region and rarely of interest to travelers. Yet we've seen many in recent months. What brings you here, stranger? What do you know about our missing supplies?"

Michael fought the impulse to shrink under the crowd's scrutiny. He'd flourished in the covert life of a dragon-horse warrior because he hated attention. Their stares were like needles prodding him back into the safe shadows.

"...*dragon-horse warriors hold their heads up and look people directly in the eyes.*"

He raised his chin and met the woman's eyes. "I serve The Collective. These people who call themselves The Natural Order are a growing threat. The Collective Council has called an army together to stop them and restore the sharing of world resources."

"How do we join this army?" The new voice was a young woman with fierce eyes.

"For now, we have all the warriors and support personnel we can train. But you can help by keeping your eyes open and relaying anything you observe that may be connected to this group's activities. Today, I'm seeking information about a member of our army who has disappeared." He activated the IC strapped to his forearm and projected an image of Diego.

Several heads shook in the negative. They hadn't seen such a man.

"He was seeking to buy supplies from the communities in this area."

"Was he at Potrerillos when the train came through?"

"What happened in Potrerillos? I heard you speaking about a train."

"Two trains," the man said. "My mate's brother said two engines were pulling a line of cars that stretched farther than he could see. People said the cars were loaded with food and other supplies. But this food doesn't belong to the people on the train. The boxes were marked for our warehouses, and the villagers attempted to take the supplies back. The men from the train had weapons—stun sticks—but the crowd was too many and overpowered them. They abandoned the supplies they'd already unloaded from the train, and all but four escaped."

Four prisoners. This was good news. Jael could probe their minds for information. "What happened to the ones who didn't escape?"

"Two were killed." The man shrugged and stared at the ground. "The people were angry. They'd been listening to the cries of their hungry children for weeks, and these men were the cause." He looked up at Michael. "That's all I know."

Michael nodded. He wasn't here to pass judgment. "Your information is very helpful." He activated the IC strapped to his forearm, then surveyed the crowd. Most were dressed for fieldwork, but one merchant also wore an IC. He held his arm out to her. "This is the information you need to contact me if you learn anything more that'll help us restore order and return your supplies."

The woman touched her IC to his for the information transfer, then grasped his hand. "My name is Terceira."

He smiled at her. "Michael." He hesitated and then opened his shirt to reveal the silver fire-retardant battle skin underneath and the dragon-horse crest emblazoned on it. "Our warriors bear this insignia. When you see it, you'll have nothing to fear. We're here to restore peace and order."

Terceira held up her IC to capture the image. "Stronger together," she said, reciting the mantra of The Collective. "Good speed to you and your compatriots, Michael." She nodded to her fellow citizens. "These hills are filled with our families and friends. We'll spread the news of your army and your need for many eyes."

He bowed and then saluted their allegiance. "Stronger together," he pledged.

CHAPTER EIGHTEEN

Bright points of light. Eyes of a million souls. Jewels nestled in a dark velvet blanket. The stars were too many to count. Just like her emotions were too tangled to sort.

"How do you not feel adrift when you're up there, among the stars?" Alyssa asked, never taking her eyes from the night sky.

"As sailors have for a millennium, we use the stars to navigate," Jael said, her voice an anchor in the vastness.

Tomorrow, the next leg of their journey would begin. They would lead more than a hundred warriors hoping to bond with a dragon horse to the nest of the wild herd.

Tonight, however, was for them—her and Jael—before the demands of duty and leadership would take precedence.

Summer's warmth still enveloped the hilltop meadow even though the sun had set, and she wished she could hold this minute for eternity. She wanted to let the world save itself while she stayed safely tucked in the circle of Jael's arms. She closed her eyes, settled back against Jael's chest, and listened to Specter tear the tender tops from the lush grass that surrounded them.

She opened her eyes again and the stars called to her. She wanted to know what it felt like to be high above the earth, far away from the realities of their mission.

"Take me up there, Jael."

"Up where?" Jael placed a line of soft kisses along Alyssa's neck. Apparently her mind was focused on a more earthly pursuit.

"I want to fly."

"We flew up here."

She'd flown several times, held tight by Jael as she balanced them on Specter's back, but she'd always insisted they stay fairly close to earth because of the one-time attack of vertigo she'd suffered after her head injury. She was ready now to let go of her fear.

"I want to really fly, up there, high above everything where you can touch the stars."

A sharp nip made the muscles low in Alyssa's belly clench, and then Jael's teasing lips stilled. She hummed against Alyssa's neck. "That's what I love about you."

"What?"

"You have such a romantic view of everything."

Alyssa could hear the smile in Jael's voice. "I don't know what you mean."

"You can't actually touch the stars, silly. Not even Specter's wings can take us that high." Warriors could be irritatingly rational.

As if he understood their words, Specter nodded and then went back to his grass.

Alyssa turned in Jael's arms to smile at her. "I want to try."

"Are you sure? It's pretty high up." Jael's blue eyes were bright with surprise, even in the soft moonlight. "But it's amazing. The air is so thin you feel breathless, but the wind currents are so strong, it feels like floating in a river." Her fingertips were rough against Alyssa's cheek. "I don't want to hurt you. If you feel even a tiny bit of vertigo, you have to tell me right away."

While Jael's fingertips were capable of igniting into real fire, they also were adept at stoking a blaze of passion that burned through Alyssa so fast and hot that just thinking about it made her tremble. She kissed that amazing hand. "I promise."

Specter left off his grazing and ambled toward them, apparently summoned telepathically by Jael. He extended his huge leathery wings, stretching them in the breeze and seeming eager for the opportunity to soar. He tugged at Jael's belt with his teeth, and she nodded.

"Give me your belt," she said, removing her own. "We'll use them to fasten your legs to the base of his wings, so if we hit a rough spot in the air flow you'll be secured."

"Like a safety harness?"

"Exactly. We'd use harnesses similar to the ones the newly bonded warriors use when they're first learning to fly their dragon horses, but I don't have one of those with me now. The belts will work just as well."

Alyssa frowned. "What about you?"

Jael chuckled. "I took a few unintentional sky dives when I was a beginner, but my legs are strong enough now to keep my seat during any of Specter's aerial acrobatics. Still, I wouldn't want to risk us sliding off if your full weight shifted against me."

She blinked at Jael. "You couldn't have fallen off. If you did, you wouldn't be standing here today."

Jael grinned and pressed her forehead against Specter's. A mental image formed in Alyssa's head, too, and she appreciated that she was including her in their conversation.

Alyssa was suddenly looking down at hands clutching Specter's mane, the earth very, very far below them. The hands began to scramble for purchase and she felt jostled, then nothing but empty air, fast-approaching ground, and overwhelming fear. Then Specter's broad back appeared under her, solid and warm.

When Jael drew back, Specter bobbed his head and curled his lip in a horsey laugh. Jael grinned, too. "That was the first time I fell off. Specter's always saved me, but I don't know if he could pick two of us out of the sky if we both slid off." She held up the belts. "So, we'll make sure you don't."

Alyssa hesitated, Jael's mental picture still fresh. She looked up at the stars, blinking, beckoning. Her desire to fly outweighed her fear. "Let's do it."

Specter stood very still, his perlino hide glittering in the moonlight. Jael strapped Alyssa's legs to his wings, then leapt onto Specter's back to settle behind her.

In tight quarters, Specter could rear and launch himself into the air, but the meadow was spacious so he cantered a short distance to lift off gently. His huge wings alternated powerful sweeps with gentle glides as he moved among the warm currents. They flew in wide circles until the ground was so far away, the trees and mountains were a dizzying, indistinct blur. Alyssa's stomach seemed to be considering a jump into her throat, and she swallowed several times to dissuade it.

"Don't look down. Keep your eyes on the stars."

Jael's breath was warm in her ear and Alyssa shivered, realizing the air had grown chill and thin. But before she could shiver again, warmth penetrated her clothes like a heating blanket against her back and she chuckled.

"What's so funny?"

"Just thinking about when winter comes." The fact that Jael could consciously turn up her body heat would come in handy during the winter months. "No need to drag out extra blankets as long as I'm sleeping with you."

She felt Jael's laugh rumble against her back. She was glad she hadn't been able to freeze that minute in the meadow, because she would have missed this one. Every minute, every hour of every day with Jael was precious. Alyssa tried not to think about what could be ahead for them. Jael was a warrior and would be in many dangerous situations.

"Stop worrying and enjoy this." A kiss brushed her cheek to punctuate the admonishment.

"Are you listening in on my thoughts?"

"You know I don't unless invited. You're just broadcasting so loudly, I can't help but hear."

"Sorry."

"I love that you don't shield me out."

Their relationship was a tightrope sometimes. Only when they were alone could they completely relax. To do that was heaven. The downside, however, was that they each could tell if the other was shielding, so it was impossible to withhold anything when they were alone. The other could sense it.

Alyssa released her hold on Specter's mane and slipped her chilled hands into Jael's warm ones. The air grew balmy around them, and Specter canted his wings to hover in the jet stream. The stars seemed so bright, so close that she actually reached out toward one.

"It took me a long time before I gave up trying," Jael said, raising her voice a bit to carry over the force of the wind. "I finally became resigned to the fact that, no matter how close they seem, you can never really touch them."

"Never say never."

Another kiss to her cheek. "I'll qualify that then. In all my lifetimes, I've never touched the stars."

Specter tensed and Jael's arm tightened around her.

"What is it?"

Before Jael could answer, an angry scream split the night. Her ears were still ringing when Specter answered with his own dragon cry. A dark shape materialized out of the night, illuminated by a plume of red-yellow flame aimed straight for them. The jet stream diverted the flame to the left of them, and Alyssa released a scream of her own and grabbed Jael's forearms when Specter folded his wings and dove downward. She'd barely registered the abrupt drop when they were sideways and curling around the pursuing stallion in a tight circle. Even Jael reached for a handhold at the base of Specter's left wing.

Specter exhaled a long blue-white flame that licked at the tip of the Black's wing.

"Bero! Why's he attacking us?" She had to shout to be heard over continuous vocal exchanges between the two dragon horses. Their shrieks filled the air like two feuding tomcats, only a hundred times louder.

"That's not Diego's Bero. That's the stallion from the nest," Jael yelled back.

The two dragon horses leveled off and circled as they measured each other. The screams were deafening. She would have covered her ears if she hadn't needed her hands to grip Specter's mane. She wasn't going to be stargazing when they took the next sudden-death dive.

The Black made the first move, darting in and back with the agility of a hummingbird. He spit fireballs at them. Carrying the weight of two humans, Specter couldn't counter the Black's quick movements, so he hovered and met each fireball with his hotter flame, exploding them before they could hit.

"Hang on," Jael yelled. "I'm going to help a little to scare this guy off."

She reached high above her head, both hands igniting into fiery orbs. Specter screamed and Alyssa felt his ribs expand in a deep inhalation before he breathed a thick stream of flame. Fire shot out from Jael's hands and met Specter's flame to form a bright, blistering wall for several heartbeats before it exploded. The percussion blew back a wave of scorching air at them.

It was enough to discourage the challenger and he disappeared back into the night, one last scream echoing in his wake.

The acrid smell of sulfur followed as they descended to the meadow in a wide, gentle spiral. Specter, still jazzed from the battle, snorted short spurts of flame and, as soon as they dismounted, pranced away to punctuate his victory with a few celebratory bucks. When Jael slapped her hands together and pointed to the sky, Specter reared and screamed before launching himself aloft.

"He'll make sure the intruder isn't hanging around," Jael said, her eyes still scanning the sky.

"Jumping stars!" Alyssa had never experienced anything like that before. Her heart was still racing, her blood pumping. She was bursting with adrenaline and…and—

The burst of emotion that hammered Jael stole her breath, nearly took her to her knees. In past lives, they called it battle lust—the unbridled arousal projected by Alyssa. But this was her sweet healer, newly anointed First Advocate of The Collective, the woman who only a few weeks ago was disgusted by the mission that would surely lead them into a war.

She took a deep breath. It had been a lifetime since she'd been part of any battle other than a practice skirmish with other members of The Guard, and she'd been holding down her own throbbing reaction. She had no reserve to absorb Alyssa's and searched for how to react. Alyssa couldn't possibly understand what she was feeling. "Are you okay?"

Alyssa's eyes were glassy with desire. "I'm jumping awesome."

Jael took a few steps back. Did Alyssa even realize she was slapping her belt against her leg as she stalked toward her? What should she do? She couldn't be rough with Alyssa like she was with Tan, and there was certainly more between them than just physical release.

Alyssa stopped her advance and raised an eyebrow. "Tanisha? Really?"

"I was just blowing off steam." Dragon's balls. She must have been broadcasting her thoughts. She hadn't done that unconsciously since she was a fledgling. "And that was before you came along. Well, there was that one other time when you had me so hot I needed a cool-off."

"After you met me?" The playful smack on her leg with the doubled belt had a bit of sting to it.

"Ow. That very first day. You wanted nothing to do with me." She caught the belt as a second blow threatened and yanked Alyssa to her. She braced for the impact of Alyssa's body against hers, but not for the quick hook that swept her leg and landed her flat on her back in the grass. Alyssa's weight pushed all the air from her lungs when she free-fell with her and straddled her hips to grind herself against the closure of Jael's pants. They both groaned.

Her last thread of control gone, Jael fisted Alyssa's blouse and yanked her down for a bruising kiss of tongue and teeth. She pulled at the tie on Alyssa's pants. "Off. Get these clothes off." She was going to combust if she didn't have Alyssa's skin against hers right now.

Alyssa batted her hands away and jerked Jael's T-shirt up to expose her breasts. She fell on them, biting and sucking until Jael had to clench her thighs together to stave off the wave of orgasm gathering in her belly. "Off. Clothes off." Her demand was now a plea.

She lifted her shoulders and had started to raise her arms when Alyssa, still sitting astride her, worked the shirt over her head. But Alyssa had other ideas. She pulled the shirt down Jael's back before she could slip her arms out and pushed her back to the ground.

"You're never going to need Tan to touch you that way again."

Though the shirt at her elbows trapped her arms, Jael knew a dozen different ways to dislodge her captor and spring free. But the fire in Alyssa's eyes—not the shirt—held her, wetted her thighs and reduced her voice to a rough croak. "No. I won't."

Alyssa stood and quickly stripped her clothes off before ripping Jael's pants open and dragging them down her hips. The cool grass pricked at her heated skin, and her breath caught in her chest when Alyssa planted a foot on either side of her shoulders and stood over her. She spread her glistening sex for Jael to see. Stars. This woman was going to drive her insane. *Please, before I combust.*

Alyssa's smile was feral, and, for a second, Jael thought she would deny her. But she could feel Alyssa radiating her hunger as Jael opened her mouth to run her tongue along her lips in a teasing demonstration. Alyssa moaned and at last knelt over her. Jael bit her thigh in reprimand for making her wait, and Alyssa grabbed a handful of Jael's hair to force her where she needed her most.

She didn't know why, but it fascinated her that Alyssa's pubic curls were the same deep red as her spiky crown. She tugged at the stiff hairs with her teeth, and Alyssa growled, her hips undulating to paint Jael's cheeks and mouth. Jael hummed as she relented and sucked at her. When Alyssa's legs began to tremble, she changed her point of attack and plunged her tongue inside. She strained against the shirt holding her arms, her fingers itching to replace her tongue, to push inside and claim her. In a small act of rebellion against the restraint, she moved up to suck again at her clit, swollen hard and pulsing, but clamped it between her teeth when Alyssa's legs began to tremble again.

Alyssa's hand tightened in her hair and jerked her away. Jael smiled at the pain in her scalp. She wouldn't have guessed such a tiger existed under Alyssa's peaceful Zen. Nor would she have anticipated her little game of denial would unleash that tiger.

Alyssa straddled her hips again, grinding her swollen clit against Jael. She grasped Jael's jaw, her fingers digging into her cheek, and bent to breathe her scream of release into Jael's mouth. Alyssa, her lover. Alyssa, the empath.

The force of Alyssa's climax slammed through Jael, bowing her body and stealing coherent thought. Alyssa was all around her, touching her in places no one ever had, thrusting, claiming, driving her beyond any place she'd ever been, sucking her into a vortex. She couldn't sort the physical pleasure from the rush of emotion that was lifting her, filling her. She was coming and coming again. Her ears rang with her own shouts. The stars pulsed and seemed to move in waves. She was flying. She was free-falling. She was dying. She was born again. She closed her eyes and drifted until she became aware of her own gasps for air and the frantic throb of her heart between her breasts. Then she smelled and felt the scorched grass under her hands and the cool fingers stroking her overheated cheek. Alyssa's eyes, filled with worry, sought hers.

"Jael, honey, are you okay? I'm sorry. I didn't know…that's never…I didn't know that could happen."

Jael weakly lifted her right hand and stared at the ashes of scorched grass clinging to it.

"Say something. Oh, please, I'll never forgive myself if I've hurt you."

The hard-bitten warrior in her felt light, floating in a sense of unfamiliar wonder. She met Alyssa's troubled gaze and struggled for the words to describe it.

"I…I think I touched the stars."

CHAPTER NINETEEN

The hundred or so who would remain behind framed the trail that led out of the encampment, saluting to show their support and offering an occasional shout of encouragement to the last group—the one led by Jael and Alyssa—departing for the nest. There were a few tears, too. Many friendships and some deeper relationships had formed during the days they'd labored together, and The Guard had been honest. The bonding was fraught with deadly danger, even for those traveling as support personnel for the bond candidates. Some wouldn't return.

Jael leapt astride Specter, wingless in the daylight, and cantered from the beginning of the line to the last transport burdened with the supplies they'd need for the next few days. It was partly a display of leadership and partly because she wanted to be sure Alyssa had found a comfortable spot in the convoy of foot soldiers and supply transports. She wasn't surprised to find her perched on the seat of the medical transport next to a sullen young woman who her officers had reported as trouble no matter what area she was assigned.

She was struck again by their contrast, First Warrior to First Advocate. No matter how righteous her mission, she destroyed and killed people. Alyssa healed them—emotionally as well as physically—and she'd apparently gathered this wayward fledgling under her wing. She was sunshine to Jael's darkness. That sunshine warmed even her emotionless commitment to duty when Alyssa smiled up at her.

"Hi."

"Everything okay here?" She maneuvered Specter to walk along-side their transport.

"I think so." She gestured to the young woman, whose attention was glued to the transport's controls, even though it wasn't necessary. These things practically drove themselves. "Jael, this is Toni. I borrowed her from the stable master to help me since Uri and Nicole are traveling with the other groups."

Toni spared her a guarded glance and a weak salute. "First Warrior."

"Antonia." Jael snapped a return salute and Toni's face colored. Jael's message that she knew of Toni—Antonia in her performance reports—had hit home. Alyssa raised an eyebrow and opened her thoughts to Jael. *Not helping. She needs to feel like someone's on her side.*

Jael frowned at her recruit, whose eyes were again fixed on the transport controls. The scowl on her face, however, probably had nothing to do with the machine. If Jael was truthful, her indirect warning was simple jealousy. It was silly to envy the young recruit for being able to ride next to Alyssa, but in all her lifetimes Jael had never experienced this constant need for Alyssa's company, this ever-present ache to touch her. It threw her normally well-ordered world off-kilter.

Please. For me?

Jael nodded slightly and cleared her throat. "I apologize for the oversight. I should've assigned someone to you when I reallocated your assistants. It appears, however, you've found an able replacement."

The sunshine returned with Alyssa's smile. "She's been assisting the veterinarian, so she already has some medical experience. She was an easy choice."

Jael nodded more firmly, holding Toni's gaze when she glanced up again. "An excellent selection then."

Toni straightened and snapped a proper salute. "Thank you, First Warrior. I'll do my best."

Jael acknowledged her salute. "I'll leave you in good hands then, First Advocate." She flexed her knees to urge Specter to the front of the procession, riding high on the wave of projected affection that followed her.

❖

"Are we going to sit here and starve while they ride off with our rations?" The woman threw her hands up at the large group gathered in the Potrerillos temple.

"We've sent a message to the Regional order keepers. What more do you want us to do?" The old man threw up his hands, mocking her.

"Go after them," the woman said. About a third of the group nodded their support of that idea.

"They're armed." The group eyed Will suspiciously. He professed to be on their side, but he'd been traveling on the train.

"The butcher has several kill sticks, and we have the two stun sticks we took from their men." At least half nodded agreement with the man who spoke.

"They're not going to let you close enough to press a kill stick or a stun stick to their bodies. They have other weapons—guns," Will said.

"Guns?" Very few remained and were only legal for a handful of agents specially licensed to use them in situations like killing a rogue animal that hunted people rather than its natural prey.

"I've seen them," Will said. "Not just a few, but boxes and boxes in a car in the first train. I think most of the believers don't know about them, but a group of men who are commanded by The Prophet's advisor do. One of them bragged to me that they'd been trained to fire them."

Michael listened quietly. Jael had been astute to send him. Terceira had obviously messaged ahead about his visit there. The suspicious group gathered here had offered him a chair the instant they looked into his distinctive mismatched eyes. And they quickly released Diego and Will from their bindings when he vouched for them. Well, he vouched for Diego.

Finding him had been easy enough.

When night fell and the dragon horses had eaten their ration of fire rocks, Bero had wasted no time. Compelled by his bond, he launched into the sky and Michael leapt onto Apollo to follow. The clearing where Bero landed was very close to Potrerillos, as he'd suspected. Bero screamed for his master. Worried that the racket would terrorize any citizens within hearing, Michael managed to convince him, through Apollo, that an extra ration of fire rocks was waiting for him at their base meadow. He watched as the dragon horses lifted off and headed home, Bero a dark shadow in the night sky and Apollo glinting gold in the moonlight.

Now, they needed to take care of some things before dark fell again and their steeds returned. Another day apart wouldn't sit well with Bero, and he was likely to land in the town square in search of Diego.

The group of citizens looked at them expectantly, and Michael signaled for Diego to speak for them.

Diego nodded. "Whether you could fight them is moot, my friends."

Michael was surprised that his normally abrasive colleague spoke so gently. Diego, however, had grown up in a rural community like this one. Though they were strangers, these were his people.

"The solar trains are very fast," Diego reminded them. "You don't have transports capable of catching up to them."

Quiet curses rippled through the group, and a man Michael sensed was a very old soul stood. "Tell us how we can help."

"The Collective Council has heard the cries of your hungry children, and a special army has been called to deal with this. We've been training at an encampment not too far from here," Diego said. "Spread this word."

"The strange screams and bright flashes we have seen in the nighttime?" The woman's question was a mix of fright and hope.

"You have nothing to fear. It's only training maneuvers," Diego said, smiling.

"If that was your racket, you'll at least scare those believers so badly they'll be filling their pants with their own dung." The old man's gruff observation drew chuckles despite the serious nature of the meeting.

"How long before the supply shipments are restored?" The woman who asked was quietly nursing an infant in the corner of the room.

Diego pointed to the shattered screen of his IC, so Michael activated his to project a holomap of the area. He touched the map to mark the valley where the dragon-horse army was based.

"That is where our army has been training," Diego said. "We have little fresh food left, but we'll share our ample supply of protein chow. You can help by putting the word out to the other communities. Each can send one transport with a list of any critical medicines they need and a count of citizens they need to feed."

"And what will we eat when you have no more?"

Michael touched his IC to transfer the information to one worn by a man who stepped forward, then looked up to share a feral grin with Diego. At Diego's nod, Michael stood and faced the citizens. "You'll eat from the supplies that will be returned to you after our warriors raid that train and soil the pants of a few of those so-called believers."

❖

Although they'd left at dawn, any fatigue from the monotony of their journey was forgotten in anticipation of the bonding. They'd met at the base of the nest mountain with the other two groups by mid-afternoon, and Second had the temporary camp well in hand. Trusting her cousin to handle the logistics of setting camp for nearly two hundred, Jael could no longer resist her persistent thirst for Alyssa's presence. She was exactly where Jael anticipated, helping Tan organize the largest of the temporary structures.

While the faces milling about the campsite were filled with eagerness, those setting up the field hospital were solemn. By dawn, the beds they were preparing would likely be filled with wounded and dying.

Heedless of the people working around them, Alyssa wrapped an arm around Jael's waist and pressed into Jael's side. She spoke quietly. "Do we really need this many beds?"

"Honestly, I'm not sure," Jael said. "There's never been a mass bonding like this that I'm aware of. The confusion when the candidates rush the herd will either give them an advantage or spell disaster. There's no way to predict how the herd will react."

Alyssa shuddered, and Jael pulled her into a full hug. She kissed her on the forehead and wished for the millionth time that this uprising would suddenly melt away so they could fly off to the privacy of her meadow of flowers and mountaintop home.

"I'm thinking there's a reason Specter is the only horse you brought with us."

"I didn't want to draw the herd's attention before the bonding by bringing all the others, but Specter and I will engage the stallion so he won't interfere."

Alyssa tightened her arms around Jael. "Please, please be careful."

Jael smiled down at her. "No worries. The wild stallion is impressive, but he dines on sulfur rubble and his flame is no match for Specter's."

"You won't hurt him, will you?"

"Only if I'm forced to. Judging from the size and quality of this herd, he's a strong sire. We want to cull his herd but leave him and enough mares to replenish their numbers."

"Alyssa, excuse me." Nicole set down her end of a long box she and Furcho carried between them. "This box isn't marked, except for these numbers. I'm not sure where to put it."

Alyssa scanned the huge, open room and waved Toni over. "Toni's a whiz with the inventory program, and she set up most of the labeling."

Toni approached warily. "Yes, First Advocate?"

Alyssa grasped her shoulder and gave her a gentle shake. "What did I tell you?"

"Alyssa." Toni blushed as she corrected herself. "How can I help?"

"This box apparently is only partially labeled. Can you consult the inventory and tell us what's in it?"

Toni's gaze flicked from the numbers on the box, to Alyssa, and then to Jael. "Pyres," she said softly, referring to the lightweight but heat-resistant metal frames on which bodies were laid for cremation. "I thought it best to only number that box in case it might freak out some people."

"Very good thinking," Jael said. This recruit did have potential. The low marks on her performance records didn't match up with the intelligent young woman who apparently was blossoming under Alyssa's tutelage.

❖

An afternoon shower made returning to the rendezvous clearing before dusk much harder than the previous night. Michael slipped in the mud and then blinked at the hand Will held out for him. He hesitated, then accepted the offer. Will was strong and his grip firm. His intentions seemed pure, but Michael had been fooled by people before—people who were friendly until they discovered he was third gender. Maybe they were being fooled now into taking a spy right into the heart of their army. No matter. Alyssa and Jael would be able to decipher his motives before he could harm their mission.

They had been detained in Potrerillos much longer than anticipated. The citizens had many questions, and Will had supplied them all with much-needed information about The Natural Order.

Also, the two believers were given a proper cremation so they could start their next life with a cleansed spirit. One man had died from a head injury caused by a rock thrown during the train riot. The other had suffered a heart attack when the stun stick shocked him. Neither was a deliberate killing, but the citizens regretted it just the same. Michael and Diego had each lit a pyre, giving the citizens a glimpse of their powerful gift. Some still weren't convinced.

"What good is magic against guns?" one man asked.

"These gifts manifested with the rise of The Collective," Diego said. "Just as The Collective is stronger than the fractured society centuries ago, these gifts are stronger than the guns and other weapons of mankind's violent past."

"Rock, paper, scissors," Michael added, referring to an old children's game. "Our flame will melt bullets before they can touch us. Our empaths can discern their true intentions, and our telepaths can hear their thoughts before they act. These are the weapons of peace."

"And if they want war?" another asked.

"We're armed for that, too," Diego said.

The citizens nodded. "Stronger together," they chorused, their voices ringing with confidence. The citizens had nothing to offer except their support as The Guard departed on their quest. Michael thought it better than food or weapons.

Now, dusk had turned to twilight and twilight to dark as they waited in the damp meadow. Will stiffened beside him when the dark shapes grew larger as they neared and the eerie swoosh of the dragon horses' wings moved the air around them and sent small denizens of the hillside scrambling into the undergrowth for cover.

"Jumping stars, giant bats?"

Michael laid his hand on Will's forearm to steady him. "No. Dragon horses. Our transport back to camp."

Bero screamed and landed with a thump, shooting flame with each exhalation. His wings, still unfurled, twitched with irritation. Diego immediately stepped out to meet him, but Bero shot a blue stream of flame at his bonded. Diego stopped it with a fireball of his own. "I'll clip your wings if you scorch my good boots, hombre." The affection in his tone softened his threat. Bero's tail swished, but his wings folded and he roughly pressed his forehead to Diego's.

"You can ride with me," Michael said. "Bero can be temperamental and probably won't accept a second rider tonight."

"They can fly with someone riding them?" Will's eyes were silver in the moonlight. "We're going to *fly* to your camp?"

Michael smiled at Will's excitement. He didn't smile often and it felt…different. Will's boyish enthusiasm warmed him. He quit smiling. Will seemed open and friendly now, but that would change when Will learned his secret. "Yes, unless you're afraid of heights. If you are, we'll have to leave you here to help pick coffee beans or find your own way back to the Third Continent."

Will didn't acknowledge the edge in Michael's declaration, because Apollo picked that minute to land lightly and trot toward them, his golden hide shimmering in the diffused light.

"Stars, he's beautiful. I've never seen such an animal. What's his name?"

"This is Apollo." Michael pressed his forehead to Apollo's, pictured him carrying both him and Will back to camp. When he stepped back, Apollo eyed Will, then sniffed him.

"Does he belong to you? Is that some kind of greeting—pressing your forehead to his? He won't buck me off up there in the sky, will he?"

Despite his caution, Michael chuckled as he leapt onto Apollo's back. It was hard not to like Will. He extended a hand to help Will swing up behind him. Diego and Bero had already launched into the sky. "One question at a time," he said as Will's arms curled firmly around him. "Hold on tight."

CHAPTER TWENTY

The sun's last rays were fingers of pink and orange, slowly lessening their grip on the surrounding mountains. The warrior candidates were dark, silent shadows standing downwind among the trees that ringed the huge plateau where the wild herd spread out to graze and snooze. Alyssa, Uri, and Nicole joined hands in a meditative circle and closed their eyes.

"Picture with me a calm sea, gently lapping against the side of a boat," Alyssa whispered.

Uri snorted. "Are these sea horses we're looking to calm?"

Nicole stifled a giggle and Alyssa opened her eyes to glare at him. His eyes, also open now, twinkled back at her. She shook her head and smiled. She sometimes forgot that her assistants were empaths, too, and he could sense her nervousness. His bit of humor, indeed, broke the tension and soothed her nerves.

"Okay. Let's try again." She closed her eyes and traveled mentally to Jael's meadow. "We are in a mountaintop meadow that is thick with juicy grass and tasty clover. Wildflowers, a myriad of colors, wave in the gentle breeze."

She had no idea if her projected calm would affect the wild horses. When she tried it with Specter, Jael confirmed that his mind held the picture Alyssa was projecting, but so did Jael's. So they didn't know if he was mirroring the picture from Alyssa's mind or from Jael's because she, too, was picking it up from Alyssa. It was just too confusing.

Still, they agreed that she should try. Even the slightest advantage as the bonding candidates rushed the herd would be helpful.

The horses would be vulnerable only while their wings sprouted, bony spurs emerged along the ridge of their necks, and rock-crushing teeth formed. Each warrior would have only a minute, maybe three, to creep among the herd to find the bond that called them. Then the warrior had to grab that animal's ears to pull it down and touch foreheads as its dragon ascended. If they were a minute too late and the transformation was already complete, the animal would attack rather than bond.

Incineration by one of The Guard steeds would be mercifully almost instantaneous. Without fire rocks to supplement their diets, the flame of the wild horses would burn their target slowly but severely.

So she and Jael hoped Alyssa could project a calming emotion that would slow the herd's reaction and give the warriors a fraction of a minute longer to find a bond.

If Alyssa couldn't affect the herd, at least she would soothe the men and women preparing to risk their lives to bond with a dragon horse. She breathed deeply, pulling strength from her connection to Uri and Nicole. The breeze rustled the flowers of the meadow in her mind. Or was it the movement of the candidates as they crept out of the shadows? A hawk's cry split the air. Tan's signal. She struggled to stay in the meadow, but the scream of the wild stallion's dragon and Specter's answering challenge snapped her out of her meditation. She ran to the edge of the plateau, Uri and Nicole on her heels.

The next fifteen minutes were the longest and most shockingly chaotic she would ever witness.

The great stallion stood over the seared bodies of three downed warriors and held a fourth in his rock-crushing teeth as he spewed a red-yellow flame around the helpless warrior. Another scream of challenge from Specter, closer than before, and the stallion launched into the sky to intercept.

The moon had yet to rise and the night settled like a suffocating blanket, bursts of flame rending its dark fabric to reveal macabre scenes. Alyssa struggled to fix her mind with meadows and wildflowers while her vision was filled with human torches stumbling, some rolling in the grass in agony. Their battle skins—fire-retardant unitards—were no match for direct flame. Blue-white fireballs met red-yellow flame as warriors scrambled among the herd. Tortured screams of the wounded blended with the enraged calls of the horses that transitioned, unbonded, into dragons.

Great wings fanned the scent of scorched grass and sizzling flesh as the dragon horses, fully transformed, lifted off. Some carried warriors. Many did not. A dark shape fell from the sky, hitting the ground with a muffled thud. Alyssa covered her eyes when a second plummeted to the ground, and she realized they were warriors who had lost their hold as their beasts plunged skyward.

"Alyssa." Uri spoke gently, his large hand squeezing her shoulder. "We're needed on the field."

She lowered her hands. The moon was rising and sporadic fires still illuminated the plateau. Tan stood in the middle of the field, Phyrrhos glittering like a copper penny next to her, as she directed the medical team and stretcher-bearers. If Phyrrhos was on the field, where was the wild stallion? Where were Jael and Specter? Her heart jumped a few frantic beats.

"Alyssa?" Nicole's face was wet with tears but her voice and emotions steady as she held up Alyssa's med kit.

As much as she wanted to find Jael and wrap herself in Jael's strength, she had others depending on her. She took the kit and gave Nicole's hand a quick squeeze. "Thank you. Let's check in with Tan."

The battlefields she'd witnessed when Jael had shared images from past lives came to mind as they crossed the plateau. The stench of blood and bowel and burning flesh was nauseating, and Alyssa realized the fires scattered about were bodies, human and equine. Medics knelt next to wounded warriors, while Furcho and Raven grimly incinerated the animals too badly damaged in the fiery chaos to fly away.

"Why are they killing the horses?" Uri asked.

"If they don't kill the damaged ones, their own herd will turn on them and do the job when they return," Tan said, never taking her eyes from the moaning man she knelt beside. "Our flame is much hotter and merciful. They flash-burn the brain so that death is almost instantaneous. It just takes a bit longer for the body to completely incinerate."

Tan helped her patient sit up and motioned for Uri to take over for her. "You've lost an ear," she told the warrior, "but you're lucky your other burns aren't that bad. This is Uri. He'll bandage your head and get someone to help you to the temporary infirmary." She stood and turned to Alyssa. "I need to be aloft. Second can't handle all those newly bonded alone, and we're shorthanded with Diego and Michael still gone."

"Jael. Do you know where she is?"

"Why don't you ask her?" Tan said.

Alyssa wheeled around, scanning the field. No Jael.

"No." Tan tapped her temple. "With your mind. She'll hear you."

"But I'm an empath, not—" Before Alyssa could finish, Tan sprinted to Phyrrhos and they leapt skyward in one smooth movement. "—a telepath. Daughter of a dung beetle!" She'd never understand Tan. What was she supposed to do? Just close her eyes and think *Jael*?

I'm here.

She jumped at the voice in her head, and it took her a minute to decide if she'd imagined it. *Are you okay?*

Behind you.

She turned and fell into Jael's arms. *I need you.*

I'm here.

After a minute, she released her hold on Jael. She ran a shaky hand over her face. She was surprised to find her cheeks wet with tears. "When I saw the other Guard, but not you—"

"I was looking for the wild stallion. I'm afraid he's injured somewhere in the forest, but it's impossible to find a black dragon horse when there's only a quarter moon. He blends right into the shadows." Jael touched her cheek, catching a remaining tear. "Are you okay?"

Alyssa nodded and offered a weak smile. "I am now. I just needed to see you, touch you." She caught Jael's hand and gave it a squeeze. "I need to get to work."

"First Advocate." A male medic stood at her elbow. "I'm sorry, but we need your help over here, quickly."

He led them to a dark figure on the ground. Jael opened her hand and held a fireball aloft to push back the night. Alyssa choked back a gasp. The torso and face were so burned, the wounded warrior was unidentifiable. Still, she sensed something familiar in the desperate emotions that washed over her as the warrior struggled to breathe. She at least was sure her patient was female. She dropped to her knees beside the suffering warrior. "I need a portable ventilator," she barked at the medic. He should have already done this.

"I tried." His words were clipped with urgency. "The patient is combative."

Alyssa laid a comforting hand on the warrior's thigh, below the burn damage, and projected calm. "You need to let us help you breathe easier," she said gently.

But when the medic knelt with the intubation tube in his hand, the warrior raised her right hand. Her fingers had been completely burned off, but a weak blue flame rose from her palm. It was clearly a threat.

"You have to let us help you," Alyssa said. Each gasp sounded like it could be the woman's last. She turned to Jael. "Maybe her ears are so damaged she can't hear and understand that we're trying to help."

Jael extinguished the fireball in her hand. Before she knelt at the wounded woman's head, she already knew what she would learn when she probed her thoughts. Only another warrior would recognize a plea for the sweet release of death. Heedless of the charred skin and sightless eyes, she gently placed her fingertips at the woman's temples.

First Warrior?

Her heart tore when recognition hit her. No. Not this one. She steeled herself. *I am here.*

I...I did it. I bonded...a young filly...so beautiful.

I knew you would. You were my most promising recruit.

It felt...I can't describe it. We lifted off and were flying, but Jason... above us...he fell...I tried...tried to catch him, and he pulled me off. Aria...my filly...was coming to catch me...an unbonded wild one got me first.

Alyssa touched her shoulder. "We need to intubate now. Can you hold her hands?"

No! The young woman's chest heaved with the effort to breathe.

They want to help. The ventilator will breathe for you.

I...I can't see. When I fell...I can't feel my legs, but I can tell my back is all busted up...fingers gone. Please...I beg...a warrior's death...help me...next life, another chance.

Jael nodded. She'd asked the same in another life and her sergeant had mercifully complied. She silently summoned Specter. *You have made me proud, my young warrior. I will be quick if you are sure.* She felt the body under her hands relax.

I am sure, First Warrior.

Then I will ease your suffering and release you from this earthly life.

She stood and drew a deep breath before looking into Alyssa's eyes.

"No." Alyssa could sense it, but she couldn't accept it. "It may take months, but I can save her. She would be disabled but alive."

"She understands that, but she is a warrior. She asks for release, and I have to honor that. She suffers with every minute that we delay."

Alyssa couldn't stop the sob in her throat, but she backed away, pulling the medic with her. She couldn't hear their telepathic exchange, but she felt the woman's desperation fade even though her breathing had deteriorated to quick, shallow gasps. She'd honored the same request more than once when she worked in the hospice, but those were people who had no chance to survive, and she'd only shortened their suffering. Still, this was not her decision to make.

Jael stood at the warrior's head and Specter landed lightly near her feet. He spread his wings and ducked his head to touch his foreleg as Jael brought her fist to her left shoulder. A final salute. White-hot flame swirled in her palms as she raised her hands, and Specter's ribs expanded as his lungs filled. The downed warrior exploded into flame, but they continued the inferno until Specter's breath was expended and little more than charred bone fragments remained where the warrior had been.

Jael's face was a grim mask, and Alyssa went to her. Jael's shields had never been so impenetrable. The silence was alarming, but Alyssa would not be dissuaded. She pressed her face to Jael's neck and wrapped her arms tight around her body. Jael was stiff, her arms limp at her sides.

"Who...who was it?" There were more than a hundred candidates, and Alyssa knew only the ones she'd treated in her clinic for training scrapes and burns. Just the same, she needed a name so she could mourn this one.

A long minute passed, and Alyssa was beginning to think she wouldn't answer. When she spoke, low and hoarse, Jael's words were a swift dagger to her heart.

"Bast. It was Bast."

"Do you know what my name means?"
"No."
"It means born of the sun." Bast held out her hand and a small fireball appeared over her palm. "I was born for this."

No, no, no. Not the young warrior so eager she'd begged Alyssa for an excruciating treatment so she could return to training quicker.

Why hadn't she refused? Bast would still be back at the main camp, recovering from her training injury.

"If the First Warrior says it must be to protect The Collective, then I will not regret doing what must be done."

"I knew her," Alyssa managed to choke out.

Jael's posture softened. Her arms closed around her, hands stroking, and Alyssa wept. She wept for the young life that had ended too early, for the raw pain she knew dwelled behind Jael's shields, and for the misguided badly born who had forced them onto this tragic path.

CHAPTER TWENTY-ONE

I have news about your young man, Kylie."
Kyle raised her eyes to her father's. His gaze held no expression. "Will? Is he all right?" When Cyrus had summoned her and Ruth to his train car, she had an uneasy feeling it wasn't for something good.

"No. Those unnatural infidels apparently captured him and two others of our believers." He glanced at Ruth, and she took Kylie's hand in hers. "I regret to tell you that their funeral pyres were reported yesterday."

"They…they killed him? The Collective wouldn't do that." Kyle wouldn't believe it. "They're against violence. They wouldn't take a life intentionally."

Cyrus cocked his head, his expression gloating. "You're talking about the citizens who stormed our train, assaulted us, and stole our provisions."

Kyle bit back a retort. The Natural Order had stolen those supplies from the citizens. She didn't believe Will was dead. She'd know it. Just like she felt somehow that her brother had passed to the next life but her mother hadn't. Still, it would be better for her father to think she believed him. She leaned into Ruth and lowered her eyes. "Are you sure?" she whispered.

Cyrus was about to answer when a knock sounded at the door. He blew out an impatient breath. "Come."

The door slid open and Simon, followed by a man Kyle recognized as one of his henchmen, entered.

❖

They had flown back to the main camp and caught a few hours of sleep before heading off to the bonding camp. The arduous climb to the bonding encampment had finally silenced Will's enthusiastic questions about dragon horses. Not that Michael minded answering them, but he was normally a solitary person and needed time alone to sort things out.

He glanced over at Will. The day was sweltering hot even though the sun was only a few hours risen, and they'd both shed their shirts. Michael wore a racer-back undershirt to cover the surgical scars where he'd had his mammary glands removed for a more masculine chest. Will's bare chest was smooth and muscled, like a Greek statue. A slash of dried mud flaked on his cheek, and his blond hair was short, but shaggy and in need of a trim. His square jaw and beard stubble a shade darker than his hair made him ruggedly handsome.

Will would have been a formidable warrior if he'd been gifted. Apparently, he wasn't. He hadn't even blinked, however, when Michael and Diego had ignited the two funeral pyres with flames that shot from their hands. He told Michael later that his friend Kyle was a pyro, so he'd seen it before. Was Kyle another handsome male, maybe a lover? Michael mentally shrugged. What did he care anyway?

Michael had never experienced an attraction—to male or female— that could overcome his insecurity about revealing his differently equipped body to another. He'd decided he was born third gender because he had a greater mission as a warrior. Jael had confided once that she'd never found a soul mate in all her lives. A warrior's life was not conducive to home and family, she said. But a warrior's life was perfect for him.

Still, the solid feel of Will against his back as they flew through the night, the accidental brush of Will's beard against the back of his neck, and the scent of his sweat had been unsettling.

Ahead, Diego halted and crouched. Michael put his finger to his lips in a signal to Will for silence. Diego turned and silently communicated with a series of hand movements, then melted into the forest. Michael whispered to Will, "Don't say anything. Just follow my lead."

They could hear it now, something moving toward them. They waited until a man rounded a turn in the trail and slid to a startled halt.

'Jumpin' stars!" He slapped his hand to his chest. "You guys nearly sent me to my next life. I wasn't expecting to run into anyone."

Michael eyed the man. "We didn't anticipate anyone either. What brings you to this mountain, friend?"

The man glanced about, obviously sizing up his options. He was outnumbered and they were in his path. His eyes found the dragon tattoo that curled around Michael's bicep and shoulder, and he relaxed. "I'm Ricardo. You're one of The Guard, aren't you?"

Michael didn't answer and the man shrugged nonchalantly, like it didn't matter.

"Medical supplies." He gestured up the trail he'd been descending. "They need more medical supplies." He shook his head, the gesture exaggerated while he nervously tugged the cuff of his left sleeve farther down his wrist. "A lot of people were hurt, burned, you know. One man was bit clear through his forearm by one of those beasts."

"They must not need much if they sent only one person," Michael said.

Ricardo blinked at him, hesitating as though he didn't understand. "Oh. I'm not to carry them back." His laugh was forced. "I wouldn't make a very good pack mule, don't you know. I'm just a messenger. I'm supposed to tell them to send more up, along with several additional transports so they can bring the wounded down to the main camp."

Will shifted next to Michael. "Say, do I know you from somewhere? You look familiar."

"Maybe you've met my brother. He travels around a bit," Ricardo said, moving to sidle around them and continue down the trail.

Michael grabbed Ricardo's left forearm to forestall him, easily confirming what he'd suspected. "What's this?"

Ricardo jerked his arm away and spun toward his escape route down the mountain, only to bounce off an immovable object. Diego, a stump of a man, had circled around and planted himself in Ricardo's path.

Will wrapped his muscled arms round Richardo's chest from behind, pinning his arms, while Michael grabbed his shirt cuff and ripped his sleeve open up to his elbow.

"Individual communicators aren't permitted in our camp," Diego said, watching Michael remove it from Richardo's arm and activate it. "Funny you should have one."

"They can't expect us not to keep in touch with our families. Madrecita isn't well. I have to check on her."

"We're so sorry your mother is ill." Diego's brow furrowed with concern. "Michael?"

"It's standard issue. I'll be inside in less than a minute."

Diego turned back to the man. "You see, Michael is a communicator engineer. He probably designed the one you were wearing."

Michael nodded to confirm it. "I'm in. Checking transmissions."

The man struggled against Will's hold on him. "Hacking is illegal. That's my personal stuff in there."

Diego spread his hands in an apologetic gesture. "We only want to send a get-well message to your mother. Right, Michael?"

Michael activated the holoscreen and a picture of each of The Guard members flashed by, followed by video of the chaotic bonding and, finally, Jael and Specter incinerating a person lying on the ground. "Apparently, Madrecita is well enough to watch vids of our dragon-horse army."

Ricardo stomped down hard on Will's foot and wiggled free when he loosened his hold. He'd gone only a few steps when a wicked thirty-centimeter knife thunked into the trunk of a banana tree one step ahead of him and he skidded to a stop.

"Oh, that wasn't smart, now was it?" Michael flicked his fingers and a blue-white flame hovered at the end of his index finger. "Either Diego or I could have incinerated you before you were a minute down the path. You're lucky, though, that Diego likes to play with blades, too. They're less…instant." He cupped his hand to roll the flame into a fiery sphere. "If I'd been forced to throw a fireball, you'd have been here one minute, then—" The sphere doubled in size, then flamed out with an abrupt whoosh. "—gone the next."

Diego yanked the large blade from the tree and held it up. Its polished surface glinted in the sun. "Beautiful, isn't it?" He touched his finger to the tip and a bead of blood sprang forth. "So sharp you don't even feel it slicing your skin."

"Did I mention that Diego is a master smithy? His specialty is custom knives and exhibition swords."

"Swords are okay, but I really love carving knives." Diego sheathed the big blade and pulled out a folding knife that produced a razor-thin, nine-centimeter blade when he flicked his wrist. He looked at Ricardo. "Want to feel how sharp it is?"

Sweat ran down Ricardo's face and his voice shook. "I...I was just sending some pictures home to entertain my mother."

Michael cocked his head and pretended to think about that as he flicked his fingers, absently lighting and extinguishing, lighting and extinguishing a slim flame. "Then you won't mind explaining that to the First Warrior."

"Sure, no problem. I'll do it as soon as I come back from the main camp." Ricardo tried to edge around Diego, but Diego moved with him.

"You know, we haven't been to the temporary camp yet, so why don't you show us the way?" Michael said. "I'm sure we can send someone else for the medical supplies and extra transports." He looked at Will and jerked his chin toward Ricardo. Will grabbed the back of Ricardo's collar and forced him up the hill.

The holo-vid was dark and grainy, with flashes of light that illuminated things too fantastical to believe.

"What trickery is this you've brought me?" Cyrus threw his hand out dismissively.

Simon's henchman didn't flinch. He stood relaxed, but his hand rested on the grip of a weapon holstered at his waist—not a threat but a possessive caress. "Prophet, this is no trickery. My brother has infiltrated those who are gathering an army to assault The Natural Order. He transmitted this vid only a few hours ago."

"Winged horses that breathe fire." The men glanced over at Kyle's soft exclamation.

"A perversion of nature just like that army, if you can call it that." Cyrus growled.

"If this is all they have, then our path will be easy." Simon's tone was mocking. "Our weapons will pick them out of the sky like big sitting ducks before they get close enough to throw their flames."

The vid began to repeat and Kyle watched intently. Every fiber of her screamed to be part of the scene she was watching. She should have been there. She would have been there if she'd managed to escape her father sooner. Did The Collective know that her father's men had restricted weapons? She had to warn them. She filled with an overwhelming urgency. She had to go now. She'd already wasted time waiting for a window of escape. She picked up an empty serving tray with the remains of her father's dinner and edged toward the door. Simon stepped into her path, his hand tightening around her forearm.

"Going somewhere, Kyle?"

She wasn't surprised that he ignored the softer version of her name that her father and Ruth insisted on using. She had never fooled him. He knew who she was. "I was taking Father's dinner tray back to the kitchen." She turned to Cyrus. "Would you like me to bring more coffee?"

Cyrus stared at them for a half minute, his face hardening. "No. Return to your quarters." His eyes pierced into hers. "Nothing you saw here leaves this room, girl."

She ducked her head and let her arm go limp in Simon's grasp even though she wanted to wrench free of his claw and slap the smirk from his face. "Of course, Father."

Simon motioned to his henchman. "John, escort her to the kitchen, then to her quarters."

Kyle pulled free, careful not to drop the tray. "I know the way."

Simon tilted his head and regarded her with undisguised distrust. "It's for your own safety." His lie was deliberately obvious. "Now that we know the unnaturals are planning to move against us, we must protect our women and children." He turned to his henchman. "Post guards outside the women's quarters," he said. "Any woman who leaves those quarters must be escorted."

Cyrus sighed. "Don't you think you're taking these Collective idiots too seriously?"

"Not at all," Simon said, turning back to Kyle. "We can't let them steal our defenseless women. Who would cook and clean or take care of our other needs?"

His leer made Kyle want to vomit. She would die before she let him or any of them touch her intimately.

CHAPTER TWENTY-TWO

Alyssa wearily ran the skin regenerator over what seemed like the hundredth burn she'd repaired that day. The last time she'd slept was the night before they left the main encampment, and the work had been nonstop—setting up camp, the bonding, and then treating the hundreds of injuries suffered during that hectic half hour.

The night had been a river of critical medical emergencies. She'd worked side by side with Tan, who had returned as soon as Raven and Furcho joined Second to manage the newly bonded.

The morning, however, had brought a steady stream of the new dragon-horse warriors with more minor injuries. Their bonds fresh and still forming, the warriors were antsy to return to the field even though their dragons had shed their wings with the daylight.

"Hold still." She snapped at the young man whose shin was a long, weeping blister.

"How long will this take? I have to check on Sunfire and get a ration of fire rocks and—"

"If I accidently run this regenerator too deep or over good skin, you'll really be injured, and I'll confine you to the clinic for a week." Truthfully, it would only scar a little worse, but she was too bone tired to regret the exaggeration.

"I'm a dragon-horse warrior. I don't have time to lie about in a hospital." His tone was both indignant and desperate.

"You will obey the First Advocate, no matter what she prescribes." Despite her weariness, Alyssa had felt Jael as she approached behind her. Not for the first time and surely not the last, she wished they were alone with Jael's breast under her cheek, Jael's hands stroking her back. She wished they were lying in Jael's field of wildflowers, without a care, without war hanging over their heads and darkening their future.

Jael's order, however, worked. The young man froze.

"Oh, for star's sake. You can breathe. Just don't move your leg, please," Alyssa said. For the next quarter hour, the only sounds were the background noise of Uri, Tan, and Nicole treating others in the large ward and the hum of regenerators. Finally, the last of the blister was dissolved and replaced by new pink skin. She straightened and flexed her aching shoulders. "Get a packet of aloe gel from the medic by the door and apply it twice a day," she said wearily. "Also, ask him for a calf glove and *wear* it for at least a week. I don't want to see you back in here with a tear in that new skin or strictures because you didn't care for it."

"Yes, ma'am. Thank you." The young man stood and saluted Jael. "First Warrior?"

"Fire rocks won't be distributed until after the dinner hour. Go catch some sleep before training begins tonight."

He shifted his feet reluctantly and stared at the wall in the direction of the meadow where his bonded would be grazing.

"You can take your bedroll out to the meadow," she said gently. "Bed down near your bonded. He'll keep the others from stepping on you while you sleep. It will help him rest, too, to have you near."

He nodded eagerly and snapped another salute. Jael returned his gesture. "Dismissed," she said.

Alyssa sank forward from her low stool to rest her arms and head on the cot her patient had just vacated. Immediately, strong hands began a celestial massage on her tense shoulders. Jael smelled faintly of sulfur.

"You need to rest," Jael said gently. "Our tent is ready, and a soft, thick sleeping pallet is waiting for you."

"Oh, stars, that sounds wonderful." Her words were muffled, but she was too tired to raise her head and too focused on the unnaturally warm hands kneading her stiff muscles. "What about you? You've been up since yesterday morning, too."

"I've got a few more things to handle, and then I promise I'll join you within the hour."

"Uh, excuse me. First Advocate? I mean, Alyssa?"

She finally straightened, immediately regretting the loss of Jael's touch, and blinked sleepily at Toni. "Yes?"

Toni looked as worn out as Alyssa felt. "Sorry to interrupt, but—" Her shoulders slumped and she stared at her feet. "The ones who didn't make it…where should we erect the funeral pyres?"

Alyssa stiffened. "Where did you—"

"Uh, behind the clinic, under the trees."

Without a word, Jael strode out the door, and, after a shared glance, Alyssa and Toni followed.

Among a hundred and twenty candidates, fifty-seven had successfully bonded. Thirty-eight were injured and unable to bond. Those numbers were a testament to their expert training and would have been celebrated, except for the twenty-four charred and broken bodies covered by their bedrolls under the shade of the banana trees. And the ash and bone that had been Bast's earthly body.

Jael knelt at the feet of the fallen, bowing her head reverently. Then she worked her way down the line of bodies, uncovering a hand of each to clasp as she murmured something in a tongue Alyssa didn't recognize. An odd mix of pain and pride softened Jael's angular features and washed over Alyssa. Her heart ached with Jael's pain, but her mind struggled with the pride. Even the promise of rebirth didn't justify the senseless loss of this life.

At last, Jael stood and walked past them. Uncertain, they followed her to the edge of the plateau, shading their eyes from the sunlight with their hands. She gestured to her left as she spoke to Toni. "Erect the pyre frames at the north end of the plateau, next to the rock face. The Guard will take care of the rest."

"Yes, First Warrior." Toni turned to go.

"Toni," Jael said softly.

She turned back.

"Pass the word that the pyres will be lit just after dusk."

"Yes, First Warrior."

"Jael—" Alyssa wanted to somehow shoulder part of Jael's burden.

"Go. Rest. You might be needed tonight. Some will have trouble as they grieve the loss of their friends."

"And when will you rest?"

"Only after my duties are fulfilled," she said grimly.

When would that be? When the pyres were lit, or when this mission was done? She started to protest, but Jael's shields were thick, the mental silence looming between them like a huge, empty, silent chasm. She didn't have the strength to cross it, and instinct told her to leave it for now. She brushed her hand down Jael's arm. "Then come as soon as you can and rest with me, if only for an hour."

She started for the path that led back to the clinic and the encampment farther downhill. Now that her mind had registered rest as the goal, her body seemed to embrace it. Every step felt like she had lead in her sandals, like she would fall asleep before she could reach her bed. That's why she didn't see him until Diego clasped her arms to keep her from stumbling headlong into him. She blinked at them.

"Diego? Thank the stars you're safe."

"I was unavoidably detained. We're looking for Jael."

Her brain sluggishly registered that Michael and a man she didn't recognize were behind him. The stranger held tight to the collar of a man she did know. He was one of a handful of locals who'd stumbled upon the main encampment and begged to work at menial chores in exchange for food and medicine for their families. "Ricardo?"

"Advocate!" He jerked free, but the stranger quickly grabbed his collar again and shook him. "Tell them you know me. Tell them I didn't do anything wrong."

Something was amiss here. She looked to Michael and Diego. "What's going on?"

"Did you send this man to the main encampment for more supplies?" Michael's question held no judgment, no emotion at all.

She rubbed her forehead. Her fatigue made it hard to think.

"It wasn't her," Ricardo said quickly. "It was a guy. A big guy."

"Uri?" Alyssa searched her memory. Uri wouldn't have sent anyone for supplies without checking with her first.

Ricardo nodded emphatically. "Yes. That's his name."

The moment he said it, she could feel that he was lying, and it must have shown on her face. Both Michael and Diego nodded.

"Jael?" Diego repeated his question.

"She's on the plateau, preparing for the funeral pyres," she said grimly, turning back to the trail. She couldn't deal with another thing until she'd rested.

❖

Jael watched the workers erect the last pyre frame, her back to Michael and Diego as they approached. She'd heard them the moment they'd encountered Alyssa. She didn't turn to greet them but reached out to Michael with her thoughts.

Tell me.

We have captured a spy, but we believe he already has relayed our location and the nature of our army.

I'll deal with him later. Lock him down somewhere and summon the rest of The Guard.

Yes, First Warrior.

❖

The harsh sun gave way to dusk, and the moon was rising in the east quadrant by the time all twenty-five pyre frames were complete. In the center of the field, the newly bonded warriors—outfitted in silvery unitard battle skins—stood in loose formation with their dragon horses beside them. Support personnel gathered at the edge of the woods ringing the plateau and lit torches as the night darkened.

The ache grew in Jael's chest as the six members of The Guard personally carried the twenty-four bodies and laid them on the black slabs of compacted ultra-flammable material that topped each pyre frame. Each snowy sheet emblazoned with a black dragon-horse symbol and draped over the pyres was her personal failure, casualties before they'd even reached their first battlefield. The last was a sharp blade that would scar her very soul.

Though it was only Bast's charred bone fragments, the box she personally placed onto the twenty-fifth pyre felt like it held all of her failures. She fingered the silken sheet—there had been too many of these in her lifetimes—and then carefully draped the pyre. The symbol on Bast's shroud was red. It was Jael's own, taken from her battle pack. She could order another to be made for when her time came. She gathered her regret and used it to fuel the anger that caught flame and began to burn in her gut, then turned to her waiting army.

"We are here to honor the bravery of our fallen." Her voice rang strong across the wide field.

The seven dragon horses of The Guard swept low in formation over the field, dark figures in the night sky, and Specter landed lightly between the pyres and the waiting army. When the remaining six flew over again, Specter's spot in the arrow formation remained open—a nod to the missing wingman. He spread his great wings and screamed at the sky, releasing a terrible column of blue-white flame. He lunged into the sky but flew straight up rather than follow the others. Soon, he was but a speck among the stars.

The night hummed with a low-level harmony as Furcho stood next to the first in his group of four pyres and cupped his hands together to form a large fireball. "Avyrl, House of Candlish of Region Five, Third Continent. Good speed on your journey." He raised the fireball overhead and flung it, igniting the pyre.

Diego cupped his hands in the same fashion. "William, House of Blackman, Region Seven, Third Continent. Good speed on your journey." He torched the pyre.

Every pyre lit to purify and release the souls for their next life burned a new mark on Jael's soul.

When the heat of twenty-four pyres forced The Guard to move back and stand as the front rank of the new army, Jael remained, scorched by the fire and backlit by the inferno. She bowed her head to cup her hands and stared into the fireball for a long minute before she lifted it skyward.

"Bast." She swallowed as the rest caught in her throat.

I beg...a warrior's death...help me...next life, another chance.

"House of Saleh. Region Two, Fourth Continent. Fly unfettered, my young warrior." Though Bast's soul already had been freed hours before, Jael had felt her hovering, waiting for the others. *Stronger together, my warriors. Go in peace.* She flung the fireball at Bast's pyre and then stepped back, finally acknowledging the scorched scent of her clothing. She addressed her army.

"We mourn their absence in this life yet celebrate their fulfillment of this journey." She raised her arms to the sky. "Glorious will be the day when all is as it should be, and we are reunited."

"Glorious will be the day," the warriors echoed.

She paced before the army, searching for the words that always seemed to come easily to her before battle. But the cloying smell of the pyres, the echo of Bast's words in her head, and a bitter anger she couldn't yet name held her in its fiery grip. Her army needed her wisdom, not her raw, barely controlled fury. "Warriors, report for flight training."

Second, Tan, Raven, and Furcho herded the new warriors into groups and prepared to instruct them. Michael and Diego awaited her orders.

"Where's the prisoner?"

Diego pointed to a large tree where Ricardo sat, his hands tied behind his back. Michael released Ricardo and dragged him to stand before her. She studied Ricardo's face in the light that flickered from the pyres. He bowed his head under her hard gaze.

"Please, I didn't do anything."

His whining felt like nails scratching at her ears. "Diego?"

"We encountered him on the trail, making his escape."

"I was going to get supplies for the clinic."

"He had an IC strapped under his sleeve, and Michael found a video he'd recorded of the bonding."

"I thought you might want it later, to commemorate the event," Ricardo said, flicking a glance at her. "I, uh, I was making it to give to the First Advocate. She told me that she keeps a journal, and I thought maybe she'd like a copy to imbed in her journal." He seemed pleased with his new story.

Michael snorted. "You told us that you made it to send to your mother."

Ricardo scowled at him. "Her, too."

"Enough." Jael closed her eyes and tried to settle her anger. His thoughts wouldn't lie. She opened her eyes and reached for him. He jerked away from her hands, his face a mask of terror.

"No, please, I saw what you did to that wounded soldier."

"Hold him."

Diego and Michael each took an arm and held him fast between them.

Jael grasped his chin. "I am a telepath. If you're telling the truth, then you have nothing to fear. If you're lying, I'll know in an instant."

He struggled, but she spread her hands on either side of his head like a vise. His thoughts were simple and the truth easy to find. Rage burned through her brain. Men like this one were ripping apart The Collective, denying food and medicine to children, enslaving women, spreading the same greed and manipulating power that had infected her past lives. She was a warrior who had at last sought peace, and The Natural Order was wrenching that from her. She released his head and dragged him by his collar as close to the pyres as the heat allowed and threw him to the ground.

"I find you guilty of treason, a traitor to The Collective." The words were a growl barely escaping her clenched teeth.

His fate sealed, his true nature surfaced and he spit at her. "The days of your perverted Collective are numbered. The Prophet will return our world to The Natural Order, where men rule and women like you are recognized as unnatural."

She raised her hands and flames arced above her head. "In the name of The Collective, I sentence you to a cleansing death and a new life in which you will pay restitution." His scream echoed through the night. Her anger had tempered her flame so that his execution wasn't instantaneous like Bast's death. For that, *she* would owe restitution. Every action had a consequence. But she couldn't think of that now. She had an army to train.

CHAPTER TWENTY-THREE

Alyssa was stunned, the man's scream reverberating in her ears. She'd roused from her nap too late to see Jael before pyres were lit and had been making her way across the field after the haunting memorial, intending to soothe the pain she knew Jael held bottled inside. Then a blast of fury from Jael had nearly thrown her to her knees. The visions Jael had shared of her past lives were shocking, but they'd been a dispassionate movie silent of emotion. This…this murderous anger frightened her. She watched in horror as Jael passed judgment and torched a living, healthy man without hesitation.

When Jael turned and their gaze met, it stole her breath. She saw nothing of her tender lover, the thoughtful leader of The Guard, the patient instructor of young recruits. She saw eyes bright with battlefield savagery, a gaze that held no recognition before Jael leapt onto Specter's back the minute he touched down and launched into the night sky.

The slap of terror from the man in the split second when the first touch of flame seared his skin before it mercifully consumed his brain lingered and soured her stomach. She doubled over and vomited its contents onto the ground.

"Alyssa?" Nicole was at her side.

She shook her head and pulled away. "Can't do this. I can't do this."

Nicole hesitated, worry filling her eyes. "Let me help you to your tent. Then I'll go find Han for you."

"No. I…I need to be alone. This is all too much." What little rest she'd had that afternoon had been restless and broken, and the shock of Jael's fury, of the man's terror had hammered her weakened shields. Even Nicole's gentle concern was sandpaper on her raw emotions. "I'll be okay. Need some solitude to regroup."

Nicole let her go, but Alyssa could feel her concern as she stumbled in the direction of her quarters. Inside the tent, she fell to her knees, sobbing. She cried for young lives too soon aflame upon the pyres. She cried for her lover stolen by the cold fury she'd last seen in Jael's eyes. She cried because she knew she wasn't strong enough to bear this. She'd failed Han, failed The Collective, and she'd failed to be strong enough to stand at Jael's side. How could she have ever thought they might be soul bonded?

The tent and Jael's things scattered about had been a comfort earlier. Now they only tore at her. Jael's scent, Jael's clothes neatly stacked in the corner, Jael's lingering essence permeating everything. She stumbled back out into the night, but the flames of the pyres were too bright, the screams of the dragon horses too loud. She turned back and found an entrance into the dark, quiet forest. She didn't know where the path led, only that it led away from the dragon-horse army and the stranger she'd seen when she looked into Jael's eyes, stark and as deadly as hot, blue flame.

The mountain peak was barren and windswept, much like Jael felt inside. She hadn't forgotten the darkness she carried inside, but so many years had passed that she'd been surprised when it surfaced. She'd welcomed it, sought it even, in past lives when she'd waded into battlefields wielding sword and knife, when she and her dragon horse had incinerated entire regiments of enemy soldiers into a pile of ash, and in times past when, like tonight, The Collective called on her to be judge and executioner. She'd never regretted the darkness. The greatest weapon in her arsenal, her dark side didn't hesitate and felt no guilt. Until today. When her eyes met Alyssa's and her dark challenged Alyssa's light. She could do nothing but flee, lest she taint the only pure soul she'd ever met, ever...loved? She slumped against the boulder at her back and closed her eyes. Yes. She loved Alyssa. But the fear on Alyssa's face—fear of her—burned deeper than the flame that had executed the traitor.

Her path had always been clear. The mantle of warrior had always rested comfortably on her shoulders, no matter the hardship or pain. Now, she hadn't even reached the battlefield and she'd already lost her taste for it. She wanted her high meadow of wildflowers. She wanted to wake up each morning to the affection in Alyssa's eyes, not the swords that hung on every wall. She was so tired. And she was so frustrated. She jerked to her feet and screamed at the stars.

"Have I not served you without question? Have I not given you my loyalty, my earthly life over and over again? How many times must I win peace for you? When will it be my turn for peace?"

Your reward is not ours to grant. It is yours to find.

❖

"Miss?"

Alyssa jerked awake at the hand on her shoulder and immediately regretted it when her stiff neck and back clenched in a painful spasm. She'd walked for hours in the dark until she could go no farther, then finally collapsed against the trunk of a banana tree. At some point, she must have fallen asleep because it was daylight now. A rock or a root was digging into her back, and she was staring up at the face of a young boy.

"Do you have anything to eat, miss?"

She started to tell him she wasn't hungry but realized he was asking for himself. She hadn't thought to bring anything when she stumbled into the woods. She closed her eyes, battling back memories of the man's scream and Jael's fury.

"Miss? Are you okay?"

"Yes. I'm sorry. Just a little stiff from sleeping on the ground." She struggled to her feet and brushed the dirt from her clothes. Her hand ran over a lump, and she retrieved a rather smashed pro-chow bar from her pocket. The boy stared at it and swallowed. She held it out. "Here. It's not much, but that's all I brought with me."

He shifted his feet in an eager dance. "Are you sure?" His eyes never left the food.

"Positive. I'm not hungry. You eat it."

He stuffed it in his pocket and looked up at her. Short red hair and green eyes weren't the norm in this quadrant, so she'd grown used to the locals staring when they saw her. "I seem to be a little lost." She cleared her throat. "And a lot thirsty. Are we near your village?"

"No, miss. The village is a half hour that way." He pointed down the trail. "This is my uncle's coffee ranch. Only my family lives here. Come, I'll show you. We have water for you to drink."

They'd hiked for about ten minutes when the forest opened into a muddy clearing with a modest house surrounded by several outbuildings. A withered old woman sat on a low stool and tended a small fire in front of one shed while two gaunt oxen grazed in a shallow ditch, tethered only by thin ropes wrapped round their horns and knotted at the other end around large rocks. The boy led her to the adobe-sided house, and Alyssa was surprised to find the inside was clean and modern. She left her muddy shoes with the pile of other shoes outside the door and padded barefoot onto the cool, beautifully tiled floor.

"Mami! I found a lady."

"Ari! What have I told you?"

"Sorry, Mami." He rushed back outside to swish his mud-caked feet in a pan of cloudy water, then dried them on a rag next to it.

Alyssa extended her hand. "I'm Alyssa. I'm afraid I got lost walking around at night and your boy found me."

"I'm Serena." Her hand was callused, like Jael's but different—probably from farm work rather than handling flame.

Ari rushed back into the room. "She gave me food!" He held up the pro-chow bar. "But she's thirsty."

"It's not much," Alyssa said.

"Thank you." Serena cut her off with a wave of her hand. "The children have had nothing for two days. We've stripped the trees of their fruit so we could eat. We've got nothing for market now except the coffee beans." The woman took the bar from her son.

"Last week, we ate a snake my uncle caught," Ari said.

Serena gave him a sharp look. "Go get the other children." She laid the food bar on the table and disappeared into the kitchen. When she returned, she carried a knife and handed Alyssa a tall glass of water.

"Thank you." Her throat was raw, probably from crying, and the water was cool.

Ari reappeared with four girls of varying ages, and they watched as Serena carefully cut the bar into six even pieces. "Eat it slowly and chew it as long as you can," she said. She gave one piece to each child, then held up the last to the tallest girl. Alyssa estimated her to be twelve or thirteen years old.

"This is for grandmother," Serena said. The girl nodded and took it, darting out the door in the direction of the old woman Alyssa had seen outside.

Their precious food in hand, the children scattered in different directions.

Serena regarded her. "You're an Advocate."

Alyssa nodded. She mostly forgot about the tattoo curling up her neck and along her temple that identified her as belonging to the temple. "I was at an encampment high up on the mountain and lost my way in the forest at night."

Serena shook her head. "The mountain isn't safe at night. Giant flying things that breathe fire after the sun goes down are there. The sky was alight with their flames last night."

Alyssa's throat tightened at the thought of the pyres. "Yes. I know."

Serena stared at her for a long minute. "You came from there?"

"Yes. But the flames are nothing to fear. The Collective is gathering an army in the mountains to stop the badly born who have taken control of the supply shipments."

"This army, the mountain beasts belong to them?"

"Yes. No. I mean, they're wild horses by day, but they grow wings at night. They call them dragon horses. The army raided the herd last night to tame some so they can go after the badly born."

Serena looked doubtful. "Flying horses?"

Alyssa shook her head. "Hard to believe, isn't it? I wouldn't have if I hadn't seen them myself."

"Why would they need these flying horses? Surely they have transports to chase these people."

"The warriors and the dragon horses are gifted—they're pyros." She stared down at her hands. "They believe the fire they wield is necessary to purify the badly born so they can be reborn on the right path, recover their right place among The Collective."

Serena tilted her head and looked thoughtful. "You don't believe this?"

"They will incinerate live people." She shuddered. "I've seen it. It's horrible. There must be some other way to restore The Collective."

Serena's expression hardened. "My sister's son fell ill with a simple childhood ailment, but there was no medicine and he died last week. My sister cries all night and stares at the wall all day."

Ari slumped in the doorway, frowning at his feet. He came to Serena when she motioned to him. She pulled up his loose T-shirt to reveal gaunt ribs and abdomen bloated with malnutrition. "These people are hoarding food that belongs in the bellies of my children. Their deaths are surely more merciful than a slow death from sickness or starvation."

Alyssa glanced out the window at two oxen that had worked their way out of the ditch and were eating the weeds in the sparse lawn.

Serena shook her head. "We cannot. Slaughtering our oxen would be the same as a fisherman burning his boat to stay warm. The coffee beans are all we have left now that the grove is stripped of fruit. The mountain is often too muddy and steep for the transports. Oxen are still needed to carry the heavy sacks down the slopes."

There had to be a better way. "You could pretend to join them just long enough to get the food and medicine you need. There are more of us than there are of them. We could infiltrate and convince their followers to return to The Collective."

Serena jerked her hand in a slashing movement, her eyes angry. "You cannot reason with madmen. They might have stolen our food, but we will not give up our dignity, too. They value men over women. Men with light skin like their leader. Their women are little more than servants and the dark-skinned men their oxen." Ari grabbed his mother's hand and held it in his in an attempt to calm her.

Like Jael, this woman seemed to have an answer to discount each of Alyssa's suggestions. "May I have a pen and paper?"

"I'll get it," Ari said, and ran out of the room.

Serena stared at the window, jaw clenching and lips drawn into a tight line.

"I'm sorry," Alyssa said gently. "I'm sure you've done all you can." Ari returned and she scribbled a quick note with the materials he provided. She held it out to Serena. "Take this note and go immediately up the mountain to the high plateau. They're probably moving out of the temporary camp today, but the warriors won't leave until after dusk. Even if the support troops are gone, the warriors will have pro-chow in their personal packs. Give this note to one of The Guard. They'll give you what food they have, as much as you can carry."

"You will not return to them?"

"No. I need to find the nearest temple and consult with the leadership there. There has to be a better way, and I intend to find it."

"Ari will take you there."

"But Mami, I want to see the flying horses."

Serena gave him a hard look. "Your sister will go with me to the camp. The Collective has given us a great opportunity to help this Advocate in her mission. It is a warrior's honor to be her escort."

Ari straightened and his small chest swelled. "Yes, Mami." He nodded to Alyssa. "It will be my honor, Advocate."

Jael stumbled into the tent. She needed months to adequately train the newly bonded warriors and their dragon horses, but The Natural Order was only about fifty klicks south at this very moment. The timing was unfortunate, but the opportunity to cut the head from the serpent and end this insurgency quickly was too coincidental to pass up.

It was barely past dawn but the tent was empty. Had Alyssa even slept? The covers of their pallet were neatly tucked as though no one had made use of it, and she cringed at the memory of Alyssa's shocked expression when she'd seen Jael's fury. Maybe she'd gone to Nicole's tent because she didn't want to sleep next to an executioner. Jael's bleary mind tried to process that bitter thought. She hadn't slept in two days. Or was it three?

Jael shed her boots and clothes in a pile next to the bed. She was more than mentally and physically exhausted. She was emotionally drained. Sleep. She needed sleep. She pulled the blanket up to her shoulders and relaxed, burrowing her head into the pillow. She missed the gentle weight of Alyssa curled against her side, but at least the pillow still carried her comforting scent. Tonight, she'd lead her untrained army of recruits on their first, and hopefully only, raid. Then she'd worry about tomorrow.

Chapter Twenty-four

The solar scooter she and Ari rode to the village was a sharp contrast to the oxen grazing along the badly pitted road, and Alyssa marveled that such rugged, undeveloped areas still existed amidst modern technology.

The village was more of a town than Alyssa anticipated. Ari's slim shoulders weren't much of a handhold as he expertly wove in and out of traffic, so her thighs ached from gripping the seat by the time they pulled to a stop in the market square. People were rushing about, urgently sending messages on their ICs, and a man nearly knocked Alyssa down as she climbed off the scooter and straightened her stiff body.

"Sorry, sorry," the man said before hurrying on.

"Something's happening," Ari said. "There are never this many people in the square—especially since the vendors have had little to sell lately."

"Let's go inside. Someone in the temple will know," Alyssa said, pulling Ari out of the path of another speeding scooter.

The temple, however, was nearly as chaotic as the market square. Alyssa grabbed a woman's arm as she dodged to pass them.

"Can you tell me where to find the Chief Advocate?"

The woman barely spared her a glance, but pointed and then hurried on. Alyssa took Ari's hand and tugged him toward the indicated doorway, which she suspected led to the rooms reserved for administrative office space and counseling appointments. She exhaled a breath of relief when Ari shut the door behind them. She was still weak from little rest and no food in the past twenty-four hours, and the high excitement of the throngs gathering in the market had felt like a battering ram slamming against her emotional shields. The open doors down the hall revealed no one, but Alyssa could hear arguing from a room at the end of the corridor.

"Maybe we should hear what they have to say," a male voice said.

"You've read the news accounts. These people are heretics and anarchists," a woman said. Her voice sounded young but bitter. "Even worse, they're callous thieves. They're trying to trade food and supplies for our souls."

"Yes, and plenty of people out there are hungry enough and sick enough to do just that. The young souls, especially, who have no memory of past lives will be swayed to their side," the man said.

A loud snort preceded the woman's reply. "The men, maybe. The women won't be so anxious to sell themselves into the domestic slavery these people espouse."

"The ones with hungry children will be vulnerable, even though they know it's wrong." The weariness in this third voice tore at Alyssa, and when she stepped into the doorway, she quickly identified the source as an older woman with the purple sash of the Chief Advocate draped over her shoulders.

"Perhaps I can help if someone will tell me what's going on outside." The three Advocates stared, and she turned her head slightly to be sure they could see her tattoo. "I'm Alyssa, Advocate, Region Four, Third Continent, and this is my young friend, Ari." She still wasn't comfortable introducing herself as First Advocate, even though The Collective Council had decreed it.

The older woman stood and extended her hand. "I'm Camila. You're a long way from home."

"I'm part of a, um, delegation called together to deal with this crisis."

The male advocate sat back in his chair. "Good. Then it's out of our hands."

"I'm Deputy Advocate Emilia." The woman extended her hand in greeting and the man frowned at her use of her title to point out her seniority over him. Emilia gestured toward the man. "And the rude one is Victor." Emilia's greeting projected a slightly amorous interest, and Alyssa projected a more sisterly emotion back at her. Emilia frowned, her expression puzzled.

"Have you made contact with any representatives of The Natural Order?" Alyssa asked.

"Their train pulled into town a few hours ago," Victor said. "Several of their believers have been tacking up notices around town, summoning everyone to the market square tonight. The word has spread that the train is loaded with supplies."

"A few people tried to see inside one of the train cars, but they're guarding them," Emilia said.

"I could get in. Mami says I'm very fast and clever."

Emilia gave the boy an indulgent smile. "I'm sure you are, but if there are supplies in there, we'll need many people to unload them." She turned back to the adults. "And if they won't share them when that hungry crowd gathers tonight, I hate to think what will happen."

Camila looked to Alyssa. "What does your delegation plan to do?"

"It's very hard to explain." Alyssa didn't want to talk about the dragon-horse army and their objective to incinerate every last badly born. "I'm hoping to negotiate some sort of truce before the delegation has to act."

"How can we help?" Camila asked.

Jael was in motion before her eyes opened and her sleeping brain registered the reflex.

"Stop. It's just me."

The strangled words took a few seconds to register, and then she loosened her arm around Second's neck. "I thought you were in here reviewing maps and strategy. We only have about four hours until dark."

She'd slept the day away. Dung. She was getting too old for this. She felt uncharacteristically off-kilter. She needed to ground herself. She needed to see Alyssa. Clothes. She needed to dress. She ran her tongue over her gritty teeth. She needed to clean up.

Second's hand closed around Jael's arm, her expression understanding. And why wouldn't Second understand? They were clones and, like twins, shared more similarities than differences. "Skip the sonic shower. I found a waterfall about a klick away. Come on. I'll show you. A real bath will clear your head." She wrinkled her nose. "And, if it doesn't, you'll at least smell better. Then you can find Alyssa and apologize."

Jael frowned. "Apologize for what?"

"It doesn't matter. She obviously didn't sleep here with you, so you must have done something to piss her off. Shower, find her, and apologize. Your mind won't be clear and fully on tonight's raid until you do." Second's smile was sad. "Trust me, I know from experience. You don't have time to argue. Just do it."

Less than an hour later, her hair was still damp from her bath, but she was clear-headed, refreshed, and on her way to find Alyssa. She slowed as she approached the clinic—or rather where the clinic *had* been. A man and a woman were loading the last of the temporary building's panels onto a trailer while Tan talked with two medics next to the open door of a medical transport that held two of the more seriously wounded. Tan lifted her hand to signal Jael, then concluded her conversation with the medics and strode over. "I know your brain has been controlled by your ovaries lately, but I needed Alyssa at the clinic today, not warming your bed."

Jael frowned. "You haven't seen her?"

"No. And I was hoping to catch a few winks—" Tan grew still. "Wait. She hasn't been with you?"

"No. I haven't seen her since last night." Jael scanned the camp. Almost everything had been disassembled and loaded onto transports to return to the main encampment. After tonight's raid, the dragon-horse warriors would fly to the meadow near there so the wild herd could return to their high plateau. A cold weight began to form in her chest. Where was she?

Second hopped off a chow wagon and waved the driver on down the mountain. "You look better," she said as she approached. Her steps slowed. "What's wrong?"

"Alyssa's missing," Tan said.

"Missing?"

Jael spotted Nicole on the edge of the meadow, shooting nervous glances their way as she shouldered her personal pack. When their eyes locked, Nicole started toward them and Jael met her halfway. "Where's Alyssa?"

"I was hoping she was with you." Nicole looked worried. "Last time I saw her was last night. She was, uh, she was—" She stopped and bit her lip.

The cold in Jael's chest was growing, its weight crushing her lungs. She grabbed Nicole's head and tore into her thoughts.

"Can't do this. I can't do this."
"Let me help you to your tent. Then I'll go find Han for you."
"No. I...I need to be alone. This is all too much. I'll be okay. Need some solitude to regroup."

She abruptly disengaged and stepped back. Nicole gasped, and Tan wrapped a supporting arm around her as she sagged.

"Stop it." Second grabbed Jael's shoulders and shook her. "You could have hurt her."

Jael grabbed fistfuls of Second's shirt. "Something's happened to her."

"This is my fault. I shouldn't have let her go off alone," Nicole said, her face pale.

Second covered Jael's hands and gently pulled them from her shirt. "This is nobody's fault. Alyssa is an adult. A very resourceful adult." Her gaze and voice were calm and steady. "She traveled more than half a continent alone to find you. She bears the Advocate mark, and the locals will honor that." She tapped Jael's head, then her chest. "Trust me. If something had happened to her, you'd know it."

Jael closed her eyes and breathed deep, struggling to center herself. In all her lives, she'd never felt this kind of soul-deep fear. She touched Nicole's cheek. "I'm sorry. I hope I didn't hurt you. Alyssa would hate me, if she doesn't already."

Nicole's smile was thin. "It wasn't your probe. I'm an empath and I wasn't prepared for...your distress. Just find her, okay? She doesn't hate you. Her love for you is confusing her. You aren't the enemy, but she's still sorting that out."

Jael nodded. She'd faced battle and death many times in her previous lifetimes, but she'd never felt the hopeless panic that threatened now to consume her. She reached deep and unsheathed the only weapon she had to battle it. The darkness turned her icy fear into hot fury. "Tonight, the pyres that burn will belong to this Prophet and his Natural Order."

Chapter Twenty-five

The burly believer stood, legs spread and arms crossed over his wide chest. "The Prophet doesn't conference with women."

Alyssa tamped down her irritation at his arrogance. "Camila is a Chief Advocate for The Collective. She speaks for the citizens in this quadrant of the region."

"I am authorized to let you speak to Ruth. She can explain to you the role of women in The Natural Order." The sun was winking its last over the tops of the surrounding mountains, and night was falling fast. The believer half turned from them, his attention shifting to several men climbing a ladder to a platform bolted to the top of one train car. "But it'll have to wait until after the gathering."

"Of all the arrogant, idiotic—"

"Emilia watches all the news bulletins. She said this group's 'natural order' bases leadership on gender, like in ancient times," Camila said.

Citizens were beginning to crowd onto the long loading platform next to the train and the wide grassed strip abutting the train cars that extended beyond the platform. Word of the supply train had spread fast, and more than half the region's population had turned out.

Alyssa grabbed Camila's hand and pulled her through the throng. "Come on. I'm not giving up."

When the high-powered spotlights illuminated the platform, Cyrus was glad for the dimmer lenses he wore. He strutted from one end of the platform to the other, relishing the feel of the crowd's attention riveted to his every move. He stopped center-stage and tapped his IC to activate the amplifier.

"I come to you tonight, asking that you open your minds and your hearts to a life-saving message." His voice boomed into the moonless night. "Unprecedented winter storms, then tornados and mudslides in the Third Continent. Devastating drought in the Second Continent. Unrelenting rain and floods in the First and Fourth continents. Millions of citizens have been killed by these catastrophic events."

He paused and ducked his head in a show of grief he didn't feel. "My mate and my son were killed in a mudslide." He wiped at nonexistent tears and cleared his throat. He could have been an actor, but this was more. He was The Prophet. He was the voice of The One. "Without warning, the side of a mountain collapsed and buried our entire hometown and most of its citizens." He paced the platform.

"These plagues of nature have devastated crops. Widespread famine threatens because the limited production of our protein manufacturers cannot sustain our population." He balled his hands into fists and held them out. "The World Council has shown itself impotent in the face of these disasters. The Collective solution is to spread our scarce food supplies to every corner of the earth so that we'll all starve together."

The crowd shifted restlessly, and many eyed the freight cars. Simon murmured into his IC, and believer guards discreetly moved into position next to each car.

Hands still raised, Cyrus opened his fists in a beseeching gesture. "Overcome with grief at the loss of my family, I asked myself: What can be done? I climbed to the highest peak near my home where the air was not clouded with the smoke of funeral pyres and filled with the cries of my neighbors mourning their families. I fasted until the vision came to me, clear as crystal."

He smiled to himself and lowered his hands. He had their rapt attention now. "I have spent my life studying the history of our world, and I realized that we are simply repeating mistakes made by our ancestors because we have forgotten…no…we have ignored a simple truth." He raised his hands and shrugged. "All humans are not created equal."

A murmur ran through the crowd and Cyrus raised his voice to make his point. "In nature, only the strong prevail because it is necessary for the evolution and survival of the species. All are not created equal.

It is The Natural Order of things, and we humans have rejected it. All are not created equal in nature, and our stubborn resistance to this fact has disrupted the natural flow of our universe."

"He speaks lies."

Alyssa leaned around Camila, but saw only a few faces turn their way. The backside of the train had been dark, and the few guards posted there were peering between the cars at the crowd on the other side, so they climbed atop the railcar adjacent to Cyrus's stage. "I don't think they heard you," she said.

Camila tapped her IC and repeated her accusation through the amplifier. "He speaks lies."

Cyrus glanced their way but didn't acknowledge them. "Are you strong enough to embrace the truth, to acknowledge The Natural Order and live it, my brothers and sisters? Those of you who join us will share the resources bestowed on believers who no longer refuse our natural path."

"And what of those who refuse your blackmail?" Camila asked. "Will they go hungry because you and your followers are thieves who have raided the distribution centers and stolen the food meant for their children?"

The railcar swayed slightly and Alyssa twisted to look behind them. "Uh oh. This doesn't look good, Camila." Guards were scrambling onto the railcar's top and making their way single file along the narrow roof toward them. "We need to get out of here."

Camila, in an athletic move that belied her mature years, leapt from their car onto Cyrus's stage. Alyssa measured the distance. Camila was taller and had long legs. No way she'd be able to make the same jump. She turned and balanced herself, then swept the feet out from under the first man. He grabbed at the man behind him and they both tumbled off the car.

"Heh. Even Jael fell for that move once."

The next guard, slender and dark-haired, spread his arms to hold the others back. It was a standoff, but Alyssa only needed to hold them back long enough for Camila to speak.

"You know me. You know I speak the truth of The Collective," Camila said. "This man is to be pitied. His grief has driven him insane."

"I am The Prophet," Cyrus roared. "I am chosen to restore The Natural Order."

"This train is filled with supplies," Camila said. "If you'll help unload it, you'll be given what your family needs. The remainder will be inventoried and redistributed to the rest of the region."

The crowd moved forward, intent on their mission. The guards slid open the doors to the cars and more believers jumped out.

"This can't be good." Alyssa tried to project calm, but her attention was divided between the guards still waiting to jump her and what was happening below.

Cyrus screamed. "Only those who follow my truth will receive the bounty of The Natural Order."

"Dung, you say." A barrel-chested man raised his fist to Cyrus. "We'll take back what is ours and send you on your way." His declaration was met with supporting shouts from other citizens as they surged again.

"No. Stop. This isn't the way to solve this." The din of angry shouts swallowed Alyssa's words.

The believer reinforcements were armed with weapons outlawed so long ago that the villagers didn't know to be afraid. They began firing upon the advancing citizens, felling many with their bullets. The mob rushed the guards anyway, hurling rocks and wrestling the closest ones to the ground.

"Cease or the Chief Advocate will sacrifice her life for your insurgence." The thunderous declaration vibrated through the night and the melee stilled. Alyssa gasped. Cyrus had his arm around Camila's throat and a handgun pressed to her temple. His madness was a cold, impenetrable wall, and she felt without a doubt that he would carry out his threat. The citizens backed away, releasing the believer guards they'd captured.

Cyrus's eyes gleamed, spittle dripping down his chin with every vicious word. "You have made your choice to live outside The Natural Order, and now you must live with the consequences. Let it be recorded. The faithful of The Natural Order will thrive, while its enemies—"

His last words were lost in a great swooping sound that filled the night. Alyssa ran down the car, prepared to leap onto the stage. She didn't have a plan for freeing Camila, but she wasn't about to waste the distraction she knew was coming. At the last minute, Cyrus turned to her, Camila still held fast in his grip, and Alyssa skidded to a stop.

Camila's gaze, calm and steady, held hers. Alyssa gestured at the sky and shouted to her. "Our reinforcements."

Cyrus heard, too, and when he looked upward, Camila grabbed the opportunity to reassure the citizens. "Don't be afraid. The defenders of The Collective have arrived. Move back, but do not—" Her last words were choked off as Cyrus tightened his arm around her neck and fired a bullet into her IC that was broadcasting her words. Blood dripped from Camila's arm.

Only the swoop of wings and the thud of sharp hooves on the loading dock broke the stunned silence that followed the gunshot.

Specter settled on the platform, his great wings still extended in a display of power, and the icy weight in Jael's chest lifted. Alyssa stood, apparently unharmed, atop a railcar, though eminent danger surrounded her. Second, astride Titan, and Tan, fierce in her war paint and mounted on the glittering Phyrrhos, settled on the roofs of nearby buildings, and Jael's focus narrowed to the man on the adjacent railcar and the woman he held in a choke hold.

She reached with her mind. The woman's mind was eerily calm. She was an old soul. Camila. The village's Chief Advocate. His thoughts, however, were a jumble of insane rants. He was Cyrus. He was The Prophet. He was The One. He was deciding to turn his weapon on Alyssa.

No. I am the one you should fear. Look at me.

He frowned at the foreign whisper in his mind, but turned to stare at Jael.

"I am Jael, First Warrior of The Collective's Guard. Release the Chief Advocate immediately."

He sneered at her, but even amplified, his voice couldn't match the cold calm of Jael's. "I'm not afraid of your contrived illusions. Flying horses, indeed."

Specter raised his head and screamed, emitting a stream of hot flame. The citizens moved away but didn't run. The believer guards raised their rifles and readied to fire on him and Jael.

"No!" Alyssa's stricken cry barely penetrated the darkness that steeled Jael's course.

"In the name of The Collective Council, I pronounce you guilty of violating the directives of The Collective to hoard for your own cause at the cost of life and health to your fellow humans. I also find you guilty of heresy and conspiracy to spread heresy." She lifted her hand and palmed a pulsating blue fireball. "I sentence you to immediate death and restitution in your next life."

A gunshot sounded, and Jael's fireball barely melted the bullet Cyrus fired before it reached her. A second gun report and Camila crumpled and tumbled off the railcar. Cyrus jumped after her, screaming when Jael's flame licked at his face as he disappeared behind the railcar.

To arms!

Jael's call brought a hail of dragon horses and their warriors down on the train. The pandemonium of battle erupted. Ear-splitting dragon screams competed with the report of automatic weapons. Citizens screamed and fled. Molten lead dropped from the sky as bullets melted in the flames that spewed forth to envelop the train and incinerate the believers where they stood beside it.

Amidst it all, Jael registered only one thing. A dark-haired guard sprang forward and tackled Alyssa so that they both dropped to the ground. Gunfire rang against the metal car and kicked up the dirt around them as they rolled several feet before the guard was up and dragging Alyssa down an alley too narrow for Specter's wingspan. A half-dozen believers chased them, and Jael incinerated the last one before he could corner the building. She cursed and leapt from Specter's back to follow.

❖

Alyssa kicked and scratched, but the guard's arm encircling her waist and lifting her off the ground held tight. After two quick turns, he ducked into a recessed doorway, where he pressed Alyssa so tight between the rough adobe wall and his long body that she could hardly breathe.

"Stop. I'm trying to help you."

The harsh whisper was female, and Alyssa suddenly realized she felt no malice or deception from her. "I can't breathe." The woman shifted back and Alyssa relaxed. She heard footsteps run past the street where they were hidden and keep going. She waited a minute, then looked up into eyes as blue as Jael's. "You don't have to carry me. I can walk."

"I hope you can run, because if those believers catch us, we're both dead."

Alyssa frowned. "But you were one of the guards trying to get us off the railcar." She gasped. "Camila. I have to go back."

"No." The woman tightened her hold around Alyssa's arm, then relaxed it again. "I'm sorry. I'm afraid it's too late to help the Chief Advocate."

Camila's calm gaze flashed before her, and Alyssa wiped at the tears stinging her tired eyes. "This is my fault. I should have listened to Jael. I shouldn't have convinced Camila to try to negotiate with a madman."

"Even I didn't realize how mad he has become." Sadness flashed across the woman's handsome features. "She'll be rewarded in her next life, right?"

Alyssa studied her captor's strong jaw and buzzed hair, realizing now that she was probably in her mid-twenties but could easily pass as a teenaged boy. "Yes," she said softly. She placed her hand over the one that still gripped her arm. "I'm Alyssa."

"Hi. I'm Kyle." She released Alyssa and edged forward to peer each way down the street. She grabbed Alyssa's hand and tugged her from their hiding place. "Come on." Kyle's hand felt unnaturally warm, like Jael's.

"That's far enough." They'd only gone a few steps when the cruel voice sounded behind them.

Kyle turned slowly and moved between Alyssa and the man holding a gun on them.

"I'll admit that cutting your hair and dressing like a man threw me off at first. But, unlike your delusional father, I never trusted you. I knew you'd make a break for it at some point, deviant that you are."

Running footsteps approached. "If we can get to a rooftop, I can get us a way out of here," Alyssa whispered.

Kyle lifted her hands, palming a fireball in each. "More deviant than you know, Simon."

He fired. The first fireball melted the bullet midway between them. The second melted the gun in his hand, and he screamed with pain.

"They're down that street," a voice shouted.

Kyle and Alyssa ran past Simon, where he knelt in the street, slapping at his burning sleeve. They heard gunshots and screams behind them—the believers chasing them or someone the believers had wounded. No time to find out. They ran blindly, turning so many times Alyssa had no idea how to get back to the train depot.

In this part of town, houses were arranged in a maze of short blocks separated by cobblestone streets and narrow alleys. There were no flat roofs or outdoor stairways. Alyssa wished, for the first time, that she'd trained with the warrior candidates so she'd be in better shape. "We need to get back to the business district where the buildings are bigger and we can find a flat roof." Alyssa stopped, bending over and gasping. She couldn't go any farther without a minute to catch her breath.

Kyle skidded to a halt a few paces ahead of her and turned back just in time to duck as a fireball flew past her head. She barely had time to throw one of her own to deflect a second headed straight for her.

Alyssa straightened and spun around. "Jael!" Stars, she'd never been so glad to see tall, dangerous, and sexy in her entire life. Then she saw the fireball in Jael's hand, swirling as blue and hot as the murderous glint in her warrior's eyes.

"I am Jael, First Warrior of The Collective's Guard."

"Jael, honey. It's okay."

Jael's eyes showed no recognition as they looked past Alyssa and fastened on Kyle.

"In the name of The Collective, I pronounce you guilty of heresy, conspiracy to spread heresy, and kidnapping the First Advocate of The Collective."

Alyssa backed against Kyle to shield her when Jael lifted her hand and the fireball grew larger. "No. Jael, look at me. Kyle was helping me escape. She didn't kidnap me."

A swoosh of air and Specter's hooves clattered against the cobblestones behind them. Alyssa shoved Kyle against the wall on their left and stood in front of her. They wouldn't be able reach Kyle without going through her.

"I sentence—"

Alyssa closed her eyes to Jael's monotone and filled her mind with every special moment they'd shared. Their first kiss at the creek. Jael warm against her back and chuckling when she attempted to touch a star. Them making love under a star-studded sky. Them sitting on the steps of Jael's cabin, the mountains at their back and a riot of wildflowers at their feet.

She opened her eyes.

Jael's brow furrowed. "I sentence you—" She blinked and seemed to search for the rest of the words.

"Jael, look at me." She smiled when Jael's eyes darted to hers, and she projected every ounce of love and affection she felt for this First Warrior, for her lover, for the soul that she knew now was the only one who would ever complete her. Jael was hers to claim. "I love you. Do you hear me? I love all of you—your darkness as well as your gentle heart. Most of all, I love your wisdom. I'm asking you to use that now and listen to me. Kyle is not a believer. She defended me against them."

The hard lines of Jael's face softened, and Alyssa was flooded with Jael's relief as she went to her. Jael buried her face against Alyssa's neck as they clung to each other. "You are my soul-bond," Alyssa whispered against Jael's ear. She captured Jael's mouth with hers—a kiss deep and urgent—to seal her claim.

CHAPTER TWENTY-SIX

The night sky was beginning to fade, and Kyle shifted nervously. She expected Simon and reinforcements to show up any minute now. When she turned slowly to regard the dragon horse, lean as a greyhound and ghostly white, he fluttered his huge wings impatiently. Stars above, she'd never seen such a creature. He studied her, too, small spurts of flame shooting from his nostrils as he breathed.

She tentatively cleared her throat and glanced back uncomfortably at the intimidating First Warrior and the beautiful First Advocate. The First Warrior broke off their kiss but tucked Alyssa against her side as she looked up at the sky, then past her, to the dragon horse.

She turned as the first swoosh of air buffeted her, just in time to see him lift off and disappear over the rooftops. Sun and moon, he was beauty and power, and every fiber of her being wanted to follow him. The urgency she'd suffered for months made sense now. She was destined to be here, to be part of this. When she turned back, Jael was watching her.

"I'm Kyle," she said. She took a deep breath and her words came out in a rush. "I've been trying to catch up to you for a long time, but Cyrus captured me every time I tried to get away. I don't really know why, but I felt...I felt like I had to...I had to be here."

Jael cocked her head. "You felt The Calling?"

"Yes!" She hesitated. "I guess. What's that?"

Jael shook her head. "We'll talk about it later, when we have more time. We need to get back to the depot."

"You're not still intent on frying me, are you?"

"She saved my life, Jael. She's gifted. A pyro."

Jael's face softened when she looked into Alyssa's eyes, and Kyle wondered if anyone would ever look at her with such devotion. An apparent decision made, Jael turned back to her.

"I am Jael, First Warrior of The Collective."

"I kind of got that when you were about to cook me."

"Will you give me your thoughts?"

Kyle knelt. "I will give you and The Collective my life."

Jael nodded and placed her fingers along Kyle's forehead and temple. She closed her eyes and plunged in. She saw Cyrus, Ruth, Simon, and how Kyle had defended Alyssa against him. After a moment, she was satisfied and gently withdrew.

"I am in your debt," she said to Kyle. "So I sentence you to guard the First Advocate whenever I'm not around."

"I don't think so," Alyssa said, slapping her hand against Jael's stomach.

"Really?" Kyle looked doubtful.

"Let it be recorded," Jael said, sealing the order. "Now, let's find our way back."

❖

After a few blocks, they only had to follow the stench of burned flesh and scorched metal to return to the depot. The noise and confusion was the same, except people were running to the train, not away. Shouts of "medic" and "another transport" replaced the sound of gunfire.

They paused on the loading dock. The ceaseless activity moved like a giant beast waking under the first soft rays of dawn. The aftermath of battle was never pretty, the losses never acceptable to Jael.

Second materialized at Jael's side. Her face was grim, but her salute snapped with pride.

"Report."

"Twelve civilian casualties." Second glanced at Alyssa, her eyes apologetic. "Their Chief Advocate was among them." She returned her gaze to Jael. "About a dozen more injured but should recover. Twenty of the badly born are on their way to their next lives."

"Our warriors?"

"No fatalities. A handful suffered burns when they were splashed with melting bullets. Three were hit by bullets that managed to get through. Four dragon horses suffered injuries, but nothing they can't recover from. Michael and Raven have flown the army back to the main camp."

"What else?"

"Furcho and I are organizing redistribution of the stolen supplies."

Jael didn't miss Kyle's head jerking around at the mention of Furcho. She'd seen Kyle's memories and knew he was an acquaintance. Kyle wisely kept silent while Second finished her report.

"The town has a small hospital, but I'm sure they could use Alyssa's help until we are ready to return to camp."

Jael's mind was dissecting with surgical precision what Second hadn't yet reported, slicing immediately to the absence of two key members of The Guard.

"Cyrus? The man who calls himself The Prophet?"

Second nodded curtly. "Cyrus and a handful of his henchmen are missing. Furcho had tracked him to the temple and was about to send him to the next life when he grabbed a boy and used him as a human shield. He disappeared into a dark alley, and nobody has seen him or the boy since. Apparently, at least a few local citizens have bought into his dogma and helped them escape."

"Tan and Diego?"

"They're looking for him."

"Any prisoners?"

"A handful of women who were hiding in the fourth car. We're holding them there for you to interrogate."

Jael nodded. There was no time to waste, but still she hesitated. She had never faltered in the face of duty, but while her command brain itched to probe the prisoners for information, her heart yearned to remain at Alyssa's side.

Alyssa lips brushed against hers. "Go and do what you must. I'm going to see how I can help at the hospital."

Jael eyed their new recruit. "Let's see your flame."

Kyle obediently stepped back and flicked her fingers. The blue-white fireball burned strong in her palm. A natural and very strong pyro. A flame that hot was rare for someone untrained.

"Don't leave her side. Not even for a minute. If anything happens to her, you'll have to answer to me."

"Yes, First Warrior."

Jael touched the blush of sunset ever-present on Alyssa's cheek and memorized the evergreen of her eyes. It seemed impossible, but she'd swear that underneath the smell of sweat and smoke, she still detected the scent of honeysuckle and summer rain. No one had ever shone light into her darkness, but Alyssa had. Jael realized that none of her many lives had prepared her for this soul-deep bond that tied her to this fiery-haired, feisty First Advocate. "I love you." The words sprang from her heart and glided off her tongue easier than she'd ever imagined. "I'll only be a few hours, and then I'll come find you."

Alyssa kissed her again, a tantalizing brush of tongue against hers. Anything more and she would throw duty to the stars and whisk her away to someplace private where they could both expend the adrenaline still flowing from the night's skirmish.

"Stop," Alyssa whispered. "It's hard enough without you looking at me like that."

Later.

I'll count on it.

"Jael." Diego strode toward them, his face grim over the blanket-swaddled bundle he carried in his arms. *It's not good.*

Jael closed her eyes for a few seconds. She saw into Diego's thoughts and wrapped an arm around Alyssa to draw her closer. "Report."

"Tan is still on Cyrus's trail, but he left you a message in a house on the outskirts of town." Diego's bundle whimpered when he shifted it to hand a smaller, bloody package to Jael.

Jael unwrapped it slowly. Inside was a small hand, a box of matches resting in the palm.

"Oh, no." Alyssa paled and reached tentatively to touch the bundle in Diego's arms. "NO. No. It can't be." Diego gently moved the blanket to expose the face of the child he carried, and Alyssa gasped. "Ari. He found me when I was lost in the jungle and escorted me here."

"Tan administered a strong painkiller, but he needs a surgeon as soon as possible," Diego said.

"How could they do such a thing?"

Jael had seen savagery much worse than a hand cut from a child. She carefully moved the small hand aside to reveal a message inked on the cloth wrapping.

You cannot stop us. First we'll cut off the right hand of your Collective. Next, we will cut off its head.

Find them. And stop him. Alyssa, her jaw tight and anguish etched across her features, took the bloody package from Jael. Her voice shook as she spoke aloud for everyone to hear. "Do whatever you must to stop this madman and protect The Collective." She looked up, her gaze boring into Jael, her words now steady and certain. "Do you hear me, First Warrior? Do what you must."

Jael felt her darkness test its tethers, eager to be unleashed. Not yet. But soon. She squeezed Alyssa's shoulder gently.

"As you command, First Advocate."

About the Author

D. Jackson Leigh grew up barefoot and happy, swimming in farm ponds and riding rude ponies in rural Georgia. Her passion for writing led her to a career in journalism and North Carolina, where she edits breaking news at night and writes lesbian romance stories by day.

Her awards include a 2010 Alice B. Lavender Award for Noteworthy Accomplishment, a 2013 Golden Crown Literary Society Award for paranormal romance, and a 2014 Golden Crown Literary Society Award for traditional romance. She also was a finalist in LGBT erotic romance in the 2013 Rainbow Awards and a 2014 Lambda Literary Awards finalist in traditional romance.

Write to her at author@djacksonleigh.com or follow her at facebook.com/d.jackson.leigh or www.djacksonleigh.com.

Books Available from Bold Strokes Books

Pedal to the Metal by Jesse J. Thoma. When unreformed thief Dubs Williams is released from prison to help Max Winters bust a car theft ring, Max learns that to catch a thief, get in bed with one. (978-1-62639-239-7)

Dragon Horse War by D. Jackson Leigh. A priestess of peace and a fiery warrior must defeat a vicious uprising that entwines their destinies and ultimately their hearts. (978-1-62639-240-3)

For the Love of Cake by Erin Dutton. When everything is on the line, and one taste can break a heart, will pastry chefs Maya and Shannon take a chance on reality? (978-1-62639-241-0)

Betting on Love by Alyssa Linn Palmer. A quiet country-girl-at-heart and a live-life-to-the-fullest biker take a risk at offering each other their hearts. (978-1-62639-242-7)

The Deadening by Yvonne Heidt. The lines between good and evil, right and wrong, have always been blurry for Shade. When Raven's actions force her to choose, which side will she come out on? (978-1-62639-243-4)

Ordinary Mayhem by Victoria A. Brownworth. Faye Blakemore has been taking photographs since she was ten, but those same photographs threaten to destroy everything she knows and everything she loves. (978-1-62639-315-8)

One Last Thing by Kim Baldwin & Xenia Alexiou. Blood is thicker than pride. The final book in the Elite Operative Series brings together foes, family, and friends to start a new order. (978-1-62639-230-4)

Songs Unfinished by Holly Stratimore. Two aspiring rock stars learn that falling in love while pursuing their dreams can be harmonious—if they can only keep their pasts from throwing them out of tune. (978-1-62639-231-1)

Beyond the Ridge by L.T. Marie. Will a contractor and a horse rancher overcome their family differences and find common ground to build a life together? (978-1-62639-232-8)

Swordfish by Andrea Bramhall. Four women battle the demons from their pasts. Will they learn to let go, or will happiness be forever beyond their grasp? (978-1-62639-233-5)

The Fiend Queen by Barbara Ann Wright. Princess Katya and her consort Starbride must turn evil against evil in order to banish Fiendish power from their kingdom, and only love will pull them back from the brink. (978-1-62639-234-2)

Up the Ante by PJ Trebelhorn. When Jordan Stryker and Ashley Noble meet again fifteen years after a short-lived affair, are either of them prepared to gamble on a chance at love? (978-1-62639-237-3)

Speakeasy by MJ Williamz. When mob leader Helen Byrne sets her sights on the girlfriend of Al Capone's right-hand man, passion and tempers flare on the streets of Chicago. (978-1-62639-238-0)

Venus in Love by Tina Michele. Morgan Blake can't afford any distractions and Ainsley Dencourt can't afford to lose control—but the beauty of life and art usually lies in the unpredictable strokes of the artist's brush. (978-1-62639-220-5)

Rules of Revenge by AJ Quinn. When a lethal operative on a collision course with her past agrees to help a CIA analyst on a critical assignment, the encounter proves explosive in ways neither woman anticipated. (978-1-62639-221-2)

The Romance Vote by Ali Vali. Chili Alexander is a sought-after campaign consultant who isn't prepared when her boss's daughter, Samantha Pellegrin, comes to work at the firm and shakes up Chili's life from the first day. (978-1-62639-222-9)

Advance: Exodus Book One by Gun Brooke. Admiral Dael Caydoc's mission to find a new homeworld for the Oconodian people is hazardous, but working with the infuriating Commander Aniwyn "Spinner" Seclan endangers her heart and soul. (978-1-62639-224-3)

UnCatholic Conduct by Stevie Mikayne. Jil Kidd goes undercover to investigate fraud at St. Marguerite's Catholic School, but life gets complicated when her student is killed—and she begins to fall for her prime target. (978-1-62639-304-2)

Season's Meetings by Amy Dunne. Catherine Birch reluctantly ventures on the festive road trip from hell with beautiful stranger Holly Daniels only to discover the road to true love has its own obstacles to maneuver. (978-1-62639-227-4)

Myth and Magic: Queer Fairy Tales edited by Radclyffe and Stacia Seaman. Myth, magic, and monsters—the stuff of childhood dreams (or nightmares) and adult fantasies. (978-1-62639-225-0)

Nine Nights on the Windy Tree by Martha Miller. Recovering drug addict, Bertha Brannon, is an attorney who is trying to stay clean when a murder sends her back to the bad end of town. (978-1-62639-179-6)

Driving Lessons by Annameekee Hesik. Dive into Abbey Brooks's sophomore year as she attempts to figure out the amazing, but sometimes complicated, life of a you-know-who girl at Gila High School. (978-1-62639-228-1)

Asher's Shot by Elizabeth Wheeler. Asher Price's candid photographs capture the truth, but when his success requires exposing an enemy, Asher discovers his only shot at happiness involves revealing secrets of his own. (978-1-62639-229-8)

Courtship by Carsen Taite. Love and justice—a lethal mix or a perfect match? (978-1-62639-210-6)

Against Doctor's Orders by Radclyffe. Corporate financier Presley Worth wants to shut down Argyle Community Hospital, but Dr. Harper Rivers will fight her every step of the way, if she can also fight their growing attraction. (978-1-62639-211-3)

A Spark of Heavenly Fire by Kathleen Knowles. Kerry and Beth are building their life together, but unexpected circumstances could destroy their happiness. (978-1-62639-212-0)

Never Too Late by Julie Blair. When Dr. Jamie Hammond is forced to hire a new office manager, she's shocked to come face to face with Carla Grant and memories from her past. (978-1-62639-213-7)

Widow by Martha Miller. Judge Bertha Brannon must solve the murder of her lover, a policewoman she thought she'd grow old with. As more bodies pile up, the murderer starts coming for her. (978-1-62639-214-4)

Twisted Echoes by Sheri Lewis Wohl. What's a woman to do when she realizes the voices in her head are real? (978-1-62639-215-1)

Criminal Gold by Ann Aptaker. Through a dangerous night in New York in 1949, Cantor Gold, dapper dyke-about-town, smuggler of fine art, is forced by a crime lord to be his instrument of vengeance. (978-1-62639-216-8)

The Melody of Light by M.L. Rice. After surviving abuse and loss, will Riley Gordon be able to navigate her first year of college and accept true love and family? (978-1-62639-219-9)

Because of You by Julie Cannon. What would you do for the woman you were forced to leave behind? (978-1-62639-199-4)

The Job by Jove Belle. Sera always dreamed that she would one day reunite with Tor. She just didn't think it would involve terrorists, firearms, and hostages. (978-1-62639-200-7)

Making Time by C.J. Harte. Two women going in different directions meet after fifteen years and struggle to reconnect in spite of the past that separated them. (978-1-62639-201-4)

Once The Clouds Have Gone by KE Payne. Overwhelmed by the dark clouds of her past, Tag Grainger is lost until the intriguing and spirited Freddie Metcalfe unexpectedly forces her to reevaluate her life. (978-1-62639-202-1)

The Acquittal by Anne Laughlin. Chicago private investigator Josie Harper searches for the real killer of a woman whose lover has been acquitted of the crime. (978-1-62639-203-8)

An American Queer: The Amazon Trail by Lee Lynch. Lee Lynch's heartening and heart-rending history of gay life from the turbulence of the late 1900s to the triumphs of the early 2000s are recorded in this selection of her columns. (978-1-62639-204-5)

Stick McLaughlin: The Prohibition Years by CF Frizzell. Corruption in 1918 cost Stick her lover, her freedom, and her identity, but a very special flapper and the family bond of her own gang could help win them back—even if it means outwitting the Boston Mob. (978-1-62639-205-2)

Edge of Awareness by C.A. Popovich. When Maria, a woman in the middle of her third divorce, meets Dana, an out lesbian, awareness of her feelings brings up reservations about the teachings of her church. (978-1-62639-188-8)

Taken by Storm by Kim Baldwin. Lives depend on two women when a train derails high in the remote Alps, but an unforgiving mountain, avalanches, crevasses, and other perils stand between them and safety. (978-1-62639-189-5)

The Common Thread by Jaime Maddox. Dr. Nicole Coussart's life is falling apart, but fortunately, DEA Attorney Rae Rhodes is there to pick up the pieces and help Nic put them back together. (978-1-62639-190-1)

Jolt by Kris Bryant. Mystery writer Bethany Lange wasn't prepared for the twisting emotions that left her breathless the moment she laid eyes on folk singer sensation Ali Hart. (978-1-62639-191-8)

Searching For Forever by Emily Smith. Dr. Natalie Jenner's life has always been about saving others, until young paramedic Charlie Thompson comes along and shows her maybe she's the one who needs saving. (978-1-62639-186-4)

A Queer Sort of Justice: Prison Tales Across Time by Rebecca S. Buck. When liberty is only a memory, and all seems lost, what freedoms and hopes can be found within us? (978-1-62639-195-6E)

Blue Water Dreams by Dena Hankins. Lania Marchiol keeps her wary sailor's gaze trained on the horizon until Oly Rassmussen, a wickedly handsome trans man, sends her trusty compass spinning off course. (978-1-62639-192-5)

Rest Home Runaways by Clifford Henderson. Baby boomer Morgan Ronzio's troubled marriage is the least of her worries when she gets the call that her addled, eighty-six-year-old, half-blind dad has escaped the rest home. (978-1-62639-169-7)

Charm City by Mason Dixon. Raq Overstreet's loyalty to her drug kingpin boss is put to the test when she begins to fall for Bathsheba Morris, the undercover cop assigned to bring him down. (978-1-62639-198-7)